LANDSCAPE WITH THE FALL OF ICARUS

A NOVEL

ACKNOWLEDGEMENTS

I owe many thanks and much gratitude to the following individuals who have assisted in the birth of this novel:

to Keith Henderson, Managing Editor of DC Books, for believing in this work and for your unfailing support leading up to its publication;

to Kenneth Radu, Fiction Editor of DC Books, for your care, attention to detail, and constant encouragement in helping me revise the manuscript. Your sharp artistic eye, abiding love of literature, and faith in my writing have only served to make this novel better;

to Matthew Firth, fellow writer, editor, and great friend who first published my fiction in Canada: a profound thanks for jump-starting my writing;

to Sabina Walser for reading through the first draft of the manuscript, and for your wise comments, observations, and suggestions;

to Howie Klarer for taking the author's portrait, and for the great conversations and friendship.

Finally, grateful acknowledgement to the following publications where portions of this novel first appeared in print or on-line: *Front & Centre # 30* (Black Bile Press, 2016) and *Montreal Rampage*, where several excerpts appeared in the form of anecdotes and personal-opinion pieces by way of my weekly column, "Montreal Then and Now."

ZSOLT ALAPI

LANDSCAPE WITH THE FALL OF ICARUS

A NOVEL

LIVRES
DC
BOOKS

Cover design by Philippe Barey.
Cover art: *Landscape with the Fall of Icarus,* Pieter Bruegel the Elder,
Wikimedia Commons/Public Domain.
Author photograph by Howie Klarer.
Book designed and typeset by Primeau Barey, Montreal.
Edited by Kenneth Radu.

Copyright © Zsolt Alapi, 2020.
Legal Deposit, Bibliothèque et Archives nationales du Québec
and Library and Archives Canada, 1st trimester, 2020.

Library and Archives Canada Cataloguing in Publication
Title: Landscape with the Fall of Icarus : a novel/Zsolt Alapi.
Names: Alapi, Zsolt, 1950 – author.
Identifiers: Canadiana 20200185667 | ISBN 9781927599501 (softcover)
Classification: LCC PS8601.L25 L36 2020 | DDC C813/.6–DC23

For our publishing activities, DC Books gratefully acknowledges the financial
support of SODEC and of the Government of Canada through Canadian Heritage
and the Canada Book Fund. *Nous reconnaissons l'aide financière du gouvernement
du Canada.*

Société
de développement
des entreprises
culturelles
Québec 🔲🔲   Canada

Printed and bound in Canada.
Interior pages printed on Enviro Book, an environmentally responsible paper
containing 100% post-consumer recycled fibre, processed chlorine-free and
manufactured using biogas energy.
Distributed by Fitzhenry and Whiteside.

DC Books
5 Fenwick Ave., Montreal West
Quebec H4X 1P3
www.dcbooks.ca

To Suzanne and Zachary,
for believing.

CHAPTER 1

"About suffering they were never wrong,/The old Masters. . . ." Auden had written. Standing in the Bruegel room of the Kunsthistorisches Museum in Vienna, though that painting, *Landscape with the Fall of Icarus,* is not there, I thought of those lines. The bumpkin farmer, unaware of everything but his plowing and the furrows he is cutting into the earth, is at the center of that painting, dominating the foreground. Below him the merchant ship sails with its cargo of bounty, also oblivious to the slight splash among the waves, the disappearing form, one wing already under the water, the other crumpled, about to disappear, and the legs, all akimbo, a flailing, failing gesture.

So goes the allegory, though perhaps Bruegel meant it differently, thinking more on the grand scale of human suffering. But as I remembered that painting, I thought of all the poignancy of the artistic imagination falling, unnoticed, disappearing, swallowed by the waves.

I was standing with Elizabeth then before Bruegel's *Tower of Babel,* she in Europe for the first time, marveling at everything, me trying to show it all to her through my eyes. I wanted to draw her attention to some details near the top right corner, so I raised my right hand and pointed, completely caught up in the moment, when a mechanical voice blared out from the speakers concealed in the ceiling:

"Achtung. Die Hände aufmachen. Sofort, bitte."

Two museum guards explained sternly but politely that the condensation and moisture from my gesture might possibly warp the painting.

Later, Elizabeth and I laughed about it over wine in some *Heurige* before we went back to our hotel.

Now, there is no Elizabeth, nothing but the memories. I think that moment was another nail in the coffin of my pursuits—my love of the singular and the sublime.

I think now (for I have nothing but time to think) about how I had come to be afflicted with this—curse? obsession? What shall I call it? All that has ever driven me to despair, given me solace, started the fire that burned for so long, that still smoulders, even now, despite everything.

I don't know when it began, perhaps when I was a child in Budapest after the war. At the age of five, I would wait for my father every day, it seemed for hours, by the Chain Bridge over the river, the Parliament building rising huge and mythical on the opposite shore. Was my mother there? I don't remember her much. But I can still see the carved lions, four of them crouched in pairs by the bridgeheads. As my father explained to me, people eventually realized that the lions had no tongues. The sculptor, János Marschalkó, was ridiculed despite claiming that the animals' tongues didn't naturally stick out, yet he eventually suffered a nervous breakdown. And as the legend goes, the English architect, Adam Clark, who thought he had built the perfect bridge, committed suicide, being the first to jump off it. That story had shocked me then and continues to inform my life even now.

When I was told about my impending discharge from the Institute, the first thing I thought about doing was to dig out the old photo album I had kept after my father's death and try to find a picture of that bridge and the lions. By looking at the faded pictures of the dead in their old-world attire, I wanted to re-enter that crawlspace of memories stored in some attic, of yellowed postcards with meticulous *Hohschule* handwriting. There was, I remember, a picture of my grandmother, Gisele–*Gizi*–they called her. She is eighteen, though she looks closer to thirty. Perhaps it's the hair done all up in a bun, her long dress, her thighs and flank an enticing hump under the black cloth. She is making *kifli*–croissants–for *him* (as the faded handwritten caption underneath states), the man who was to become my grandfather.

She is staring uncertainly from behind the mixing bowl at the photographer who has captured her shy girlhood, her wanton desire to feed a man, the symbolically phallic croissants coming magically to life in her hands dripping with butter, risen in splendor, piping hot. They had five children, my father being the second oldest. He looks so serious in the family portrait, an adult with worries even at the age of sixteen, wearing the same look I came to know as a child: accusatory, sad, despairing, betrayed.

The day they finally discharge me from the Institute, I have my last in-house session with Dr. Rheinblatt. He keeps going back to the issue of my family, of something about the pattern of failed love, the early death of my mother, of losing roots. I think he means well. Dr. Rheinblatt is a Freudian, so he wants to know everything about my past, my neurosis, everything that induced me to do what I had tried to do. Thus, he has dug, not without success, into the past and unearthed most of the ghosts, leaving them to wander in a foreign land that has become my home, disembodied shapes as fragile and tenuous as the hold I have over my reality that I reinvent for his interest and analysis every time.

He has determined that my father was obsessed with order, and that my conflict is having tried to instill this same order onto the chaotic landscape of my imagination. For the good doctor is convinced that I am suffering from both low self-esteem and delusions of grandeur, unable to participate in the everyday world by living an ordinary life with ordinary people. The part about my father may be correct, since he was orderly and painstakingly thorough to the very end. I remember after he told me the story of the lion without the tongue, he had said:

"Being perfect is important. Order above all is what matters. *Ordnung,* the Germans called it." However, he was also quick to tell me about the horror of watching the Nazis enter Budapest, of how his heart sank with each grinding thump as the Panzer divisions drove down the *Duna Korzó.* He also told me how they had blown up several of the bridges during their retreat from the Eastern front to keep some distance between the relentless approach of the Soviet "liberators." I came to live in these stories of his youth, of terrible and happier times, covering me in almost the same way they blanketed my father from the reality of exile in North America.

"You can't blame the past, but only try and understand it," Dr. Rheinblatt says to me, though I suspect he'd feel cheated by one of his patients coming to him with no stories of past indiscretions, injustices, or sorrows. In fact, I want to counter with a similar saying, the famous one by George Santayana, but Dr. Rheinblatt wouldn't like it since he believes I use my bookish knowledge to erect a barrier between myself and my immediate reality, hiding behind the words of others to keep from speaking my own truths. Perhaps he is right, but how can he know that this dialogue has become so mixed over the years that they have become inseparable? "So, who can you blame?" I want to ask him. "Who can you blame for all this....?" But even my thoughts and intentions trail off as a question mark.

At the end of our last meeting prior to my discharge, he keeps the discussion pretty general and practical. He wants to know what my immediate plans are. Where will I live? How will I manage the daily tasks? Will I call my son? Friends? (I tell him I have none, but he scoffs at this). He wants me to be a success in the world, he tells me. He knows or seems to know what I am capable of, that I still have a destiny awaiting me. He is fully confident in me, my intelligence, my ability to cope, faith renewed.

"And, most important, is the medication. I've phoned in your prescriptions to the pharmacy and there will be a nurse visiting you twice a week at first to make sure you are on track. Then, there is the schedule of the follow-up appointments, the group sessions, and the community sessions."

He shakes hands with me almost solemnly, as I pass through the electric doors into the parking lot where the bright, insistent sunlight forces me to squint, causing a brief moment of dizziness and panic.

CHAPTER 2

Once outside, I walk along Pine Avenue in the warmth of the early spring day. This world is not a child's delight, as I think of Cummings' famous poem, but rather, filled with the fumes of cars racing toward some destination. Finally, I turn up Cedar, up Côte des Neiges, and veer left onto the Boulevard. This is the road I had taken for over twenty–five years, and I know it well, though it all seems oddly different now.

I walk until I come to my apartment in NDG below Sherbrooke. How long have I been away? I don't remember. When I open the door, the place is much as I had left it. I have scant use for furniture, just an old armchair next to a reading lamp, an antique coffee table (from my father), a rug, and the walls of books. The light is flashing on the telephone telling me I have messages.

I look at the dust bunnies along the floor ("pussy hairs" Elizabeth and I had called them, our French pun) and the fine dust on the spines and covers of the books. By force of habit I check the messages. Two are probably solicitors who have hung up, three are from Nico, saying he is coming into town at the end of the week and I should call him as soon as I get home. The last is from someone unknown. This one interests me the most. It is the sound of someone listening, (for what? I wonder), followed by a sigh, a woman's voice, and music playing in the background which I later remember is a piece from Schubert sung by Dietrich Fischer-Dieskau.

I find some tea in the pantry, though little else, so I make a cup and carry it into the living room and pick up the old photo album I had left on the coffee table. There is a photo that I come back to again and again. It's a picture of my sister and me at the Budapest Zoo. We are sitting in a horse and buggy, and I am holding the reins. She has her hair done up in braids and is wearing a summer dress with floral patterns. I am wearing shorts and high leather boots. We are both staring solemnly into the camera, unsmiling, our expressions sad and intense. Looking at the date under the photo, I notice that it is the summer of '56, shortly before our mother's death and months before we were to leave our country forever for the promise of North America.

I cannot speak for my sister or know what she was thinking when that picture was taken, but I see myself as that young boy, and it is his story that unfolds before me, almost as if he were a stranger, a third person in a story into which he has been abstracted, lacking the voice to tell it in his own words. It goes something like this:

Three old ladies knitting in a room filled with remnants of antique Empire furniture. Two overstuffed armchairs, a sofa, and a coffee table. They drink ersatz coffee from the last pieces of china left in the flat, speaking noisily in German. The boy sits apart, gazing out the window and watching the few trucks rumble down the wide streets five flights below. One lady knits, shakes her head in his direction and turns, addressing him in Magyar in that tone of condescension and mock friendliness grownups use towards children:

"So, Stephen, how is it to be without your poor, dear mother?"

The older lady wearing spectacles, his grandmother, puts down her cup onto the saucer, almost chipping the porcelain.

"Anna," she says urgently, "be quiet..." finally, continuing in German, "Sei still, er weisst es nicht!" Then, a further barrage of words, which he hears, his eyes filling now with tears whose origin he doesn't understand, but they continue to fall, shaking his small body.

"Come, Stephen," his grandmother's bullish tones reach him as she takes his left hand (the right fist is wet, tucked into his eye), "into the kitchen with you." There she slices two pieces of the light rye. On one she carefully ladles a tablespoon of honey from an earthenware jar. The

other piece she butters generously and places on it a very thin, smallish piece of meat, then tells him smugly:

"Pariser wurst... just for you, and honey for you. Eat it now, before I gobble it first!" She makes as if to eat the baloney sandwich while he reaches for it with both small hands, his eyes still moist but serious now as they hold her own attempt at a roguish smile which, even as it folds into tired crease lines, echoes the vacuity of the youthful features before it.

"Yes, that's it. Eat all of it, like a good boy, Stephen...."

*

The boy and his sister sat in the yard waiting. Today, their father had told them, they would see their mother who was being brought in from the city hospital to where they were vacationing. The doctor said the country air might even do her some good, that she might stay for a few days if she felt better.

The farmer who owned the house where they were staying came into the yard with a large milk bottle in his hand and passed by them on his way toward the barn. The children, tired of their wait, walked up to him and asked what was in the jar. Laughing, the farmer showed them a bottle containing watery milk with a half-drowned mouse inside, desperately trying to stay afloat. The mouse's fur was slicked down from the moisture, making it appear all skin and bones. Its eyes were terrified, and the legs flailed desperately against the side of the glass trying to obtain a foothold. Periodically, it would emit a sharp scream as it redoubled its efforts to survive.

The farmer laughed at the look on the children's faces.

"It's to scare away the other mice," he said. "I catch a few each day and put them into the barn to warn the others that something isn't right. So far, we've had a lot fewer of them invading the larder."

Just then, the ambulance entered the yard. The children ran to it, eager yet afraid to make any move to disturb the planned progression of events. Their father approached the doctor and the attendants, whispering to them. The woman on the stretcher was thin, pale, and drawn from the cancer. She grimaced in pain when the stretcher jolted along the rough dirt of the courtyard. Before they entered the house, she signed to the bearers to wait. Then, she looked at her children who were watching her from just a few steps away.

"Come..." she said, drawing back the blankets and extending her arms. The children went to her and felt her breath upon them for an instant before she was removed into the house. They remained in the yard, small, in the glare of the summer sun.

After supper, the boy went by himself to play. He had been in the barn for only a few moments when he heard the scream. It sounded like a person in pain, like something he had heard just a short while ago. Frightened, he nevertheless went to the corner where he had heard the noise. He saw the milk bottle, covered, lying among the sweet-smelling straw. When he finally dared approach closer to look inside, he saw that the mouse was dead, sunk to the bottom of the jar.

That night, the boy awoke from his sleep, afraid. The room was still, save for the steady breathing of his sister in the bed beside him. Just when he was finally ready to doze off again, he heard a loud cry from the other room. There was the sound of other voices and hurried whispers. Steps approached his door, then stopped. The thin moon had finally entered the room, so that by its light he could see the figure of his father standing by the door, staring at him. This disturbed the boy, although he did not betray himself through any movement or outcry. After some time, the door closed, quietly, and he heard his father sobbing as he moved down the passage.

*

The father walked with the two children through the park, one on each hand. It was a brilliant afternoon, the summer sun hot upon their backs and the sweet odour of magnolia coming to them from the banks of the river. The man stopped, and for a long time looked at the children who were quiet, attentive to him. Then he spoke in a rush, fighting against the humming in his ears and light-headedness: "Your mother died last night. You will never see her again."

The girl, the older of the two children, began to cry. The boy looked from her back to their father. His father looked down at the girl helplessly, watching her tears, himself numb from his own inability to do or say anything.

"Quiet," he said to her. "It's no good to cry, nothing can bring her back." They approached the kiosk where a man in a gaily coloured cap sold ice cream. The father placed his order and gave the first cone to his daughter. Still crying, she accepted it, finally busying herself with its consumption between sniffles.

As the man gave the second cone to his son, the boy lost hold of it and saw it drop to the ground. He began to cry. The father, losing patience, took him roughly by the hand, pulling him up from the ground. Then, he removed his daughter's ice cream from her hand and hurled it into the bushes. Now both children were crying. Desperate, the man felt like leaving them, to run away forever.

"Shut up now! Shut up! Can't you! How can you both cry about ice cream at a time like this?"

But the children cried even louder, and the tears came down his own face as he hurried from the park, almost dragging them behind him toward the noise and life of the nearest thoroughfare.

*

Finishing the last morsel of rye with honey, he stands outside the kitchen door, listening to the chatter of the old ladies. They have switched from German back to Magyar, and he can understand their voices again. They talk about her, and he sees them walking through the park and his mother asking him:

"How much do you love me, Stephen?" A game they used to play all the time. But this time, he wants to think up something extra–special for her.

"Enough to have a carriage of eighteen white horses come calling for you to come meet me!" And as he tells her this, he can actually hear the gallop of hooves on the pavement and see them approach, in splendour, the entrance to the park.

Then, all fades, and he remembers being dragged by his father homeward, the ice cream spilled on the ground, both he and his sister crying.

The ladies are quiet, only the click click of their needles breaks the silence. The boy goes to the pantry and takes the milk bottle, then hesitates, checking for something inside the bottle by shaking it. But the milk he pours into his glass is white and thickly translucent, and the scream he still hears in his mind fades into the complacency of another afternoon.

CHAPTER 3

The phone rings insistently, and I can see it is long distance, so it must be Nico again, but I am not ready to embrace his worried voice and slip into his world of practicality and concerns. When it stops, the light comes on, a persistent beacon calling me back into the immediate world, but instead I am traveling again, not into the past of old photos and memories of the dead, but through the display of the books in my living room. In the quiet of the apartment, they seem like the comforting murmur of familiar friends, talking in unison about the same thing though their actual words are obscured.

I know I have read all of these books, but I'd be hard pressed to have to tell anyone about any specific plot, character, or event, though snatches of lines, mostly from poems, come back to me as I scan the covers. Sometimes I wonder if it's been worth it all, what was my life's work, or, perhaps more fittingly, the job I fell into, though it was partly acquired through my own machinations.

When I was fourteen, my cousin invited me down to visit her during her freshman year at university at a state college in Binghamton, New York. She was majoring in comparative literature, and she was the first one to read me poems, some of which we used to memorize and recite. I still remember two of them in their entirety: Poe's *Annabel Lee* and Kipling's *Gunga Din*, though the former for some reason would give me nightmares.

My cousin, Emma, showed me around the campus and took me to one of her classes. I remember being terribly embarrassed at fourteen to be among young adults five or more years older than I, but more than that was the magic of sitting through a class by the

Wallace Stevens scholar. I don't think I understood much, but his analysis of "The Emperor of Ice Cream" still haunts me to this day. It was at that moment that I decided on my eventual profession. At eighteen I discovered a love for poetry, particularly for the poetry of Rimbaud and Baudelaire (whom I read in translation), the music of The Doors, and the works of Hart Crane, whose *Collected Poems* I now take off the shelf. With the shock of memory, I read my notes next to the underlined passages, many of which strike me as completely obscure from the distance of more than three decades.

To continue my ambition to teach English, I won a full ride scholarship to Dartmouth College, an Ivy League institution (not to be confused with the Institution where I had so recently spent my time) located in the New Hampshire countryside. It was not a happy time, and I left it near the end of my first semester, though the strangeness of the place and the experience of being there is still etched in my memory:

There was that small town across the New Hampshire border into Vermont, Bellows Falls—Fellow's Balls, the boys called it. This was where the guy who was twenty-one or who had a good fake ID went on Friday night whiskey runs. For the others, there were the kegs that rolled in after 5:00 p.m., once the last classes of the day were finished.

I learned very little at Dartmouth, though it was Ivy League and everyone told me how privileged I should feel to have a full academic ride. I was eighteen when I arrived there, having read a lot, but knowing very little about the ways of the world. The two upper classmen who had the "suite" next to my single made it their mission to teach me. Robbie was the Master of the Revels. During Frosh week, he made us chug pints until some puked or passed out. He took it personally if a keg was returned undrained. No one knew much about him or even what his major was, except that he was from a moneyed family from the Berkshires.

After his seventh pint, Robbie quartered a watermelon. He said: "It's red, boys, just like the inside of a pussy. Watch me eat." It was something awful to see. Robbie was big and broad with a Neanderthal forehead. He had thick, fat lips—cunt-lapper lips, he called them. Robbie dug in. His tongue darted like crazy in and out of the pink flesh. He started spewing seeds and pieces of melon flesh all over the floor. His chin and face were covered with melon juice, black and white seeds, some green rinds. Robbie lapped away like a man possessed. Even his designer glasses fogged up from the effort.

Finally, he stopped: "That, boys, is what eating pussy is like, but more delicious. One day, if you're lucky, you'll get some and have me to thank for teaching you. Try a piece." He offered another untouched quarter to those of us left standing. Somehow, none of us wanted any.

Jake was his roommate, a swimmer who had almost qualified for the U.S. Olympic squad. He majored in finance, skied the Rockies every winter, and had a mother who was into antiques. Their room looked like a den out of a nineteenth century Victorian bildungsroman. There was an armoire in one corner and a velvet sofa that seemed to be made of silk. On the day I arrived, Jake had a large Persian carpet draped over a rope between two trees. He saw me lugging a box of books up to my room.

"Hey, Shit-shorts.... come here.... I got a job for you."

"What?" I said, "I'm busy."

"Listen, you little prick...you do what I tell you, or you're going to be one sorry motherfucker. Now get your ass over here and start beating. I know you got to be good at that."

He then gave me a ski pole and told me to start beating the rug to get out the summer mould and mildew. Jake watched me, flexing his arms. They looked big, and now some other guys had gathered around, laughing. I started to beat the rug, but then looked him square in the eye, ignoring the others. I took a tremendous swing, missing the rug entirely, and wrapped the pole around one of the tree trunks. There was silence.

"Sorry, guess I missed." Then, I turned and went back to my box of books as I felt their eyes bore into my back. I never turned back to look at him but walked upstairs to my room at Richardson Hall.

They came to call me The Ghost. I guess it was because I always walked through the campus at night. I seldom went to my classes and spent much of the days sleeping. Night was another matter. I became fully awake, and restlessness drove me along the bank of the Connecticut River that ran through the north side of the campus. One day I found the tower. It was actually small, with maybe about twenty-six stairs leading to the top turret. But it was a place to sit, to be, and nobody ever came there. I had just started reading Joyce in the only course I thought worth attending, and it came to be my Martello from whose top I looked across the vast sea of trees, the scrotumtightening green of New Hampshire's firs and maples.

There, I first read Crane's poems, and, by moonlight, "The Broken Tower," whose lines haunted me. Although it was only mid-September, I shivered under the blank gaze of the moon. The night breezes, the noises of the woods, the starkness of the night with its stars. I felt Hart's tears in those lines, his longing for the embrace of death, of love, as if he, knowing his own brief tenure on this earth, the call of the sea, the black ocean split by the ship's prow, sailing back from the Caribbean. And leaping into Her arms. I was eighteen, longing for romance, for the painful embrace of my own life.

And so, after forty-six days I reentered the world again. Departure was no less easy. The Dean of Arts called me into his office. Under a portrait of Daniel Webster, he told me what a mistake I was making, of how I was cheating my parents, my country, the university, and, above all, my future. Here was an opportunity given to so few that I was throwing away. Had I no shame? After all, the university had invested so much in my promise. After an hour I left.

Now, almost touched by some odd grace of fortune, I became in my last days no longer The Ghost, but someone whom everyone wanted to speak to and be around. Robbie and Jake took me to their frat house for a farewell celebration. Everyone looked at me like some rare being, come back from the dead. If I had displayed visible wounds, they would have wanted to feel and verify them. I went back to the tower one last time that night. I rolled a joint and slowly smoked it, watching the stars, the heavens unfolding over the broken world.

I got a ride across the border into Vermont with Dan (the Man), who was making the Friday afternoon booze run for the others in the dorm. We bid each other an almost formal farewell, shaking hands on the outskirts of the town that led toward I-87. Four more rides landed me in Burlington where I found a small hotel. It was late at night when I arrived and there was a young woman at the reception looking bored and (so I thought) eager.

We talked for a bit. Her name was Amy-Jo, and she had a small pug-face with a strong body, round breasts, and deliciously full lips. Amy-Jo was a farm girl trying to make it in the city. She drove an old heap every day to Mater Dei College to attend courses in business management. Amy-Jo had plans for her life. She was going to work eventually in a metropolis, maybe even New York.

I asked her about what she did on the weekend or on days she wasn't working. I asked her about boys and, because I had read my Kerouac, I asked her what she really wanted out of life, about her dreams and deepest desires.

"A good life," she replied, "with all the trimmings. Someone to love, a family, maybe some kids, a house in the country eventually. I want a job where I make piles of money. I know I can do it. My marketing teacher says I have a real gift for making money. And you?"

I told her about leaving Dartmouth, about my dreams to see the world and to write.

"*You left an Ivy League school? Are you crazy? You don't know what you've thrown away. Can't you go back? I'm sure they would take you back if you asked enough.*"

"*But I don't want to go back. It really wasn't for me. I'm sure that after four years there, I could have gotten a job as a junior exec. for Reader's Digest. The guy next door to me in the dorm... his father was a Veep there. I want to live at the heart of life.*"

"*The what? What are you talking about? Listen. I grew up in a family of five kids. My dad worked from morning until night on the farm. Dropped dead at the age of fifty, right there in the barn. Josh, my brother who was eleven, found him on top of a bale of hay, his face purple and his tongue hanging out. He was still clutching a pitchfork in his hand. The sheriff had to pry his fingers off, they were so cramped and stiff.*" *She began to cry.*

"*You must miss him, I guess. I'm sorry.*"

"*The bastard,*" *she blubbered,* "*he felt me up after I turned twelve. I can still feel those calloused fingers on my tits. I hated the fucker!*"

We were both silent for a while. Finally, I spoke:

"*Say, Amy-Jo, when do you finish up here? Tomorrow's Saturday. Why don't we spend it together?*"

"*I'm coming off a five-night shift. I'm tired, man, really beat.*"

"*I've got the room upstairs for the next day. You can crash there for a while. Maybe we can smoke a number and do something together.*"

"*Oh yeah, like what?*"

"*Anything. Talk. Make the beast with two backs. You pick.*"

"*Go to sleep, Dartmouth boy. We'll talk by and by. It's awful late.*"

She tossed me the keys and I went up to my room. It was on the third floor and smelled of must and mildew. Even the sheets seemed damp, since it had been raining for the past two days, Amy-Jo had told me. I went to the old, cracked tub to run myself a bath. There was a stray, dark pubic hair near the drain and the sides of the tub had faint brown rings from age and neglect. I ran the taps and rusty water came out as the pipes began to knock loudly. I washed the tub out as best I could, ran a steaming bath, got in, and lit up a spliff.

Time passed. I guess I must have dreamed about Amy-Jo, her pug-face, and promising breasts. She had used the passkey and walked into the bathroom, shedding her clothes along the floor, standing above me in the cramped bath, her curly bush level with my mouth. With a groan, Amy-Jo lowered herself onto my up thrust manhood. The water splashed out of the tub on all sides of us. She locked her lips onto mine and sucked on my tongue wildly. She moaned, gasped, gnashed her teeth. I half expected a bark. I felt a warm tingle from the small of my back up into my stomach and then into my groin. I quivered like a leaf. There were whistles, bells, and more bells ringing.

It was the phone that woke me up, that and the fact that the water had cooled down somewhat. I opened my eyes and saw my erection at the bursting point. The ringing continued, insistent. I got up, out of the bath. My penis went flaccid, turning into a dull ache that cramped into my stomach like a tight fist.

"Hello, what is it?"

"Hey, Dartmouth boy. It's the front desk. What the fuck? Room 306 is complaining about the noise from the pipes and running water. They also say they smell something as if things were burning. Say they can't sleep. It's after three, you know. Keep it down or I'm gonna have to throw you out. All right?

"Sorry, but I fell asleep in the bath. How you doing, Amy-Jo? Still awake?"

"Barely. Now seriously, keep it down up there."

"And you, are you coming up later?"

"Time will tell. Bye."

"Ciao, bella."

"What?"

"Nothing. Bye."

Dawn came slowly, reluctantly. I had dozed a bit and felt groggy. I couldn't sleep any more and willed the phone to ring or for a soft knock on the door. Finally, I got out of bed and felt around in my backpack until I found the book. I opened it at random, and then dialed the front desk.

Her gruff, sleepy voice answered:

"Good morning, reception."

"Don't say anything, Amy-Jo, just listen to this. Something I wrote for you last night." I then read her "Voyages" tenderly, my voice trembling. After, there was a long silence.

"You really wrote that for me? No one has ever done anything like that."

And then the line went dead.

I shot back the bolt on my door and waited for the door to open. Well, Hart, your poems will serve someone some use today. Falling into a deep sleep, I awoke much later with a start as I heard the sound of a Norton 650 firing up outside my window. The driver wore a leather jacket and a red bandanna covered his long hair. He adjusted his sunglasses and lit a cigarette, balancing the big machine with his left boot planted in the gravel. Amy-Jo ran out of the office, her breasts swinging, her nipples hard in the morning air. She jumped on the back of the bike, kissed his leather-jacketed shoulder once, and buried her crotch into his backside. They roared off down the road.

I packed my bags slowly and went downstairs to check out. Someone named Madge was at the front desk. She was barely twenty, a mousy girl with thin, wispy hair who smiled at me shyly through braces. I nodded to her and bent to the road, heading toward the highway.

There were some short rides, mostly from farmers, once I was closer to the Canadian border, and the last one left me outside of the village of Beebe. I walked a ways and then sat down by the side of the road on my pack. It began to drizzle, slowly turning into rain, and finally a hard downpour. I thought of Amy-Jo, Hart Crane, and the company of love. Amy-Jo was probably asleep in the arms of Brett the Biker after a good fuck. Hart Crane was dead, his bones washed clean somewhere in the Caribbean. And what about Slater Brown and Malcolm Cowley? What had they felt when they heard about his suicide? They were all ghosts now, and I too felt like the Ghost they had called me. I began to shiver in the rain, and felt the pain of their loss, of all the lost souls who had loved greatly in this sorry world. I groped in my bag to touch his book, all sodden now, washed with the salt tears of the ocean that was his shroud and with the tears of all who had passed too briefly through this life.

I whispered:

"I'm sorry I did not do justice to your words. Your poem was more for me than for someone else." Desperately, I searched the road for signs of life until finally a car came by, slowing, stopping, and letting me into its warmth. I sat back, half-closed my eyes and watched the blur of trees, sky and the indifferent sun that had returned to warm this broken world.

CHAPTER 4

The phone is ringing again, and this time I pick it up. It is Nico, my son. He sounds genuinely worried, and I feel a brief pang of guilt for this.

"Dad? When did you get home? Where have you been? How are you?"

"I got back just a short while ago. The discharge papers and follow-up took longer than expected. How are you doing? How's grad school?"

"For God's sake, Dad... this time it's about you, for once. What's going on?"

"I'm coping, glad to be home, fed up a bit, fragile, all those things." And then it slips out before I can stop it: "I miss you, Nico, I miss so many things... Sorry!"

"For what, Dad? Don't be." I hear him swallowing hard at the other end of the line. "I want to come to town to see you. How about next week sometime?"

"You're near the end of the term. You have papers to finish. Come in late May when you have more free time. I'll still be here. That's a promise." He doesn't laugh at this.

"There's so much I want to ask you. Are you on the meds? What kind of follow up are they going to be doing?" The one question he wants to ask hangs like a silent accusation in the air between us.

"I'm better. Really." I say this with more authority, more like my old self that Nico is used to. "The meds cause some drooling and the Limp Cock Syndrome, but at my age, who knows?"

He laughs at this despite himself. "You sound better, but I still think I should come." As a teacher of English and an expert grammarian,

I want to point out the danger of using modals and conditionals and their perceived nuances, but I ask him instead:

"How is the love of your life? "

"Natalie is fine. She sends her love. She's in class so she can't come to the phone."

"Ok, Nico, now listen to me. We've gone through the niceties of a concerned son talking to his suicidal father. It's over, or at least I think it is. Sure, I'm fragile, who wouldn't be after the EST, Largactil, Zoloft, and ping pong." I hear a laugh at the other end. My son loves many of the same writers and recognizes the reference to *Howl.*

"Stop worrying. I promise to be good, or if not that, at least I can compromise. The good Doctor Rheinblatt thinks I have made some progress and will be personally following me once a week during the sessions. If he can cure my sociopathic nature and misanthropy, he'll probably get a major paper out of it."

Nico laughs again and says: "Dad, you are one crazy bastard."

"I love you too. I'll call you in a few days. That's a promise."

"Sure?"

"Yes, sure."

"I love you, Dad."

"I know it. My love to Nat. Tell her she owes me some brownies on your next visit."

"Dad....?"

"It's ok. Really. I'll see you soon. Bye for now."

I love you, I think to myself long after he has hung up. Nico. My son. Tall, handsome, smart, concerned, yet happy perhaps that he is far away from me now, left to live his own life, best rid of me.

I still see him as he entered the world, torn from his mother by C-section, blue, not breathing, until they suctioned his lungs and he let out that first wail, and didn't stop for six months after that, only when Elizabeth nursed him. Our Nico, an angry red little face glaring into mine the first time I held him, wanting nothing to do with me, wanting only the breast. The little bugger never napped when we took him home from the hospital. I used to go to work and somehow manage to stumble my way through my classes and come home, only to find Elizabeth in the same chair I had left her in in the morning, still in her nightgown, Nico latched to her breast. I used to imagine that I would come home and find a skeleton with breasts instead of my wife, for she was so weak from fatigue and lack of sleep that the dinner I would prepare wouldn't even pass her lips since all she wanted to do was fall into bed once I took over.

And it was me walking him around the apartment, Nico strapped to my chest while I patted his bum non-stop and sang nonsense songs in Magyar to him until he would tire of that and wail louder and louder until I returned him to his mother. Finally around 1:00 or 2:00 a.m., he'd give in and I walked him to his crib where he'd stir restlessly until I discovered that he would finally fall asleep if I patted his bum for as long as it took. There was also the problem of our creaking floors since we lived in an old apartment building at that time. Just when I thought he had finally drifted off, I would tiptoe out of the room only to have a creaking board wake him into a full-blown crying fit that could only be soothed if he joined us in bed.

One night, I became so desperate for sleep that I actually took a throw pillow and put it under my stomach to pull myself out with my hands so that the floorboards wouldn't creak. After 15 minutes of this maneuvering, I had just shut his door and started to carefully walk off to bed when I heard his first whimpers that soon became a heart-wrenching howl. From that day on, we moved him into a "family bed" and we finally all slept, though the habit of our company became such a presence for him that even as a young child, he would insist on one of us lying down with him at his bedtime after telling him a story. "Who will join me?" he'd ask, and one of us always did, usually me.

Now, today, Nico is a young man in the prime of life, confident, gifted, and on the path to academic success, romance, and, for this I pray, a happy life. I still think of how I felt the day he moved out, keeping a smile on my face while my heart was breaking, knowing the necessity of his departure, wanting to share his joy in the adventure that would begin the adult part of his life. His first apartment, before that, his first real love, his first job, all of the firsts that make for a life.

I pick up the phone and listen to his three messages just to hear his voice again. "Our beautiful boy," as Elizabeth had called him when she first saw him through the veil of Demerol and mother's love.

Nico. My beautiful boy.

CHAPTER 5

The phone is back in its cradle, and it is now only the emptiness of the apartment, its particular silence, and outside the noises of city life. What was it that John Cage said: something about there not being anything like true silence, that the noises of life form like some bubble that sometimes stumbles out as words? And it's true. I still hear Nico's words in my mind, and I feel the fragility of my own presence in the chair where I am sitting, a hum or a trembling through my body. I can hear the beating of my heart, the working of my digestive system, the sound of my breathing, and feel the heat of my body's changing temperature flush my skin. The painful and tell-tale reminders of being alive.

I used to think that all I wanted was a place to lay my head and not be bothered by it all, that the risk of human involvement wasn't worth the trouble, words spoken in bitterness and arrogance.

I think of Elizabeth, and suddenly I am crying, crying for all the feelings I had kept hidden, for all of the memories, and for everything that had made us wide eyed with unspoken hurt and accusation in the last few months we were together.

When I was still in the Institute, Dr. Rheinblatt had asked me about the dissolution of my marriage. But how can one sum up the decades spent together, the good times, the tension involved in parenting, the eventual misunderstandings, the resentments, how it is hard to live through all of this for anyone? He did pinpoint some things, laying most of the blame squarely on my shoulders: my emotional unavailability, my jealousy over her successes, my own inertia and resentment at having to support our family throughout a large part of our marriage, and, finally, my own obsession with literature, the nature of art, suffering, and all the weighty constructs he felt I had erected as a barricade to my potential happiness.

Some of this was certainly true. Yes, I had been the sole support for our family, sometimes working two teaching gigs for extra money to afford Elizabeth the opportunity to pursue her art, even to pay for her studio where she spent a large part of her days, sometimes coming home so exhausted in the late evenings that she missed our suppers and the times I spent with Nico doing homework after my own long days. Yet Elizabeth was a loving, wonderful mother, and her relationship with Nico was always good, perhaps because it was usually I who harangued him about school, his social life, and his habits since I was around more.

I was largely happy to do so because I felt she had real talent and a true artistic vocation, yet deep within me was a resentment I could not name, based on my own inability to produce anything of worth.

"Why was that?" Dr. Rheinblatt had asked.

"I had writer's block for over two decades," I told him. "Still, I always felt I had the potential within me to write, that I had the talent, and also something to say."

"And what do you think prevented you? I've heard that if you really do have the desire and the talent, nothing will stop you, and that you will often put that first and foremost."

"Well, in Elizabeth's case her art was an integral part of her life, like breathing, loving Nico, and perhaps even me for a time. In my case, I put our family life first, parenting Nico, teaching, all the demands of our daily life. These things somehow got in the way."

"In what sense? Did you resent this role you had assumed? Did you then assume it because you were unconvinced of your own abilities and perhaps afraid to face this fact?"

"You could be right. Maybe I was always afraid to really test myself, my purported 'talent' so it became more convenient to sublimate it..."

"At which point it surfaced as resentment. Perhaps even jealousy?"

"True. I was jealous of Elizabeth, even wanting to compete with her. When she had her first vernissage, which was applauded by several prominent critics, I was there as her greatest supporter. Yet this also began our slow journey away from each other, a path that led us in divergent directions. In her case, it was to exhibit her work that took her across North America and Europe, to a lucrative career as an artist that was a vindication of her years of struggle in obscurity. I became the 'artist's husband', an afterthought."

"And you felt that what you were doing was invalid, or maybe not as grand and valid as her path?"

"For sure. It paralyzed my attempts to be creative even more; meanwhile, I still believed that it was my obligation to write, even though the words wouldn't come."

"And is that maybe why you....?"

"Tried to kill myself? It's ok to say it, since we always dance around this subject. No, not back then, since, as you know, my attempt came much later. And my desire to end my life was based on something more basic and more profound, divorced from jealousy and lack of self-worth..."

Dr. Rheinblatt ignored this last statement and continued:

"And now where are you with all of this? You say your marriage dissolved because of your failure to accept your limitations, the fact that you were maybe ordinary?"

"Interestingly put. I suppose I should accept your put-down as a compliment since you feel I am obviously strong enough to face this truth?"

"Yes, but why the sarcasm and hostility? The sooner you face your pretentions and fabricated self-image, the sooner you will be able to accept your more authentic self and reality."

We went on in these ever-winding circles, though I knew that what he said had much merit. What I never told Dr. Rheinblatt was that Elizabeth and I had grown apart over the years slowly and painfully. Maybe it began way back when my father had had to move in with us for several months as he was awaiting what was to be his final admission into the hospital. He was sick, weak, and totally disruptive to our family life, yet I couldn't deny him access to our home. Eventually, I rented a small apartment in NDG that I shared for over four months with him while Elizabeth and Nico kept living in our house. My father was too sick and weak to protest, though I think he knew he was partly responsible for the tension in our home life. Even after his death, I kept the apartment, using it as my purported "writer's studio," though it became more a place of refuge from my unacknowledged yet gradually dissolving marriage.

Over the years, we still maintained the veneer of a family for Nico's sake, and Elizabeth and I still managed an amicable relationship when we were together. In due course, Nico entered university, moved out, and was living in a flat in Verdun with a friend, so it became easier to see him without the constant tension that had become evident between us. Nico took it in stride, or at least I think he did, but with children one never really knows. As long as they feel loved (and both of us made sure of this in our own way), they can thrive, unlike those of us who fall out of love or abandon it, as was our case. For me, my apartment became both a prison and a haven: a prison where I was left to ponder my newest form of exile, this time from a relationship: and a haven where I could live or pretend to live the bare-bone existence I felt any writer should want. In fact, there was a brief creative burst during which I wrote a long confessional novel in its entirety, something I had dedicated to Nico and asked him to burn after reading, rather dramatically, in a note I left for him when I attempted to end my life.

So, to answer the question that still hung in the air from Dr. Rheinblatt, my marriage didn't come to an end through some *sturm und drang* moment, some dramatic confrontation where we unpacked our feelings replete with resentments and accusations, but rather as almost that calm moment when we sat in the notary's office on Monkland Avenue and fairly dividing our assets from the sale of our house after we had finally decided to divorce.

Not with a bang nor even a whimper.

CHAPTER 6

I feel somehow light, lighter than I have ever felt, as I wake up the next morning and I realize it's because I have slept through the night. Gone are the nausea and dizziness, the tremors and the zombie-like lethargy and depression. I make myself a good breakfast, shower, dress, and leave my apartment amidst the bustle of a weekday morning strolling along Sherbrooke in lower NDG. I walk to the Vendôme Metro and change lines until I get off at Guy, then onto the 165 bus that drops me at the corner of Cedar and Côte des Neiges. I am pleasantly out of breath as I begin the climb just behind the Montreal General Hospital. All the clichés of an early Montreal spring day surround me: the budding leaves on the trees covering the mountain, the blue sky with lazy clouds, the lovers strolling along the paths. I take a long walk over the mountain and emerge near Parc Jeanne Mance, the old Fletcher's Field of Richler's stories. I walk up Parc Avenue to St. Viateur, passing the building where I lived as a student, across from the KFC when I first met Elizabeth during my student days.

It was at the *Théâtre de Quat' Sous* on a Saturday night. My friend, Ildi, a fellow Hungarian who was managing the theater, had invited me for a vernissage of paintings, followed by the launch of a new poetry journal. It was the usual Montreal bohemian crowd of would be artists, poets, students, drug dealers, and general partygoers. Billie, the Lebanese hashish dealer, was casting the *I Ching*, trying to attract clients and women. I bought two grams of hash from him and entered the crowded theater.

After the poetry reading, I found Ildi talking with a young woman.

"Stephen, come," Ildi said, taking my arm. "A friend I want you to meet."

She made the introductions, and it was then that I first met Elizabeth.

She was small, beautiful, with flowing dark hair past her waist. She wore a dark skirt with a flower pattern, sandals, a skimpy blouse with no bra, her nipples hard against the silk cloth. She was dark complexioned, and I thought she must be Semitic or Mediterranean, and later learned that she was half-French, part Armenian with a smattering of northern Quebec Cree tossed in for good measure.

Elizabeth was one of the painters whose work was on display. Most of her paintings were nudes, self-portraits, the figures light, almost shy like one of Degas' *Dancers*. There was a simple eroticism about each painting, as if the figure of the woman was waiting for her lover to arrive, or as if she had just risen from the bed where they had just lain.

I told her how much I liked her work and asked her why she painted her figures in the nude.

"I love the honesty of the human body, naked," she answered. Her voice was surprisingly strong for someone of her size, I thought. She spoke with confidence and was not shy about the subject.

"Your paintings make me think of Lawrence's great Imagist poem, 'Gloire de Dijon,'" I told her. Normally, I would have been embarrassed talking about poetry to anyone, especially someone I had just met for the first time, but she listened intently as I recited the poem's opening lines. My voice had risen, and I think I may have blushed when I recited the lines about the lover's breasts, but she only looked at me with her infinite dark eyes and smiled.

"I love Lawrence's description of the act of love, of sex, I guess he would call it. I read *Lady Chatterley* when I was in high school and it made me so excited that I couldn't sleep. That part about her running out in the rain, naked, and him pursuing her, catching her finally, drawing her to him. I could almost see and hear how their hot bodies sizzled as they joined in the cold rain. Wonderful stuff!"

I was enraptured. She had given me a full-fledged erection when she recited this scene, one of my all-time favourites. For some moments, I remained speechless.

A book of her sketches was on display as well, and I looked through these, fascinated. Three pages depicted just a man's torso, done in charcoal, the well-defined pectoral muscles and arms coiled almost as if in menace. On the last page, there was a line inserted under the torso, a line I recognized from Yeats' "The Second Coming." Next to it were black slashes, as if the charcoal in her hand had gone mad, assuming a life of its own, and had lashed out some angry message.

Elizabeth had followed along behind me, so I told her how I found these pages fascinating, and asked her what she had meant by using the lines from Yeats where he writes about everything falling apart, but I saw Ildi shake her head quickly as she walked over to join us.

"So, how are the two of you getting along?" she asked.

"Great," Elizabeth replied, "we both seem to have an affinity for Lawrence and perhaps even Yeats." The last part contained a hint of irony. I couldn't stop looking at her but didn't know what to say. Ildi looked at both of us, amused. Finally, I managed to blurt out:

"Anybody want to walk over to my place to smoke up and listen to music? It's only 11, and the night is still young." I had meant to ask only Elizabeth, but I included Ildi in the invitation, thinking perhaps that it would make things less awkward. Ildi agreed right away, and after some hesitation, Elizabeth said she would come as well. We drained our glasses of wine and set out, slightly tipsy, laughing, walking up The Main, crossing over onto Guilbault, then across St. Urbain and up Esplanade to Parc.

I had a basement 3 ½ room apartment on Parc Avenue almost at the corner of St. Viateur. I suggested picking up some bagels, cream cheese and lox, anticipating the munchies after the hash. As we stood in line waiting for our order, Duncan, my neighbor, walked up behind us. Duncan was tall, amorphous, and generally big. He had reddish hair that looked perpetually dirty and he always needed a shave. He seemed awkward in his body, and when he saw me with the two women, he almost contorted as he stared at the ground, stealing covert glances at them. Duncan always seemed to sweat. Despite the coolness of the evening, stains darkened the armpits of his shirt.

He was studying art history and literature at McGill, though he seldom attended classes. We had become acquainted when he saw me in a local café reading Gaddis' *The Recognitions,* one of his and my favourite novels. We had struck up a conversation and discovered that we were neighbors, so we ran into each other often. Usually Duncan would drop into my place where we talked about books far into the night. He was a voracious reader and a compulsive book collector. His favourite writer was Patricia Highsmith, and he fancied himself as somewhat of a Tom Ripley, especially in his desire to live the wealthy, amoral lifestyle. Ironically, he was also a cheapskate, always short of cash and never offering to buy wine, beer, or split any of the weed during our get-togethers.

"Hey ho," he greeted us. I could tell that he found Elizabeth especially attractive, and I noticed that he glanced at her periodically as he tried to make small talk. Despite his seeming bravado, Duncan was shy around women. I debated whether or not to invite him over, thinking that he might engage Ildi in conversation while I spent time with Elizabeth.

"What are the three of you up to?" he mumbled.

"Not much. Just off to my place for a snack and to hang out."
I paid for the food and we set off, Duncan following behind. When
we got to our building, Duncan invited himself in, saying that he
had to go up to his place first but would be right down. When he
left, I asked them if they were okay with him coming over, and
they didn't seem to mind.

Once inside my place, I invited them to sit down as I dimmed the
lights, lit some candles, and put on *Paris Encounter,* Grappelli's great
collaboration with Gary Burton on vibes. I went to the kitchen and
laid out a spread of bagels, cream cheese and the smoked salmon
with some hot banana peppers and a jar of capers. Shortly after we
were settled, there was a knock on the door so I went to answer
it, finding that Duncan had changed into a clean shirt and had
half-combed his unkempt hair. He was also carrying a small book
in his hand and took me aside, lowering his voice, saying:

"Picked this up at Botrees Occult, you know, that place up on
Decelles in Ville St. Laurent? It's a rare, numbered limited edition of
the Crowley poem, *Leah Sublime,* reputed to be the most explicitly
erotic poem in the English language." Duncan was almost salivating
as he said this, his eyes gleaming. Duncan fancied himself a follower
of Crowley. He had most of his writings, and he imagined himself
as possessing the same charisma and magnetism of the "Beast." One
weekend, I had been away and given Duncan the keys to my place
as he said he wanted to have access to my music. When I returned,
I found that he had taken up the rug and had drawn a pentagram
on my floor, affixed an "altar" in the middle, and brought in some
black candles. I had managed to get rid of most traces of the pentagram, but the candles were the ones I lit that night.

"Congrats, but why bring it along now?" I asked, looking at the
book he was clutching.

"That small one with the dark hair, she's a real fox," he replied. "Her friend is ok, but Foxy there, she looks like she's ready for some sexual magick." Duncan, like Crowley, would have added the "k".

"Yeah, right... we hardly know each other, so give it a rest. I don't want you embarrassing me, ok?"

Duncan shrugged, and we went into the living room, joining the girls. They were sitting together, chatting on my futon sofa. I passed around the *sebsi,* the small clay pipe I had picked up on my travels in Morocco. The hashish was very strong, opiated. The first portion I had put into the pipe stuck together, coming out in long strings like black gum with white flecks, probably the opium. We all became instantly high and lethargic, a Paul Bowles moment. I felt my heart racing in my chest and had a brief instance of panic as sweat formed along my brow. They had stopped talking, their eyes filmy, listening to Duncan's jabber.

Duncan could go either way when stoned: either painfully shy and silent, or garrulous and manic. He prattled on, telling them about his interest in the occult. Duncan recited the story of Crowley's first meeting with Leah Hirsig, his "Scarlet Woman" and his lover during his stay at the infamous Abbey of Thelema. To hear Duncan tell it, Crowley had noticed Hirsig in a café and established eye contact with his hypnotic gaze. After some moments he had walked up to her and, without speaking, reached over and grabbed her head, kissing her fully on the lips, biting her, and drawing blood. Apparently, Hirsig got up immediately and followed him, becoming his lover and Muse for the next several years.

Perhaps due to the effects of the hashish, Duncan had a rapt audience. Ildi was staring at him with her mouth half open, her eyes glazed, slumped into a corner of the futon, while Elizabeth had her eyes half closed and was softly rocking back and forth next to her.

I was wondering how to put an end to Duncan's rant but was too stoned to do much more than put another record on the turntable.

As the eerie music of Oregon's Collin Walcott's sitar and Paul McCandless' oboe soared through the room, Duncan brandished a small book, proclaiming:

"This is The Great Beast's ode to the Powers of Darkness. He invokes the powers of the earth through sexual magick in his ode to the Scarlet Woman, Leah." With this, he thrust the small book into Elizabeth's hands.

It was the size of a small chapbook, burnt orange with a title page that seemed to have been rubbed out. The pages were of a fine parchment, blank until the third page that had Crowley's sketch of Leah sitting naked on what appeared to be some rock. Her portrait was full face, and she seemed to have a bemused grin on her face. A gaunt figure without breasts, she looked like a small boy except for the obvious feminine features of her mature face. Elizabeth stared for a while at the drawing and then spoke, her voice rising sharply:

"My God, is that a penis she's sitting on? I thought it was a rock or something."

Duncan grabbed the book from her and showed it all around, giggling maniacally. Sure enough, upon closer inspection, Leah seemed to be sitting on a gigantic penis wedged into her rectum, her bare feet casually astride a pair of oversized testicles. Under the picture in Crowley's scrawl were the words "*Alostrael the Beloved.*"

"Listen to this," Duncan crowed excitedly. "Listen to these words of the Master, an invocation of the Great Beast 666." He began reading the poem in a deep, tremulous voice:

Leah Sublime
Goddess above me!
Snake of the slime

Alostrael, love me!
Our master the devil
Prosper the revel.

He continued reciting. The others had fallen silent, almost stunned, listening to the explicit words spewing from his mouth. Duncan, aware that he had a rapt audience, became ever more dramatic in his rendering. I wanted to stop him, but all I could do was stare at Elizabeth who was tightening her fist, almost driving her nails into her hands.

Duncan continued with his reading, a litany of provocative sexual scenarios that Crowley had practiced with his mistress. The language was beyond bold, and the imagery left nothing to the imagination. At one point, he read:

Your hand, oh unclean
Your hand that has wasted
Your love, in obscene
Black masses, that tasted
Your soul, it's your hand!
Feel my prick stand!

I felt embarrassed yet fascinated as I watched Elizabeth hearing these words. What was she thinking? Disgust, disgust with the poem, with Duncan for his mania, with me for having brought her to hear this after just a few hours together? Expressionless, her eyes closed, softly breathing, she was beautiful. I wanted somehow to approach her, to talk to her, gently, to present a different version of myself than someone complicit with everything that was transpiring, but I felt almost paralyzed, helpless, unable to say or do anything.

Finally, Duncan approached the end of the poem. His voice had become powerful, almost strident, as he read out the last stanza:

I am your fate, on
Your belly, above you.
I swear it by Satan
Leah, I love you.
I'm going insane
Do it again!

And as Duncan almost yelled these words, something very strange occurred that, to this day, puzzles me. The two candles flickered as if a strong wind had blown across the room even though the windows of the basement apartment hardly allowed any air. Then, suddenly, a huge *CRACK* sounded and the glass ashtray in the center of the coffee table next to the sofa shattered into a hundred pieces. We all jumped up, even Duncan, who yelled:

"DO YOU FEEL IT? Do you feel the Presence?"

"What the fuck was that?" I shouted.

Ildi had gotten up, and Elizabeth looked like she was going to be ill.

"This is seriously fucked up," Ildi said, her voice trembling. "I'm outta here. Come on Elizabeth. Let's go."

Elizabeth got up as if in a trance and followed her. They both left, wordlessly, slamming the door behind them. I felt too shaken to follow after them. I glanced at Duncan, who seemed to be having difficulty breathing, and I went automatically to gather a small broom and a dustpan to sweep up the carnage.

"Some evening, eh?" Duncan whispered. "That Foxy felt IT, I could tell. She's an Initiate, for sure..."

"Enough already," I answered. "Now get out of here. Some evening this turned into! What the hell am I supposed to tell them now?"

Duncan had no answer, and sensing my anger, he gathered his book and crept up to his apartment on the third floor. I tried to take stock of the evening. For sure, I felt there was something between Elizabeth and myself. It had started at the gallery over discussions of her paintings and the talk about Lawrence's writing. It had even continued at my place as we spoke about books, music, art, everything that was so exciting in our lives back then. Even Ildi had taken me aside at one point and told me that she thought Elizabeth fancied me, though she explained that she had just been through a damaging breakup with a man who had been her lover for two years, a man who held some kind of sway over her and had eventually cheated on her. She had been devastated, and her notebooks with the sketches and the quote by Yeats had been her own form of catharsis and revenge. Until the poem and the exploding ashtray. So, what could she possibly think of me now?

It took me four days before I summoned up the courage to phone. I had gotten her number from Ildi, who told me that they had hardly spoken on their way home that night. When I asked her if I should call, Ildi said she didn't know, but that I could try.

"And try to be normal this time," she warned me. "No more Black Masses at midnight, and as for that messed up friend of yours... what's his name? Duncan? Keep him away from her, and I suggest you avoid him as well."

The phone rang for a long time, and I was almost grateful there was no answer, ready to hang up, when I heard Elizabeth's voice, again so thrilling that I was struck momentarily dumb. I asked her how she was, and after the cursory small talk, I said: "Look, about that evening. I honestly don't know what happened, except that things got out of control. Duncan gets that way sometimes when he smokes. All I can say is that I'm sorry, sorry that I may have ruined what had started off as an interesting evening."

She ignored my apology and said:

"And you? What about you? What does that book mean to you, and what happened there that night? Are you an "initiate" of Crowley's? That's what Duncan had whispered to me before I left."

"That's crazy. He's crazy." I said. "Sure, I've read some of his stuff. I even read his biography that listed all of his strange doings throughout his life. I actually got into it not through Duncan, though he sure tried to fuel my interest, but reading Kenneth Anger's interview about Crowley after watching his movie *Scorpio Rising*. I'm sorry if you found the language obscene. That poem is certainly outside the norm."

"But something did happen that night," Elizabeth said, "and we can't pretend it didn't. I felt some kind of force in that room. It seemed to have a hold over me. I felt you were in its vortex too."

"So, what now?" There was a long silence on the line. "Can I see you again? No more Black Arts, maybe not even any poetry... something normal, a talk over coffee somewhere?"

"I'm working in my studio. You can come over. Now, if you want," Elizabeth replied.

She lived in a top flat on Lorne in the McGill ghetto. Desperate to see her, I splurged on a cab and arrived in ten minutes. Not wanting to appear too eager, I walked twice around the block, up to Prince Arthur, over to University and down Milton to her building. She opened the door, smiling, as she squeezed my hand and drew me into her studio.

It was a large, airy room with a skylight covered with some dirt and leaves from the roof. Still, the light was powerful, and it illuminated a large unfinished canvas in the middle of the room. Elizabeth wore a smock that was dappled with paint. She had tied her long hair in a bun, securing it with a maroon bandana.

There were flecks of paint on her hands, and some even covered her left eyebrow.

We did not speak. She handed me a glass of wine as we stood before the canvass. It appeared to be a self-portrait. The figure in the painting seemed to be struggling with something, her hands clenched together, obscuring her face. It was naked, and her pubis had a full bush while there was more hair showing from one of the armpits of the raised arm. The legs were unfinished, still in shadow, and it seemed that the woman in the painting was yet to emerge fully into form. I stared, fascinated.

We stood close to each other, drinking the wine, silent. She seemed small, almost vulnerable, but also self-sufficient, contained, and apart. Alive. She looked at me with a half-smile, almost mocking, uncertain, yet fully aware of her actions. Elizabeth took the half empty glass from my hand and put it on the mantle. Then, she stood on her toes and kissed me, first on one cheek, gently, then full on the lips, tentatively, and then more fiercely. She smelled of burnt almonds, patchouli, and cigarettes, and I buried myself in her hair that had come undone, covering her small, sharp features and full lips in its strands.

Elizabeth raised her hands over her head quickly and I removed her smock. She stood before me, naked. Her body was small, lovely, tight. There was an ample covering of down on her arms, a dark shade of it covering the small of her back where her spine curved into her buttocks. I fed on her tongue, cupping her buttocks into my hands, feeling her moistness and the heat between her legs. Then, I kissed her hard, erect nipples as she moaned and took my penis into her hands, pulling me down onto a futon that was spread out on the ground. Elizabeth took me in her mouth and then swiveled so that her legs swung over my head. She had a tremendous amount of black hair covering her pubis. For a brief moment, I thought of Gustave Courbet's deeply erotic painting of a vagina, *L' Origine du monde,* as I buried my tongue deep inside her, inhaling her strong odour, tasting her wetness.

Finally, she flipped over onto her back and raised her legs high, putting them around my shoulders as I entered her. We both started a slow rhythm, gradually building in intensity. Elizabeth was moaning uncontrollably, and, despite my desire for her, I was able to continue for a long time, watching her beautiful face contort in passion. I started to thrust violently, my foot against the wall as leverage, as she came again and again, yelling so loudly that I wanted to laugh in some odd way although I was touched by her ardour and openness. I drew my penis out and lay back, still violently erect, and felt Elizabeth's soft lips on the head as she started to increase her rhythm, one hand locked around my shaft. Her long dark hair covered my stomach, and I gently held it back so that I could see her face as she looked up at me with her dark almond eyes that seemed to be both smiling and urging me on to my climax wordlessly. I shuddered as I released into her mouth again and again as she moaned and swallowed what felt like the depth of my being.

The light gradually moved into dusk as we lay locked in each other arms for a long time, softly kissing until I entered her again and moved slowly into her, over her, feeling such a warmth for her that tears welled up in my eyes and I thought this must be love, though I remained silent. After we had finished, Elizabeth made a pot of tea and brought out some biscuits, and we talked of everything while we picked the crumbs off each other's naked bodies. She asked me if I knew what that moment in my apartment had meant. I told her I didn't know, but only knew that this moment, today's moment, was the real magic. During this brief evening together, Elizabeth had made me unafraid to talk intimately, so

I regarded her loveliness in the growing dark and recited a section from my favourite Borges poem, "Happiness":

Whoever embraces a woman is Adam. The woman is Eve.
Everything happens for the first time....
Everything happens for the first time but in a way that is eternal.

In the fullness of my youth with its passions and yearnings, that epiphanic moment would haunt me at various points and illuminate the world as if I were seeing it for the first time, Elizabeth for the first time, a world of wonder through the eyes of a child.

CHAPTER 7

Later at home, I begin to feel dizzy and disoriented. I realize it is part of the mood fluctuations caused by the medications that were prescribed. I pick up a cup from the other day and have a sip of my tea. It is cold and bitter, but this lets me somehow know I am alive, tremblingly alive. I want the familiarity of something I know, so I cross to my bookshelves and take down Allen Ginsberg's *Collected Poems* and start reading at random. Suddenly, I am laughing, remembering a story I always told my students about meeting Ginsberg and Peter Orlovsky.

I am back in high school, and my friend, Jenny, whose father is the head of the English Department at the State University, is going to be introducing Allen Ginsberg, who will be reading from *Howl and Other Poems*.

"Who's he?" I ask her.

"He's a famous Beat poet."

"A what poet?"

"Beat... my father says it's a must-see event. After, he's going to be at our house for a party. You can come if you like."

We go into the Fieldhouse Auditorium that night at 7. A huge crowd has gathered, around 600 people. Before this poetic event, I had only been to coffee house readings with maybe 20 people in attendance. The crowd is mostly students, though there are older people as well. Long hair, beards, sandals, and palpable excitement. There is the strong smell of marijuana filling the halls, and incense is wafting from the holders on top of the oriental rug that is spread out on the stage, scattered with lotus petals.

Dr. Freiberg, Jenny's father, gets up to the podium to introduce the poet. He talks about his poem "Howl" as the voice of a generation and its immeasurable relevance not only to our time, but also to the future. Dr. Freiberg is eloquent, and then Ginsberg comes out, kisses him on both cheeks and raises both hands in the Buddhist sign of prayer and supplication over his head and bows to the crowd.

Dressed in a long white robe, he wears an Old Testament prophet's beard and long, wavy black hair barely covering a balding skull. Ginsberg comes out with a beautiful young man, Peter Orlovsky, his lover, so Jenny tells me. Also a poet, Orlovsky holds hands with Ginsberg and gives him a petal from the rug, putting it in his hair. They are like innocent children, lovers deeply in love. Ginsberg kisses Orlovsky on the lips and lingers over the kiss. The crowd goes wild and claps, as Jenny feverishly clutches my hand.

Then, Ginsberg takes out a harmonium, Orlovsky picks up what looks like bongos, though Jenny tells me it is a tambala, and begins a slow beat, as Ginsberg starts to chant, accompanied by the drone of his harmonium.

"*Hare Krishna... Hare Krishna...Hare Rama...Krishna... Krishna....*"

Ginsberg chants over and over again, louder and louder, Orlovsky and the crowd joining him. He is swaying now and trembling, sweating, totally into it. Orlovsky has his eyes closed and is beating the small drum skins, chanting, his long hair coming loose from its pony tail, a beautiful man, swaying like most of the crowd.

Ginsberg knows the moment is filled with magic, and holds it, holds all of us in its sway, holding the final note of his chant for an absurdly long time.

And then, just as suddenly, he is up at the lectern, screaming the first lines of "Howl" into the microphone. He reads from it for the next twenty minutes, and when he yells the "Moloch" section, I am transported with all of the others, so that I don't see Jenny or feel her gripping my hand, but only follow the passion of the words, knowing that this is what I want more than anything in the world to understand, to utter, to sing.

Ginsberg reads for over an hour and rants and berates his audience, telling us to end the war, to embrace the Great Gay Creator, and to dance in our naked secret joy and wonder. And, true to his word, he whips off his robe and the shorts underneath until he is naked, hairy, bestial, his dark genitals flapping before the crowd as Orlovsky also takes off his clothes and dances naked with his lover, free of inhibition.

Ginsberg pleads and exhorts the crowd to join him, and many do, all naked, some embarrassed, but caught up in the moment until the campus security finally makes its way up to the stage and hustles the two of them off into the wings.

Later at Jenny's house, her father playing host to the members of his Department, to poetry groupies, hipsters, and some students who have somehow managed to sneak in, I am the youngest one there. I don't know what to do, so I hold onto Jenny's hand and follow her around the house through the crowd.

"Do you want to meet him... Ginsberg?"

"Ok... yeah... I guess... but what will I say?"

She takes me up to her father and whispers in his ear, and Dr. F. pushes us through the crowd until we get inside the circle where Ginsberg is holding court with Orlovsky next to him. They are both smoking a joint, and Ginsberg is holding a bottle of beer from which he takes the occasional slug and is laughing about something someone has said to him.

Jenny's father introduces us. Ginsberg looks me up and down and smiles. His eyes seem big behind the black frames of his glasses, and his pupils are dilated from the weed. Smiling again, he takes both of my hands and pulls me down next to him on the floor while whispering something in my ear, something about a Blake-light vision, something about a sunflower and of children on the echoing green. His coarse beard brushes my cheek, and he smells strongly of body odour, incense, beer, and cigarette smoke.

I am embarrassed and mutter something about how great his reading was, something about never forgetting this moment. His eyes sparkle with glee and some inner, secret joy. I don't know what to do, so I shake his hand formally, thank him again, and turn to go after saying goodbye.

As I turn my back, I feel his fingers close on my buttock in a sharp pinch, and I hear him giggle to his lover.

And as I am thinking of this, I also think about the line I used to say to my students when I told them this story:

"So, I guess I will always be able to say that Allen Ginsberg pinched my ass."

Almost always, the class would burst into laughter when I used to say this, having built them up to this point, usually after we had finished studying "Howl" and "America."

I would always save the punch line, delivering it with perfect timing:

"And I haven't washed it since...."

Now, as I read through his book, it's like the caress of a friend's smile. I think of Ginsberg, so small and humble before his death, stooped over, wrapped in his own humanity, suffering, yet still having the courage to smile and wonder about the surprise of his own fleshless frame disappearing into infinite space.

CHAPTER 8

"Do you have friends?" Dr. Rheinblatt asks me. "I have heard you talking about books, students, failed relationships, but never about friends."

We are "In Treatment," as he likes to call it, part of the weekly ritual I have come to endure.

"Well, the clichéd answer would be that my "friends" are the dead writers whose work I read and whose wisdom I try to emulate, but that would be too easy."

Dr. Rheinblatt looks at me for a long while from behind his opaque lenses. He appears small, predatory. His nonchalance in the way he drapes his spindly Armani-wrapped body into his overlarge leather chair is deceiving. I sense he is getting ready to pounce.

"Ok, I'll say it. I'm a recluse, a hermit of sorts. I love humanity; it's people I can't stand."

He doesn't find this funny and appears annoyed. I continue.

"I don't mean to be critical, but why do you never laugh at any of my jokes?"

"Should I?"

I want to challenge him on this point. After all, he considers himself to be a Freudian. Has he never read Freud on humour? Should I tell him how I spend some of my time making up little sexual puns and off-colour jingles? Like the one about the Buddhist nymphomaniac who had cunt passion for all living things? Or how, if John Thomas is the name of Mellors' penis in Lawrence's most notorious work, then the euphemism for Connie Chatterley's privates should be "Chatterbox"?

As a teacher of English, I have become all too used to inadvertent malapropisms on the part of my students, many of whom are from diverse linguistic backgrounds and fracture the English language sometimes hilariously and sometimes pathetically. One time, I had lectured on idioms and their origins to my class, The History of the English Language, and then had asked them to write a short piece practicing these idioms to test their practical function. One student had written: "after work, most people are so tired that they only want to be a potato on the sofa," while another who had perhaps overdosed on the constant Internet barrage of sex aid products (coupled with a course she had taken on the History of Christianity) wrote the following precious rejoinder: "Viagra helps the Gentiles grow."

However, I know the cues. It's my time to be serious.

"Ok, I venture. "I guess I subscribe to Sartre's edict that hell is other people."

I can tell by looking at his furrowed brow and his barely audible sigh that this is not what he wants to hear. I am a failure in his eyes, not ready to be reintegrated into society. He reminds me of my psychiatrist when I was a student at Dartmouth. Dr. Green-something. Leaf or Field? Who can remember? Let's call him Dr. G. for short, my G-string with whom I practiced weekly auto-neuroticism.

Actually, I went to see him to be free of the U.S. Army, for my tenure in college was at the height of the escalation of the Vietnam War. Already at the age of eighteen I had a plan, which was to get a psychiatric deferment from serving.

I came in to sell him on my madness. It wasn't too hard. I was tall, gangly, pimpled, serious, a virgin, and a chronic masturbator. I would climb up into the old tower on campus and smoke dope while reading the poetry of Hart Crane, wishing I could have my own metaphoric Caribbean Sea to drown in. I admitted to Dr. G. during our very first session that I was depressed, suicidal, hopeless, that I felt I didn't fit in among the Ivy Leaguers, that I didn't fit in anywhere. Though I told him this part earnestly, deep down I knew this was a load of crap, youthful poetic angst (though I had yet—and have yet—to produce any poetry of worth). Dr. G. listened to my story and scribbled away while I spoke about my past: my mother dying when I was five, emigrating from Eastern Europe, watching my grandmother drop dead while she was reading me "Snow White and the Seven Dwarfs," living in a small apartment in poverty while sharing a bedroom with my father who was *shtupping* my seventeen year old cousin in the bed next to mine, the same cousin who'd make me push her on a raft on a lake one summer while she languorously showed me her pubis.

But who doesn't have tribulations in life? Maybe I was even normal compared to some of the others…who knows? I would wake up in the middle of the night after hearing my father get his rocks off and bang my head against the wall until it bled and raised bumps. So what? Was this a neurosis to be "worked through," as the Good Doctor claimed?

Anyway, Dr. G. put me on a heavy dose of Librium and Darvon to numb me, I guess. He also made me go for an EEG to measure my brain waves to see if my special brand of insanity could be the subject of a scholarly article: "Extracting the Erotic from the Neurotic: Sexual Deviance in Post-revolutionary Hungarian Males." The Librium gave me a nice high, and the Darvon numbed me to the point of being almost comatose. In that respect, I was no different than the other students going off to 8:30 a.m. classes. Still, it both backfired and saved me.

One day, I went to a dance, a mixer of sorts. The way this worked at Dartmouth, at that time an all male school—three thousand rabidly horny young men confined to an area of wilderness—was that once a month, women would be bused in from our "sister" colleges, places like Colby, Smith, and Mount Holyoke. When the buses arrived, the lads lined up with the football team first, followed by other sports in descending order of importance with bookish nerds like myself at the very end.

The boys grabbed and pawed them as quickly as they exited the bus. Usually there would be none left by the time the Great Chain of Being came to me and a few fellow stragglers.

That night I arrived at the venue, high on my prescribed medication, which made me feel both oblivious and emboldened. As I weaved among the drunken bodies dancing to "Sunshine Superman" (it was, after all, the late 60s), I saw a lovely young girl dancing seemingly by herself. I approached her, and in my best faux British accent said:

"I say, miss, I don't like your legs."

She stopped dancing and stared at me. I swear she was blushing all the while.

"What... why not?" she stammered.

"Because they're not wrapped around my neck."

Now under normal circumstances this would have warranted a slap across the face or at least a huffy shake of her locks and the cold shoulder. Instead, she replied:

"No man has said anything like that to me. You're fearless, bold. What's your major?"

"English," I said, "Literature," as if somehow that would explain it. The Wiser Brotherhood of Chauvinist Males lead by Henry Miller, D. H. Lawrence, and Ernest Hemingway all acknowledged me, tilting their glasses of whiskey.

"Wanna dance?" she asked coyly.

"Me wanna," I replied, and started to gyrate with her, a sensual octopus throwing out tentative tentacles.

At that point, I felt a ham descend on my shoulder. Did I just say *ham*? I meant *hand*, though it did look like a giant ham...I was stoned, you have to remember.

"WHATDAFUCK?"

I stopped both dancing and breathing. His grip was vice-like, inching ever closer to my throat.

"HEY," he said. His eyes were small, close set, pig-like. I think his name was Biff, or something like that, a two hundred sixty-five-pound offensive tackle majoring in Communications.

"Biff, I have no beef with you, so don't boff me," I ventured. My words sounded like they were coming through a wad of cotton. Biff grabbed me harder.

"HEY...HEY....," he said. Biff may have been good with the ladies, but he had a serious limitation to his vocabulary. I briefly wondered what his verbal score must have been on his SATs.

"With a hey and a ho, and a hey nonny–no," I croaked nervously, quoting the Bard, trying to extricate myself from his grip.

Biff, his bloodshot eyes narrowed to nasty slits, glared at me. He smelled of sweat, beer, and cheap aftershave.

"DON'T TOUCH MY BROAD," he screamed, picking me up bodily and carrying me to the large French windows overlooking the garden. In one swift clean and jerk, he lifted me up over his head and flung me out the open window. For a brief moment I felt weightless, floating in the autumn air. It was probably the combination of the Librium and Darvon that kept me supple and free from serious injury. I landed in some bushes and walked back to my dorm with only a few minor scratches.

When I told Dr. G. this story, he looked at me piercingly over the top of his half-crescent reading glasses.

"Hmmm," he said, "I see...."

"So now you see why I hate this place—a bunch of Alpine cretins parading as the Future of America?"

"Do you feel you are better than them?" he queried.

"Well, yeah, just slightly..."

"And what you said to that young lady, that was alright?"

"It was harmless foreplay. And what's more, she actually thought it was original. Maybe we even had a future together."

"How's your sex life?" Dr. G. suddenly asked.

I stopped, momentarily stunned.

"Not great. You do know I'm in a school with three thousand males?"

"Do you find men attractive?"

"Only the ones who don't throw me out of windows."

Dr. G. stared at me for a long time. Then he reached into his desk and pulled out a spiral bound folder.

"What do you think of when you see this?" he asked, showing me what appeared to be something like an ink-stained version of smeared road kill. Then I remembered. The Rorschach Test. I quickly scrambled to recollect what I had read about it. What was the "normal response," after all?

"It looks like two angels fornicating. Lucifer and God. The Marriage of Heaven and Hell." I may have been eighteen, but I had read my Blake and Milton.

"Ah," he mumbled. "And this one?" he asked, showing me something that looked like an elephant with a giant trunk.

"That's a large penis with a set of oversized testicles."

"I see," he said dispassionately, all the while furiously writing. "Are you sure?"

"Yes...yes I am."

"Now, tell me what it was like losing your mother at the age of five."

I realize that as I am telling this story, my voice has started shaking. I look at Dr. Rheinblatt to gauge his reaction, but he is in his chair sound asleep, his hands folded in what appears to be benign supplication.

I'm glad that I don't have to tell him the story about how years later, while appealing for a psychiatric deferment from the Army, I had written to ask Dr. G. for a letter on my behalf. It had arrived with my diagnosis: "Possibly bi-polar, coupled with schizophrenic tendencies." And after a long litany of comments and observations, he had written: "Not only is this young man not fit to serve in our nation's Armed Forces, but he is largely unfit for human society."

Nor do I have to tell him that I have framed this letter together with the one that came from the U.S. Selective Service telling me that by not reporting for induction into the Army, I am in violation of the law and a warrant for my arrest will be issued.

And that they both still hang over my writing desk together with a laminated photo of Whitman's famous portrait next to the wizened portrait of Ginsberg holding his last collection, *Death and Fame*.

CHAPTER 9

But what Dr. Rheinblatt has asked about "friends" still bothers me after I leave his office and descend Peel, turning left off of Sherbrooke onto de la Montagne. Heading south, I pass by where the Bistro had been, my first Montreal café where I would spend afternoons hoping to meet anybody, knowing no one in the city, an exile from my former life, trying to find a place that could be home.

It was there that I first met Gerald, who was balding, full-bearded, with his belly-laugh, whose eyes would light up even behind his tinted glasses, who spoke in a deep Texas bass that sounded as if it were filtered through beer and Camel plain, who made rattan chairs squeak, and who made women stare, then look away. We met at the café on an early August afternoon. I had one of the few outdoor tables to myself; the rest were taken. He asked if the other chairs at my table were occupied, and when I grudgingly said no, he and his party sat down so that we were crowded together, our knees almost touching. The two young women he was with were Québécoise, both pretty and both high. I disappeared behind my book, the first one by Mrabat (translator: Paul Bowles), my drink, and the dense smoke of my own cigarette.

They all drank beer, and the women got increasingly louder. Finally, one of them knocked over her beer and it soaked part of my book and the stub of my cigarette. They apologized, giggling, switching from French to sweetly accented English. I answered in my halting but correct French that it didn't matter and rose to go. As I walked up the street, I looked back at them. The women were still laughing, and Gerald was shaking the beer foam off the book I had left behind in my haste and embarrassment.

About a week later, I was in the tobacconist Pouparts on Ste. Catherine where I would go a couple of times a month to treat myself to a package of Balkan Soubranies which I smoked in an onyx holder the rare times when I did indulge, a habit I had affected during my stay in Europe. As I turned from the counter, a tall bearded man who seemed vaguely familiar spoke to me rapidly and followed along as I exited the store.

"I hoped I'd run into you here one day. I noticed in the Bistro that you smoked Soubranies. Only Pouparts sells these smokes, you know. I had meant to apologize for the other day....and your book, the one you left behind."

It was only then that I remembered him from the week before.

"Listen," he continued, "I'd like to buy you a beer (he pronounced it *be-ah*), you know, to make up for that lousy thing...the girls felt badly too, you know...we all hoped you would stay so we could make some restitution..."

We had strolled half way down Bishop and were standing before the Annexe, so we went in as he continued talking. He wasn't really frenetic, as I had originally remembered; rather, the very calm of his voice sort of drew you to him. I noticed that the sun's glare had darkened his tinted lenses so that you could barely discern his eyes.

He told me his name, Gerald, originally from Belleville, a small town in Ontario, now residing in Montreal, and asked me about the book, saying he had read it and loved it, and who was Bowles, and how had he come to learn the Moghrabi dialect?

I told him the little that I knew and we talked about our experiences in Europe and North Africa. I told him about Tangier, about Burroughs and the artist Brian Gysin, the new exiles, I called them, and about *The Sheltering Sky* and really feeling like that on those long, lovely Mediterranean nights, of my stop in Majorca, walking through the bars in Deià, hoping to see the poet, Robert Graves, and when someone pointed him out to me, he looked like an old Spanish peasant with his long, wispy white hair and cape, carrying a straw satchel of wine, bread, olives, and cheese up the road near the cliff. I didn't stop him, though I had meant to, but rather sailed on the *Cuidad de Valencia* toward Ibiza where I stayed for over three months.

I told him about Ibiza, the strangeness and beauty of the place, of Tomas, the kif trafficker whose house I had visited and who once took me for a buying run into the Rif Mountains of Morocco. We stopped in small villages and drank mint tea in cafes, watching the kif cutters prepare their product, lacing some with tobacco for each individual customer, and later, soldering the twenty kilos into the bottom of his VW camper that he'd drive through Europe to sell his ware.

My stories were punctuated by his "Let's have another beer," and by the third round I was telling him about the beach five kilometers between Villa Blanca and San Antonio. I'd ride there every day on my scooter. In the old Moorish tower along the empty beach, I'd sit reading Hart Crane, watching the rinds from the blood oranges I had bought fall into the aquamarine sea in slow spirals, landing, drowning, unheard in the clear water. There I had finally thrown my watch into the sea, the watch my father had given me upon my graduation because time no longer mattered and it was just the eternal moment steeped in loneliness yet infinite possibilities.

We traded stories for most of a summer afternoon, drunk on beer, yet living in the fullness of our youth, memories, and dreams.

Gerald told me of the time he had spent in Morocco where he had met Anaïs Nin in a café, spent the afternoon in her company, and had contracted a bad case of dysentery some weeks after, so bad in fact that he had to be hospitalized once he came back to Toronto. He was kept on a strict diet and regular medication, and had to maintain a twenty-four–hour stool collection in a plastic bucket that he'd have to take into the lab to be analyzed at the end of each week. One day, he told me, friends had come to visit and wanted him to go out for a meal. The doctor reluctantly agreed but told him to eat light and to avoid any alcohol. He also was to take along a bucket he used to collect his stool samples just in case he got the urge. In order to avoid obvious embarrassment, Gerald had placed the bucket in a fancy bag with the insignia of a well-known department store (I believe he said Le Château) on it.

By his own admission, Gerald could never resist "juicing," as he called it, so he disregarded the doctor's orders and threw back a few beers with his meal. Soon he felt the call and slipped off discreetly to do his business in the bucket, which he placed back into the bag and gingerly carried around town to different bars. In one particularly packed place, he and his party managed to find a table and drank some more while the crowds milled about. When Gerald got ready to go back to the hospital, he reached for the bag with his bucket and its precious cargo only to find that someone had stolen it, no doubt thinking that it contained some recent purchases.

"Can you imagine" Gerald boomed, "the guy opening the bucket in the parking lot, or better still at home to a stinking case of the runs?" His eyes grew large behind his glasses and he spewed out a huge cloud of cigarette smoke through his laughter.

During the following months, I learned more about Gerald, although some of the things, I'm sure, were half-truths or fabrications. He had worked in Toronto as a B & E man until he had ripped off the fence to whom he sold his stolen wares. He had recently arrived from Vancouver where he had been living with a French girl called Sylvie. Gerald told me that his fence in Toronto had sent one of his thugs to find him, and this person had asked

Gerald which of his fingers he most valued before he broke all of them. He had to wear a cast on both hands for several weeks. Yet Sylvia had stuck with him, and he, in turn, with her.

Later, Gerald invited me to meet Sylvie over supper at their flat on St. Urbain. Sylvie was bright, tall, not really pretty, and totally devoted to Gerald. After the thug had broken all of Gerald's fingers due to the "misunderstanding," as she called it, they went to Vancouver together where she worked as a waitress in Gastown while he stayed at home reading with both hands in a cast. She told me during dinner that she even wiped his ass and bathed him for the seven weeks until the cast finally came off. This, Sylvie said, had created a close bond between them.

But Gerald needed other women, and Sylvie reluctantly accepted this. He came to rely on me because I was working the night shift as an orderly at the time, so he was using my apartment for his escapades, sometimes several times per week. I was, he told me, the only person he respected. He loved my intellect, my "decency," as he called it, and considered me a true friend, but if truth be told, Gerald also secretly thought we might one day make a great "haul" and light out for North Africa where we could hang out in style while I wrote and he fucked. In some ways, I was his Sancho Panza, or perhaps his Don Quixote, depending on his day and his whims.

By and by we became friends. On my part, it was my persistent fascination with the "dark" side of life, with the unsavoury, shady characters that peopled my imagination. For him, it was more complex: an effort to regain some of his humanity through friendship, the humanity he had lost in morally questionable escapades, in his persistent womanizing, and his constant failure to find and plant roots.

On one of my rare nights home from not working, Gerald came by, weeping, to tell me that Sylvie, whom he had left some months ago, had called him just before leaping to her death from the fourteenth floor of her high rise on de Maisonneuve and St. Marc. He said that she must have been upset by dinner with him, a quick screw for old time's sake, and her fear that she couldn't make the payment for a new car she had recently purchased.

I was with Elizabeth by this time, and we were spending more and more time together and had even spoken about living together and marriage. I got up at his request and walked though the McGill ghetto in the early hours of the morning while he wept and embraced me, and we had ended up at his apartment on Crescent where I lay tensely awake on the couch until he finally fell asleep, though he did wake several times during the night crying out in despair. I had to go in to soothe him while he clung to me in tears.

After that evening, perhaps out of shame for his "weakness" (as he called it) and vulnerability, Gerald disappeared from my life. I did receive a note from him congratulating me briefly after I had married Elizabeth, but he never came to see either of us, and I heard through the grapevine that he had eventually been shot and killed in Ontario during a cocaine deal gone bad.

How does one sum up a life lived with others, the secrets we all hold in our souls, and the guilt we all carry around with us? Why are we afraid of the very closeness that we seek out in our relationships? Why do we flee from this very closeness to lock ourselves into the image we have created of ourselves to shut out any potential pain?

Dr. Rheinblatt will surely have a lot to say about this if I ever bring it up, but maybe just keeping these stories private yields a place where the heart finds its own memories and meaning.

CHAPTER 10

I realize that I have no photos of my family in the apartment. Where could they have all gone? I try to picture Nico, whom I haven't seen for almost six months. Would he be heavier now, more solid in his manhood? There is only the old album with its brown, tattered cover, and the photos that take me back.

Budapest, the Budapest of my childhood in 1956, was different from the vibrant, modern city it is today in the post-Gorbachev era of former satellite nations. Most of all I remember the city as a grey place, the houses—some of them gutted by the bombing—and the people with downcast eyes, dark suits, shoes with newspapers stuffed into them to provide warmth and to cover the worn soles.

Our flat, what was left of it, had remnants of Biedermeier furniture—a large dining table with only four chairs, a baby-grand piano, some paintings, a large brass bed, some Herendi porcelain, photos of the dead in old-world attire.

For a period of time seven of us shared the flat, slept in the same room, ate together, and dreamed of past times and better days, and of happier times to come. Since my father had the care of my grandmother, a lady in her mid–seventies, we were allowed to receive a package from our relatives in America once a month. There was always great excitement the day the package was delivered. Even though the content was always the same, we tore open the wrappers and feasted our eyes upon the colorful designs and mysterious writing that seemed to even the more cynical adults some cipher of hope for a new beginning.

The package always contained a tin of Nestle's cocoa for us, the children, a carton of Chesterfield cigarettes for my father, and some bars of Zest soap whose smell was an orgy of delight for our noses used to the daily odour of cabbage and boiled potato. The last item was a large plastic bottle of Pepto Bismol that our well-meaning relatives sent to my grandmother who suffered from gastro-intestinal ailments and chronic flatulence. And there was always a note enclosed—a general letter commenting on their life with the added postscript:

"Hope your gas is better, Momma."

My grandmother would read this last part with pleasure, nod her head, look at my father, and say:

"You see, *they* know how to care for me."

Then, she would take her last remaining crystal goblet, fill it meticulously with the prescribed amount of the pink liquid, and slowly sip it as she waddled off toward the bathroom. As we watched her fat rump disappear around the corner, we heard the first series of farts as they subsided into a faint roar that she discreetly obliterated by running the tap.

As soon as it became dark, we'd tack blankets over the windows and huddle together waiting for the inevitable air-raid sirens and hear the big guns as they began the shelling of the city. Occasionally, a rapid burst of machine-gun fire from the resisters would answer the steady boom of the guns, and this was sometimes interspersed with my grandmother's own bowel noises that seemed to mutter an angry response to a world that had upset her security. Her very digestive tract moaned and groaned of better times, of blood-sausage and paprika bacon, of proletariats who knew their place, of the Christian crown of St. István and the one thousand years of Hungarian culture, answering the guns that left our city gaping like her own toothless scowl.

At night, as the rest of our family sat around the kitchen table on old boxes by the light of a solitary candle, we would play our favourite game of charades. We called the game "My Future Profession in America." Each person performing the charade would have to mime the profession he chose and the rest of the players guessed what it was. Since we all felt that America was the land of opportunity, its streets paved with gold, our favourite charade was the one performed by my uncle, who was a natural actor, of the immigrant who arrives in the new-found land and runs around gathering the greenbacks as they scatter like confetti down the mysterious streets of Fifth Avenue, West 42nd Street, and Broadway. Even though we knew the routine by heart, we would take turns guessing every phrase of the story. My uncle called the skit *The Man with the Midas Touch,* after a Hungarian novel of the same name. With pleasure we uttered phrases of what we felt would soon be our new language, gleaned from a book our relatives had sent us some months previously, phrases like:

"Hello. I will now buy this car, ok?" and "Thank you. So much pleasure to do business, yes?"

Even my grandmother sometimes joined us, smiling approvingly, punctuating our language lesson with the occasional intestinal rumble while dreaming of the land of plenty, of fresh fruits, chrome counters, well-stocked grocery shelves, a lifetime supply of Pepto Bismal, and white-smocked internists who knew how to treat a European lady.

One day my father came home after work and the adults sat together for hours whispering. My sister and I could sense their excitement, and we spent a fitful night lulled by the artillery fire yet always aware of the hushed talk that continued far into the night.

The next morning, we dressed hurriedly and boarded a train, carrying with us a few duffel bags and valises. As we watched the city recede into the distance and followed the curves of the Danube passing into the gently rolling farm lands, we knew instinctively that we had left some part of us behind and America, for so long only a whispered word or a child's charade, loomed ahead. After a six-hour journey during which we almost lost my grandmother who had gone off to seek a toilet at some waystation, we disembarked at the village of *Tarcsa* in the area known as *Burgenland* and walked to the house of one of the local farmers.

Once there, my sister and I were sent to bed right after supper and told to sleep, but she and I, snuggled under the eiderdown duvet, heard snatches of the adults' conversation. We heard the words *Andau* and *Austria* and then our father's gruff voice arguing over money. Finally, we drifted off to sleep.

I remember being awakened by my grandmother and told to dress quickly. It was the dead of night and winter. Christmas was just two days away. We gathered around the kitchen stove in the farmer's hut, adjusting our boots and scarves, having a last bite of the rye bread with the bacon drippings and the strong coffee with milk. Then, we began to walk.

We walked for what seemed like hours through cornfields, marshes and snow, saying nothing. It was so still that we heard the ice snapping the corn stalks, so still that our feet crunched through the snow like the staccato of the guns we had left behind.

And then we heard it. The unmistakable sound of marching feet and orders shouted in Russian. Suddenly, the whole sky lit up with flares, what I heard my uncle call "Stalin's lanterns," as he cursed under his breath. We dived, face down into the snow as machine gun bullets ricocheted over our heads. Then, just as suddenly as they had come, the sound of the marching and gunfire faded. There was silence and the rapidly falling flakes of snow.

We walked farther. I was tired and began to cry, so my uncle carried me for a way. At one point, my grandmother said that she would go no farther, that this place was "no place for a lady of her upbringing." My father and uncle pleaded with her, telling her that we were almost at the Austrian border, but she refused to budge. My uncle told me to walk and picked up my grandmother onto his back. We marched onward and eventually saw some lights. There were people, at least twenty of them, lights, and a van with a red cross on it. Everyone was smiling. A man ran toward us, shouting in German: "*Herzliche Willkommen—Herzliche Willkommen!*"

"*Gott sei dank*," my father answered, and it was the first time I had seen him smile in a long time.

We must have looked a sorry sight to these people. My father, unshaven in his Homburg hat, his last vestige of respectability from a former life, two tired and bewildered children, and my uncle with an old lady on his back who drew herself up, adjusting her scarf, while beating time to the noise and laughter with her parasol, punctuating it with occasional bursts of gas and snatches of conversation in her immaculate German.

A man helped us into the van. It was warm, and they gave us American chocolate bars. My sister and I were in heaven! Chocolate! Even though this was not America yet, it seemed just as good. We huddled together in the van and slept, clutching our treasure, heading toward Vienna, about two hours away. We were in the West, free; the streets of the city were sparkling with Christmas lights when they woke us. Our chocolate had melted, but there would be more. Yes, there would be more in America, all the chocolate we could eat—more of everything. All the dignity any European lady could desire.

After a transition period of a few months, which we spent in a former army barrack, we were granted passage to what was to become our new home. We arrived in New York City, waited interminably in line with the other DPs, waded through the mountain of paperwork and red tape, and finally settled in a large, western New York town, Buffalo, to begin our new lives as Americans.

After we had been living in America for about five months, my father decided that it was time for us to go on our first family excursion. He had heard about a beautiful place only forty-five minutes away by bus where we could go for an outing, or what Americans called a "picnic," as he told us proudly, pronouncing his latest linguistic triumph. We'd go on a Saturday and spend the day.

The bus let us off near the large iron gates before the park's entrance. My father led the way, followed by my grandmother, and my sister and I carried the basket and miscellaneous shopping bags.

It was a lovely June day; even my father's usually somber mood had changed and my grandmother's gas seemed under control. We walked for a time through grassy fields interspersed with trees, banks of sand, and small hills. Occasionally, we passed small groups of people holding leather bags containing what looked like sticks and poles, or bending sometimes over the ground intently looking at something. We wondered what they could be staring at and what wonderful goodies their large bags contained. Sometimes these people stared at us rudely as we walked in front of them. We also heard strange noises and shouts—always the same word—followed by grunts and the sound of a large WHACK, followed by a thud and a whistle. We marveled at this strange American ritual, yet another new experience to add to our repertoire of growing impressions.

Finally, after mounting a hill, my father said:

"This is it. This is our spot."

We saw before us a small lake surrounded by a few hills of sand. Off to one spot was a large expanse of green with a tiny red flag in the center of it suspended from a long pole that rested in a hole. The flag bore the number 11 painted in bold black letters and fluttered gently in the breeze.

We walked to the middle of the green and started unloading our food. The grass was shorter here, all evenly cropped, and felt like velvet under our bare feet. My father lifted the flag from its stand, held in place within a small, white cup. He yanked out the flag and threw it onto the nearest mound of sand.

"I've seen enough red flags to last a lifetime," he told my grandmother. "Besides, by removing it we will let the others know that we have claimed this area for our own use."

We sorted through the food, enjoying the warmth of the sun and the quiet. There were the usual lard sandwiches sprinkled with paprika, fried chicken, smoked sausages, cold pork chops, green peppers, and shallots. My father opened a bottle of Tokay wine of which we were allowed small glasses. My grandmother had brought her large parasol, which she stuck into the cup where the red flag had been, to use for shade.

After our meal, she began to complain, as usual. Her stomach was bothering her and she wanted a bathroom. My father said there was none nearby, and suggested that she try the sand over on the far side of the hill. She cast one of her withering looks at him and said that she would wait.

Then, she began to complain that she had gotten food stuck in her dentures. She removed them and told me to go and rinse them for her in the nearby lake. Horrified, I ran to the water, holding her teeth at arm's length and dipped them into the dirty water. I was surprised to see some change and a few small white balls below the surface. I called to my sister and we fished out some of the balls and the money, glorying in our find. Meanwhile, we had placed her dentures on the edge of the green to dry in the sun.

Some distance across the lake we saw two men approaching. They were bent over something white, swinging large sticks. They saw us watching them and waved, shouting. We waved back.

We heard the sound of a WHACK and a small, white orb sailed toward us and landed into the water with a large splash. We saw one of the men throw his stick to the ground and grab at his hair.

Then, we heard the second WHACK and saw the white orb whizzing toward us, straight and true. We had just enough time to duck out of the way and watched in horror as the ball struck my grandmother's dentures and bound up to the hill where my father and grandmother were sitting. The ball thudded into the cup just as my grandmother's teeth shattered and flew in a hundred different directions. The man across the water was dancing and shouting, waving his stick, gesticulating to his companion. From the top of the hill I heard my father curse as the white ball came flying back toward us, landing in the water. The man who had been dancing before seemed rooted to his spot, staring. He shook his head in seeming disbelief, then started running toward us.

We were taken to a police station and questioned. There was a picture of a bald, smiling man above the Sergeant's desk that bore the legend *I Like Ike.*

Amidst much shouting and excitement, other policemen gathered around, staring at us. The two men with the sticks shook their fingers at us and shouted at the police. We understood only brief snatches of their screams:

"A goddamn hole in one...."

"Picnicking on a golf course...."

Then there was some discussion as to whether we were Reds, whether the minions of former Senator Joseph McCarthy should know about this.

My sister and I tried to translate for my father the best we could. Red-faced from embarrassment, we told them about the Hungarian Revolution and 1956, about my father who was familiar with prison, the Gestapo, and the A.V.H., the Hungarian Secret Police. We told them we were new Americans, that we didn't have golf in our country, and my grandmother needed to get home and attend to her bowels.

The crowd of people stared at us in disbelief. Finally, the supervising officer told us that we were allowed to leave and reminded us to appear in court in three days.

We walked out of the police station: my father, his face pale and set, my sister, and myself, followed, finally, by my grandmother, mastering all of her dignity. Outside, there was a poster of Uncle Sam whose finger and gaze followed our every move. *Uncle Sam wants YOU*, the poster read.

We took the bus home in silence and went back to our cheap, cold-water flat and unpacked our stuff. My grandmother drank her Pepto and confined herself to bed for two days.

CHAPTER 11

Exiles. Shelley and Byron in Italy. Joyce in Trieste. Wilde and Beckett in Paris. Auden in Austria. Márai in Switzerland, and then in California. It always fascinated me how exile somehow made Ireland live as recalled memory for Joyce, and even Beckett's Unnamable speaks with an Irish lilt. How is it that their exile gave such a rich tapestry to their imagination? Of course, I don't count myself in their company, but I have also lived in exile; in fact, I have twice been exiled, first from Eastern Europe, and then from the United States.

I arrived in Canada with green hair, the result of a bucket of house paint landing on my head. Shortly before I was called in for induction into the United States Army, I was painting my friend Lee's house, having been hired by his father out of some pity, I suppose. Lee was on the high ladder, while I, notoriously afraid of heights, was painting the trim along the porch. We had spent the afternoon smoking hash, and had rashly decided to make a half-hearted effort at working so that his father, when he came home, wouldn't think we had wasted our day.

Smoking hash and then painting, I don't need to emphasize, can be hazardous. In our case, Lee started laughing at something I'd said, laughing so hard that he tipped the bucket and a huge splotch of paint had landed directly on my head, covering the left side of my hair, face, and shoulders. I'd tried to wash it off, but it was oil-based, so the next day, when I walked into the induction center, I wore my green Army jacket with matching green locks that reached past my shoulder.

The look on the Sergeant's face registered incredulity, followed by disgust. When it was my turn to approach, he glared at me:

"So, tomorrow we'll cut off all that hair and make a soldier of you... teach you the real meaning of 'green.'" He then murmured under his breath as he filled out my papers: "Goddam faggot..." I was now officially 1-A, fit for military service. All that remained was the final step, where we were taken into a room and asked to pledge an oath of loyalty to the United States, to promise to serve and protect that nation. When it came time for me to take the oath, I refused. Two noncoms looked at me in disbelief, one of them clenching a fist as if he wanted to drive it down my throat.

"You realize what this means?" the other asked, in a tone cold as ice.

"Yes... yes, I do."

"You realize that you are in violation of section Z5204 of the Conscription Act, and that legal action can and will be taken against you?"

"Yes... I suppose..."

"You realize that you have twenty-four hours to change your mind, to report for duty tomorrow afternoon by no later than 3:00 p.m., or, failing that, there will be a warrant for your arrest put out by the District Attorney of the State of New York?"

"Ok."

"Ok WHAT?"

"Ok... SIR?"

"That's all. When you come back tomorrow, you will come back as a soldier, ready to do your duty. UNDERSTOOD?"

"I'm not deaf.... SIR."

"What did you say? GET THE FUCK OUT OF MY SIGHT, YOU PIECE OF DRIED UP SHIT BEFORE I TEAR YOU A NEW ASSHOLE.... DISMISSED."

I left the induction center and walked to the flat I shared with four of my friends. That night, we went for drinks at our favourite bar, "Brinks." I paid for drinks all around, even for the old hustler, Charlie Brown, the guy who always ate a stick of butter before coming out to drink and hustle the guys at pool. Claimed it kept him sober, though his eyeballs were a vicious yellow tint.

The next day I slept in until almost noon. Everyone had gone from the flat, out to work or classes. I looked at all of my books: Wallace Stevens' *Collected Poems,* my Auden, Mann, Proust, the others, all the voices that had been ringing in my ears those past years. I packed a green rucksack, the one I had used on my first trip to Europe, and two books: Hart Crane's *Collected Poems* and *The Jade Mountain.* I took a bus down Niagara Street to where the Peace Bridge walkway began. When I got to the Ontario side, a disinterested Customs Officer asked me how long I would be in Canada and barely listened to my stammered reply. He let me through the turnstile, green hair and all. I had just around eighteen dollars left in my wallet.

It wasn't hard to hitchhike in those days to Toronto, and, later east along the 401. I got two rides in rapid succession, the first to Kingston, and the next to Montreal. In the short space of 12 hours, I had gone from being almost a soldier to a longhaired, ex-American, now twice exiled. I rang the bell at my older brother's flat (he had left Hungary before us and emigrated to Canada) in NDG. He opened it and stared at me in amused disbelief.

"Well, I'll be damned," he said. "My little *bruder*...look at your hair...welcome to Canada, the coldest place on earth, home of polar bears, igloos, draft dodgers, and all the assholes in the world that no other nation would take."

My hiatus with my brother was brief. He has just gone through a messy divorce and had custody of his two boys, ages five and three. I was the designated baby sitter while he was at work; in return, I received food, a couch to sleep on, and a ration of cigarettes.

When the boys were in daycare, I wandered the city streets and was shocked to discover that Montreal was French, beautiful, vibrant, and totally inaccessible to me. I had no job, no money, and no prospects. Even my green hair had been clipped by an Italian barber who mumbled curses to himself as he cut.

My brother was a man with plans, always on the make, always looking for the big score. He told me:

"There are millions of morons on this earth, and I have been put on this earth specifically to exploit them."

One day, some three weeks after I had arrived, he came home and said he wanted to talk to me.

"I've bought 10 acres of land just north of St. Jérôme, around an hour and a half from Montreal. Cost me $800.00. Place is between New Glasgow and St. Calixe, or St. Câlisse, as the locals up there call it. We're going up there this weekend to start the digging."

"What digging?"

"For the pond. I'm gonna make a trout hatchery in the woods. Dig a lake and put in 6-inch fingerlings, young trout. If they're fed daily, they grow 2 inches a month. By October, they'll be ready to sell to restaurants. Big bucks for fresh fish."

"What do you know about fish?"

"What's there to know? You feed the motherfuckers for five months and then you fish them out. Easy."

"Who's going to feed them?"

"Guess! YOU. I'm sick the fuck of feeding you and watching you feel sorry for yourself. It's time you got to work. We leave on Saturday."

I arrived on the "Land," as we called it, in early May and lived there until mid-October. It was in the middle of nowhere, half a mile from the nearest village and next to a large abandoned sand-pit. My brother called in a bulldozer and they excavated a pond that filled up with greenish, murky water into which he put three thousand trout fingerlings, purchased from a local hatchery. Within a month, great pools of algae had formed on the pond, and due to the hot, humid summer and the lack of rain for almost eight weeks, I watched the level of the pond recede daily. Yet the fish seemed to thrive, and it was my job to feed them twice a day with Purina Trout Chow, something that I initially thought was a joke, but proved to be their food of choice.

I lived in the woods in a one-room cabin that we had built. The floor was plywood, and there was no furniture, only a one-burner Franklin stove, a blow-up rubber mattress and my sleeping bag. There was no outhouse, so I had to shit in the woods. I got water from the brook and walked to the village daily to get my food since nothing could be stored near the house because of raccoons and skunks. At night, I would walk into the sandpit and listen to the coyotes and wolves howling in the distance. It was some Walden.

The only person I saw almost daily was an old man, Phileas Lachance, who lived in a cabin just a bit larger than mine around a quarter mile into the woods. He was a *chômeur,* on welfare, and ran an illegal trap line where he caught rabbit and partridge, which he sold in the village to the locals. Each Saturday night, someone from his family would come by with a case of twenty-four, and they'd drink far into the night, laughing, screaming, and sometimes firing off a volley of buckshot into the sandpit. After a few weeks, Phileas asked me to join them, although it was mostly with hand gestures and grunts that I was able to answer him since my French was non-existent. Then, it became a ritual. I would go at least once a week and sit and listen to his strange patois, rapid fire rants, spoken through loose dentures and constant cigarette fumes. Slowly I started learning French, though I now know that it was mostly swearing directed at the Church and all the saints in its colorful history.

Old Phileas sold me a rifle, telling me that you needed one in this part of the world. It was an old Lee Enfield, bolt action, with a clip of six bullets that were the size of the trout fingerlings. The one and only occasion I had to use it was late one summer Friday night. The sandpit near my cabin, which was hidden in the woods, was a place for lovers and car thieves. On many occasions, while going out for an evening walk, I saw cars parked near one of the eerily surreal dunes and heard noises of lovemaking. The first time this happened, I went with my flashlight and gun and shined the light into the car, only to see a man's hairy ass bobbing up and down, followed by two terrified faces looking up at me as they scrambled to throw on their clothes and drive off, the gravel screaming under their tires.

The others who came were the car thieves from St. Jérôme. They would often arrive in two cars, theirs and the stolen vehicle. One night, I heard them moving the gate as they were getting ready to drive into the sand pit. I came out of the woods, obviously startling them, and shined the large flashlight in their direction, screaming in bad French that they were trespassing. In response, one of them pulled out a small pistol and opened fire in my direction. It was probably no more than a pellet gun, but I was so scared that I ran back to the cabin and returned with the Enfield. As they stood by the tree doing something with the first car, I approached in the dark through the woods. Suddenly, there was a huge noise, a flash of fire, and the car exploded in a great display of debris. They had apparently thrown something into the gas tank and ignited it for fun. When I saw this, I yelled at the two men standing by a large Scotch pine some twenty meters from where I was hidden. They looked in my direction, swore, and I could hear the *pop, pop, pop* of the pellet gun. I put the Enfield to my shoulder and aimed at a tree branch above their heads and pulled the trigger. The kick of the rifle was so strong that it almost broke my jaw. I saw a huge flame exit from the barrel and heard the crack of the branch that came crashing down on their heads. Screaming in terror, they ran back to their cars and raced away toward the village.

Terrified, panting, I remained in place, yet exhilarated, for about ten minutes until there was only the silence of the woods, the moonlight, and the cool breeze. I walked back to my cabin where I shivered in my sleeping bag, awake until the dawn, listening to the crack of twigs and the sounds of foreign life all around me.

CHAPTER 12

It is a Wednesday and my weekly appointment with Dr. Rheinblatt. I arrive downtown early, get off at the Peel Metro, and walk west along Sherbrooke. A beautiful spring day, the cafés are filled with the Montreal sun-worshippers, people starved for warmth after the unbearably long winter. Everyone is smoking, drinking, flirting and into the second hour of their lunch break. I think that you would never see this in most large cities, where everyone is bustling back to the office to work and produce, and realize again why I love Montreal. I pass the Musée des Beaux Arts featuring an exhibit of Inuit sculpture. With two hours to kill, I contemplate going in. I stand by the doors and suddenly remember Maria.

I met her in the most unlikely of places, the Flemish room of the Musée while I was pondering the Bruegels, killing time. I had returned to Montreal from the "Land" and was between jobs. Stepping back to admire a landscape by Jan, the son, I felt the soft yield of female buttocks brush my own as she too was lost in her own ruminations. We both smiled awkwardly at each other until I ventured:

"That one is by the son, you know. It looks like a good attempt at the *Kermes.*"

She nodded in agreement and later, as if by unspoken consent, we met outside on the wooden benches at the corner of Sherbrooke and Bishop. I took her to a small Hungarian café, the Coffee Mill, on de la Montagne and ordered their *fatányéros,* six different types of meat and sausages broiled or fried, served on a wooden plate with a huge skewer in the middle to impale the food with a mountain of roast potatoes settled near the bottom. For dessert I had their *Rigó Jancsi* and she the *Lúdláb,* a sinfully rich confection of whipped cream, cherries, pastry, and rum liquor. She told me her name, Maria, and that she was in her first year of medical studies at McGill, recently arrived from the U.S. Classes were starting next week, and she'd been in town just three weeks, taking this time to explore Montreal and get a feel for the downtown.

Maria was an enthusiastic eater, matching me bite for bite and even downing a second cup of the strong espresso. After, I gallantly offered to pay for the meal, and while she waited by the door, I pretended to go back for something I thought I had left behind, but actually returned to a different empty table to pilfer the tip left by another diner. I graciously handed our waitress who was at the cash a $5.00 tip and walked outside with Maria into the bright August sunshine.

She lived in a large 4½ on the third floor of an old triplex on Aylmer in the then cheap McGill student ghetto. Her apartment had what could be called "great potential," but she had done nothing to change its barrenness. Chipped plaster hung from the ceiling, the walls were a hideous combination of blue and orange, boxes of books and clothes were strewn everywhere. The kitchen sink was full of stacked, unwashed dishes with a bulbous, mouldy growth like some tumor sprouting from a pot that had contained a palatable stew in happier days.

She smiled at my astonishment and went to the fridge, took out a bottle of half–finished wine with the cork floating inside, rinsed out two glasses, and poured. She led me to the bedroom which consisted of two single mattresses pushed together covered with a tangle of blankets, sheets, books, and dirty clothes. She swept the mess off the bed and placed the bottle of wine on the hardcover of *A Textbook of Pathology*. Then, she took off her blouse, her skirt, and her panties to stand smiling before me, naked.

"So, let's make love," she said brightly, adding, "that is, if you have nothing better to do."

I didn't. Home was an apartment in NDG just on the wrong side of the Westmount border on Claremont Avenue that I was sharing with Judit. Judit was a Hungarian refugee, a true DP from behind the Iron Curtain. She had defected to Canada while visiting her sister and now lived on the $150.00 per week subsidy that the Québec Government gave to immigrants provided they attended French courses six and one-half hours per day, five days per week. She spoke no French or English and we had been introduced because I spoke Magyar, English, and some French, was myself a refugee, albeit from the more immediate chaos of Vietnam and the U.S., and we both needed to share a place to afford accommodations. The arrangement was supposed to be strictly Platonic, at Judit's sister's insistence.

Which, for me, it unhappily was.

The day we moved in, her relations set up a queen-size bed in one room with an old oak dresser and a comfortable armchair in the corner. They also donated a kitchen table, four chairs, pots and pans, two throw rugs, some cushions, and a short-wave radio so she could listen to the broadcasts from home.

For my part, I brought a knapsack of clothes, a sleeping bag, an inflatable mattress, a collection of Chinese poems in translation, and an espresso maker with a five–pound tin of Mario espresso coffee.

During our first month together, we rarely met since Judit was either off at school or with her relatives. When we did meet on the occasional weekend, it was to drink endless cups of coffee, smoke the Export "A"s I rolled myself, and talk about the writings of Karl Marx.

Despite having fled Communism, Judit was an avowed Marxist. She had left Hungary, she insisted, not for ideological or political reasons, but simply because she and her then boyfriend had been on a five-year waiting list for an apartment that had been denied them at the last moment. She still believed in the historical imperative, that religion was the opiate of the masses, that the workers would one day rise to slaughter the bourgeoisie, and that hetaerism (extramarital sexual intercourse between men and unmarried women) was steadily developing into open prostitution.

In vain I tried to reassure her that I was unmarried, and even after this failed, I told her that I wanted to simply share a meager third of her bed not for licentious purposes, but simply to rest my aching back since my air mattress had fallen into disrepair and permanently deflated.

All to no avail, but then came the different men.

At first it was Maghdi, an Egyptian in his thirties. Then, Ediz from Turkey, followed by Won Jun from Korea, Carlos from El Salvador, Jean–Baptist from Haiti, Guptal from Bangladesh, and others.

Each night, I heard different men cry out in different exclamations of pleasure, from the sharp guttural of the Arabic, to the high-pitched whine of the Korean. The constant staccato drumming of the bed frame against my wall was some form of cruel derision as I vainly tried to sleep on the hard, wooden floor, tortured by longing.

When I asked Judit why I couldn't join her in bed, she laughed contemptuously, saying that these others were victims of the capitalist, imperialistic wrongdoers who had raped their countries, their very souls, and it was her duty to provide them with some solace and comfort in their exile.

On the day when I first met Maria, I decided to leave. I had paid Judit my share of next September's rent. Unemployed, having been laid off from my latest attempt at sales with around $50.00 in my pocket, for the first time, oddly, I had hope for the future. I had strolled along Sherbrooke, feeling the wonderful August heat, until I came to the museum and decided to kill a few hours to think about what to do with my life, which now lay unfolding before me.

I have always been a great admirer of Jung, believing in synchronicity, signs, and symbols. Art spoke to me, as did books, literature. Strolling along Sherbrooke that day, I remembered the two poems by Auden and Williams about the Bruegel paintings. I knew that Montreal had none by the Elder, but the sons were no slouches. So it was I met Maria.

Maria had a female cat named Mitzi and a small black male she called 'Ti Guy in an attempt to immerse herself in Montreal's French aura. When I made love to her, the two cats would come into the room and watch us. Usually, after a few minutes, 'Ti Guy would become angry and jump on Mitzi furiously, biting her on the scruff of the neck and trying to hump her. The problem was that he was too short. His little bright–red dick would poke out, but try as he might, he could never work it in.

Mitzi was a vixen of the worst order. She would always be in heat and go around cooing like a demented pigeon with her ass up in the air. Eventually, she took to going outside onto the roof and disappearing for the entire night, returning in the morning completely filthy or with a dead bird that she would proudly offer her owner. 'Ti Guy would wait up for her like some cuckolded husband. After a few days, he gave up trying to hump her. Maria was cat obsessed, though both cats were wary of her and avoided her whenever possible. She would grab them and force them to sit

in her lap while we watched TV, or sometimes she would brush
their teeth to remove the plaque, as she said. They each had their
own toothbrushes. Soft bristle. The fourth day after I had moved
in, Maria said:

"You can stay as long as you want, but I have to clear it with
my roommate."

"Thanks." I was relieved. Anything was better than Judit and
her international bordello of lovers and that hard, wooden floor.

A few days later, the roommate arrived. Her name was Yolande
from South Africa. She was half Boer and half French from Cape
Town, also there to study medicine at McGill. She and Maria had
apparently met at Philip Exeter, the prep school in New Hampshire
where they had both studied.

Yolande was thin, pale, and attractive, a study in contrast to
Maria's voluptuous Italian build. She always wore long dresses that
appeared Victorian and kept her hair in a bun. She had poor vision,
so she wore wire-rimmed glasses and spoke in a soft, muted accent.
She seemed very shy when Maria introduced us.

"This here is Stephen. He's going to be staying for a bit. He has
no place to go. I hope that's ok with you." This last statement was
not a question but a declaration.

"Hi," I said. "Nice to meet you. I hope that's ok?" There was a
long pause. "You'll hardly know I'm here."

"All right," Yolande replied softly. Then, she went into her room
and closed the door.

Classes started up, and suddenly the girls became busy. Maria,
especially, did everything fast and furiously, as if there was a deadline
for all activities. She ate quickly, almost violently, and could study for
hours on end. She had a photographic memory and could remember the minutest detail of her anatomy text. She made me quiz her

endlessly on all the bones of the human body. Sometimes, lying in bed she would touch each part of me and tell me the Latin names.

Yolande, on the other hand, kept to herself, mostly locking herself in her room to study. The only time she had spoken to me was when she asked me to come with her to pick up the second–hand VW Rabbit that she bought with the money from her trust fund at the dealer's near the Metropolitain. She had never driven a standard, so she asked me to drive the car home for her and to give her some lessons after.

Yolande and I talked a bit riding the 17 bus up Decarie. She told me about her father, a radiation oncologist, her mother, an artist, and how she missed South Africa, the sun, the servants, and the slow life. Montreal, she had heard, was terrible in the winter, somewhat like New Hampshire where she had already experienced the northern cold. Becoming shy about having revealed so much, she continued to look out the window until we came to our stop.

When we got off near the dealership, we were by the Decarie Circle, and I saw the building just near the ramp leading to Boulevard Marcel Laurin. The sign on the top read "MULTIDIC."

I couldn't help myself, so I started laughing.

"What is it, what's so funny?" she asked.

"That. The sign there. MULTIDIC. What do you think they manufacture there?"

"Dildos?" She said this with a straight face, and then we both collapsed.

I finally blurted out: "What's the company slogan? 'Every woman should have one; every man wishes he had'?" We both howled at this, and she swayed against me so that I involuntarily touched her arm. Yolande blushed and drew back. Then, she adjusted her hair, and we walked toward the dealership.

The paperwork took just over an hour, and then we were heading down the 15 South toward the Villa Marie tunnel in silence. I stole a glance at her as I shifted into third and let out the clutch. Yolande had her face turned away from me and was watching the traffic in the middle lane. She had a habit of grasping her thumb between her index and middle fingers when she was shy or nervous. I noticed this time that her thumb was red from the pressure and her normally pale skin was pinker with some beads of sweat down the long curve of her neck.

When we got back, Maria was studying in bed, eating a head of lettuce, leaf by leaf, as she flipped the pages of her anatomy text. It was a warm day, a perfect Indian summer, and the French windows leading to the roof were open. Mizi was asleep near the ledge in the sun, and 'Ti Guy was curled up on a pillow. Maria wore a red T-shirt and panties. She was on her stomach, and her legs were wide apart, the shirt hitched up just to the bottom of a round cheek.

I closed the door and undressed, knelt down and started kissing my way up from the bottoms of each calf to the point where her thighs rounded into her ass. I noticed the dark patch of hair through the panties and drew the elastic back to one side, revealing a cheek and her pubic region. I slowly inserted one finger. She was already moist, and I gently bit into one of her cheeks. Marie slowly raised her hips, then resettled herself, and tore another leaf of lettuce and put it into her mouth, pretending to ignore me.

Slowly, I pulled the panties off until they were down over one ankle. I hiked up her shirt until her broad back was revealed and ran my tongue from the crack of her ass up her spine. I carefully moved her long hair to the side and kissed the nape of her neck and moved my knee between her open legs, applying slight pressure. I then slid my left hand up her side and cupped one breast, feeling the hardening nipple.

I was hard now, the head of my penis wet from anticipation. I moved it slowly over each cheek, letting the hardness spring against her flesh and then slowly brushed the tip against her anus and finally below against the soft hairs of her sex. Marie flipped another page, still ignoring me, but she had opened her legs slightly and rotated her hips to meet me. Then, suddenly, I grasped her and half of my cock slid into her as she let out a sigh.

Maria bucked up on all fours, lifting me half up in the air as she groaned:

"Come on, give it to me.... HARD!"

I knelt straight up, my hands clutching each of her hips, and I drove into her again and again. Her shirt had slid up almost to her neck and her full breasts with the erect nipples swung back and forth with each thrust.

But a frantic scratching at the bedroom door distracted me. 'Ti Guy had jumped off the pillow and, frightened by the violence and noise of our lovemaking, was desperately trying to run out of the bedroom. I pulled my penis out and said:

"Don't go away. Hold that thought."

My erection poking out in front of me like an absurd exclamation point, I opened the door to let the cat out. Standing there, I saw Yolande in a short nightdress by the door of her room, staring at me, at my swollen member.

Both of her hands were clutched tightly into fists, with both digits red from pressure, like two buttons of desire.

CHAPTER 13

I must make an absurd picture. A man past the cusp of sixty, not undistinguished, in a tweed jacket and casual cords, standing in the middle of Sherbrooke Street before the art museum, eyes squinting tightly shut with the memory, a semi-hard on in his pants. I shake the web of the years away, pull out my pocket watch, and realize it is time to head up the hill. I turn up Simpson and pass the Trafalgar school and see the young girls coming out in their short uniforms. I pass the park and what used to be the Polish consulate across from the dog walk, and then turn right along Pine Avenue, past the Trudeaus' art-deco home until I come to the corner of Peel where I follow the long drive into the Allen.

With my usual trepidation, I enter Ward 4 East toward Dr. Rheinblatt's office. When I was first brought in on that fatal day, I was hardly aware of where I was, my stomach having just freshly been pumped, hooked up to oxygen and an IV, a megadose of Largactil or Lithium, I forget which, coursing through my veins. I was put into restraints the first two nights and kept in a private room. When they saw that I had no further intention of harming myself, they put me in a semi-private room with a man from El Salvador, a Mr. Ramon El Barquez, who spoke only Spanish and a smattering of French. Like me, Senor El, as we came to call him, had tried to end his life. Something about a wife who had left him, a friend who had become her lover, longing for the old country, the usual. He was not very talkative, but the clearest memory I have of him is late one night when he tried to escape, having realized that a steady dose of therapy, depressants, and enforced leisure was not for him.

Around two in the morning Senor El woke me with his agitated mumbling and swearing. I watched him in his Johnny-shirt slowly sneak along the corridor until he came to the glassed-in nursing station near our room. When he arrived there, he got down on all fours and crept like some nocturnal animal just under the glass to avoid detection. However, halfway down the hall, the night orderly, a tall lug named Tony, came up to him and firmly took his arm to lead him back to our room. This was fairly standard procedure, as confused and medicated patients would do this all the time. I heard Senor El tell Tony that it was ok, that he was going to go back to bed peacefully. But then, Tony made the mistake of letting go of his arm.

At that moment, despite his rather diminutive size, Senor El struck Tony full on the side of the head with a wild haymaker, and as Tony went down, Senor El made a run for the door, his privates flapping in the breeze as Tony sounded the Code Blue to summon help. When Senor El was brought back in a straightjacket, we all learned that he had actually run down the four flights of stairs until Tony jumped him and grabbed his Johnny-shirt. At this juncture, Senor El slid out of his shirt and, buck-naked, ran out the front doors down along Pine Avenue until he turned down McTavish. At the corner of McTavish and Dr. Penfield, Tony finally apprehended him, not before some startled motorists coming home from a night out almost ran into the concrete embankment near the McGill Student Union Building. Once he was subdued, Senor El became completely passive, crumpling in a heap on the sidewalk where Tony sat on him until reinforcements arrived.

I smile as I think of this turning into Dr. Rheinblatt's waiting room. At 3:00 p.m. precisely, the door opens, and I am summoned into the inner sanctum. His office is bright and airy with a nice Persian on the floor, some comfortable chairs and a sofa, his large oak desk, and shelves of book. I automatically scan them, though I have been here many times before, and notice Freud's massive biography next to another volume entitled *Love's Body*.

I am struck, once again, by how he is always impeccably attired. I think he fancies himself somewhat of a dandy. He has stylish, tinted glasses, so it is hard to read the expression in his dark, birdlike eyes. He always sits behind his massive desk, keeping a professional distance from his patients, one hand occasionally stroking an onyx paperweight, the other in his lap. For some reason, I think about what he must look like naked, his thin torso covered by thickly matted hair that most likely curls along his back ending in tufts in his rather large, bat-like ears. He is not unlike a better-looking version of Nosferatu, without the claws.

"Come in, sit down, Mister... I mean Doctor.... Stephen, isn't it?" Dr. Rheinblatt knows I have a Ph.D. and wants to remind me of this, as if the mere uttering of the title will somehow erase everything that has happened. He had also learned that TRUST is an important factor in doctor/patient relationships, hence the first name.

"How have you been this past week?" he continues.

"Managing, thanks. It's a lovely day today, so I went for a walk downtown. Almost made it to the museum before our meeting."

"Still taking the meds on schedule? No adverse affects?"

"Dry mouth and grogginess, and I haven't had a real hard-on in days." Dr. Rheinblatt ignores my last remark, but writes something on a pad.

"And how have you spent your days?"

"Not doing very much. Some reading, though it is hard to concentrate. I go for long walks when the weather is nice. Some music, mostly jazz, the lighter stuff, Brubeck, Bill Evans, Grappelli.... the favourites..."

"And your family?"

"My son, you mean?"

"Yes."

"We spoke. He's coming to see me at the end of his term. He's fine. I think he has stopped worrying so much about me."

"Oh? And why should he not be worrying?"

"Because I'm in good hands." Here, I graciously sweep my hand in his direction.

"Tell me how you're feeling today, right now."

"Actually, I have a question for you." At this, Dr. Rheinblatt almost smiles, clutching his pen, poised over his pad and leans forward in anticipation. He raises his eyebrow, prompting me to continue.

"Why do you have no Jung in your office? Not even the *Portable*?"

"Why do you ask that?"

"Because we all could use more Jung. More spirit, religion, soul. More synchronicity."

"Tell me more."

"Ever read *The Magus,* by John Fowles? No? You really should you know. It's about finding the mysterious core of life and love. I believe Fowles read Jung; certainly, it's evident in the wonderful trial scene near the end of the book. As did Robertson Davies. Ever read *The Manticore*?"

"Let's talk about you, not these books."

"But these books are me, or at least an integral part of who I am and how I see the world. I talk about them for a living, you know. I also read them because they perhaps have some secrets to be deciphered. Fowles really understood the ridiculous vanity of the shells we erect around us to protect ourselves."

"Like you with your books, perhaps?"

"Touché. Chalk up one for the Good Guys."

"Why the hostility?"

"Hostility is good, no? Passivity or apathy is what you and your profession distrust the most, isn't that true?" He ignores this last remark and says:

"Tell me about the talk with your son."

"Well, he is worried about me. He wants to come, but doesn't really want to. Full of ambivalence, which is the price of deep love, I guess?"

"Do you love your son, Nicholas, is it?"

"What kind of question is that?"

"Well, do you? A simple answer will do."

"Of course, I do. I named him after the hero of the Fowles novel, after all."

Dr. Rheinblatt does not find this funny, and writes something on his pad. We fall into an uncomfortable silence, him watching me.

"You know, I do realize that we have to do this to keep my long-term disability going," I finally say.

"Have you thought about possibly going back to work?"

"That's an unfair question. Our term is ending, and then the long summer. I just want to be a cat on a hot tin roof and warm my sorry behind before thinking about inspiring young minds again."

Dr. Rheinblatt is silent, but continues to look at me as he scribbles on his pad.

"Ok. I apologize. My son. How is he? Worried? Concerned? All of the above. I feel as guilty as shit for hurting him. I hope he never thinks I don't love him."

"Then why did you do what you did?"

"Are we talking in euphemisms again? Why not say 'tried to kill yourself'?"

"OK. Then why?"

"I guess citing Kierkegaard and Camus are out?"

"Just tell me in your own words," Dr. Rheinblatt almost sighs.

"There's this great poem I used to teach to my students, by Phyllis Webb. Called "To Friends Who Have Also Considered Suicide." Wait, before you tell me again to leave off the books and poetry and to answer directly. I always loved, needed preambles. I used them to start my classes, to built up to the 'truths,' as it were. So, can you indulge me?"

"Go on."

"Anyway. Phyllis Webb. Where was I? Ah, yes. She says: '*In the end it brings more honesty and care/than all the democratic parliaments of tricks.*'"

"And what do those words mean to you?"

"That living with the knowledge of our death can also be authentic and somehow redemptive. To walk daily with death or the knowledge of our death, and to know that we are not lonely."

"I don't follow."

"I feel I'm teaching a poetry class that's not unfolding very well. What I mean, in simple terms, is that I wanted to find out if I had the courage to try this possibility."

"Courage?"

"Yes, that. And also, to feel what it would feel like after, to re-enter the trembling fragility of my own flesh and thoughts. Like some Lazarus come back from the dead, as Sylvia Plath wrote... sorry. I'll stop, if you stop writing every time I mention literature."

"Anything else?"

"Yes, I also know that books are a kind of Freudian displacement to hide the latent content. I've read him too. But the latent content is despair, if you really want to know."

"Despair. About the breakup of your marriage?"

"That, too, I suppose, but despair of another kind."

"Yes?" Dr. Rheinblatt looks interested for the first time.

"I hate to bring it all back to the books, but feeling the despair that Kafka felt to write his bizarre works. The despair of Keats knowing that he was writing against time. Hart Crane seeking the embrace of the Caribbean waters. Also, Whitman when he wrote his last poems about the delicious embrace of death. Despair about the death of the artistic imagination, about how the artistic spirit vanishes, unnoticed in the waves as the merchant ship sails calmly by."

I am greatly excited as I am telling him this. Dr. Rheinblatt is writing furiously now, and for the first time in a long time I laugh, which must sound to him like a maniac's guffaw, but for me it is a welcome summons back to my life.

CHAPTER 14

Our session has ended on a sour note, but for some reason I'm happy, happier than I have been in a long time. Laughter can do that to a person. It is truly a lovely spring day, and I feel giddy from it, perhaps the result of the medication finally working or my meeting with the good doctor. I cross Pine Avenue and wait along the divide where Doctor Penfield intersects it across from the Royal Vic, and I am suddenly struck by the memory of standing there with Elizabeth holding her hand, wanting to tell her, as if it were some unique discovery, that I love her. It must have been a romantic moment with all the traffic whizzing by, two lovers oblivious to the carnage of the rush–hour world.

What do I feel? The beginning of feelings, some strange memory beyond all of the drugs, beginning in the gut and finding visceral longing in the tremors of my hands? I cross the divide in the momentary lull of traffic and jump onto the 144 bus that has just stopped at the corner of University. I stand with the early rush hour crowd, the McGill students going off to their digs in the Plateau, the Greek and Portuguese hospital workers finishing their day shifts and heading off to their paid-up triplexes on Colonial, Esplanade, and St. Urbain.

I get off at the corner of St. Laurent and Pine and contemplate strolling along these familiar streets. A right and a quick left will take me to Prince Arthur and perhaps the Mazurka for supper, but it's too early. Instead, I go left along the Main, up past where the St. Lawrence Bakery used to be, across from the old Warsaw's, now a pharmacy, past the stone monuments with the Hebrew script that is still the same after twenty-five years when I first worked on this street.

More synchronicity. I was broke after living with Maria and Yolande for a month and hadn't contributed for some days to the food or rent. I had damned near given up trying to find something, since jobs were scarce and my French was barely functional when I saw the sign outside Brown's Department store on the Main during one of my long walks around the city. And there it was, a notice in the window, in English and French:

Wanted, short order cook, delivery man, all purpose kitchen help. Spoken French and English. Some knowledge of German helpful.

I was directed up to the fourth floor where I met Herr and Frau Schoendorf. The interview was conducted in German, and I made an attempt to speak my best and most correct. Herr Schoendorf said:

"You work ten to six, Monday-Wednesday, ten to nine on Thursday-Friday, weekends off. The store is closed Saturdays. Jews, you know." When he said the word, "*Juden,*" he almost spat it out.

He continued: "You will help my wife with the cooking. At lunch there will be sandwiches and two hot dishes. Then there are deliveries to the salesmen in the store, all four floors. You will also take coffee to the back room for the peddlers who play cards there." At this, Herr Schoendorf chuckled. I realized that he had made a joke, and so I smiled uncomfortably. Schoendorf had called them "*bettler*" with his Hanover accent. I remembered that "*bettler*" meant beggar.

"Any questions?"

"No, I think I get it. *Ich verstehe.* I understand."

"*Und du, Liebchen, was denkst du?*" But Frau Shoendorf, a sad, silent woman, had nothing to say. She nodded noncommittally and went back to cutting up tomatoes.

Herr Schoendorf walked me to the door.

"You start Monday. Be here on time."

"Yes. Of course. And thank you. *Danke vielmals. Bis Montag. Auf Wiedersehen.*"

I walked out onto St. Lawrence Boulevard and took a right on Prince Arthur toward McGill. Even though it was early afternoon, the streets were full of students walking with friends, their arms laden with books. Pretty girls, girls in flowery skirts, long hair, and no bras. I came to La Cité at the corner of Avenue du Parc and Milton and walked into the local SAQ. I had a few dollars left, Maria, an apartment with two cats and Yolande. And now a job. Feeling expansive, I bought a bottle of Mateus and a bottle of Chateau Cartier. I had just over two dollars left to my name.

Each day between ten and eleven, it was my job to buy the rolls, cream cheese, and Danish. First, I would go to the St. Lawrence Bakery where I bought Kaisers, onion rolls, rye, and the cheese and poppy seed Danishes. They all had to be Kosher. Then, I went to Biederman's butcher shop near Duluth where a thin old man wearing a blood–stained apron and a black *kippah* would give me the order of meat for the day.

"I'm here to pick up the veal that was ordered," I told Biederman.

Biederman said nothing, only laid the chops onto the sheets of paper. He wrapped them and handed them to me, mumbling something in Yiddish. I caught the last part: "*Goyim...*" Biederman spat on the sawdust-covered floor as I left.

Back at the kitchen, Frau Schoendorf unwrapped the meat and she and I would start to prepare the day's lunch. She carefully sliced around the bones, removing them, then handed the chops to me and I covered them in flour, egg-wash, and breadcrumbs.

Herr Schoendorf looked on and chuckled:

"*Wiener schnitzel* they want... what they get is cheap pork. Old Biederman is some Kasher butcher, eh? Anything for the money... that's how the Jews are."

Just then, Frankie Schoenberg, one of the peddlers entered. Frankie had class. He wore a blue blazer and had slicked back hair covering his bald spot. Frankie was from Poland, a son of survivors. He spoke mostly Yiddish, but knew a smattering of languages and spoke more than passable French. His English was something else, and we had long ago given up trying to understand it.

"*Gibt mir ein pletzle,*" he told me, snapping a finger.

"Sorry, no pretzels today. The bakery was all out. *Tout finis.*"

"*Pletzle, pletzle....* can't you get that through your *goyische kopf*?"

"*Na, ja,* Frankie, *machts nicht,*" Herr Schoendorf intervened. He took me aside and said:

"A *pletzle* is an onion roll. Hold the butter and some beef salami with mustard on it."

I made the sandwich, and suddenly there were other salesmen, peddlers, and staff. It was the lunch hour, and they all screamed to be served in at least five different languages.

"Two egg salad...."

"*Un Coke avec un Mae West....*"

"A poppy seed Danish, and one bagel with cream cheese...so then Morris said to me, if you won't put out, I'll get myself a *shikse*...so me, I said to him good luck with that, who wants your hairy old nuts and your back with the boils....I should be so lucky? Sure, he said I was his Princess...he can kiss my royal ass, I told him...and as for his *shikse,* she's just some east end slut, Lise or Hugette or whatever the hell her name is. Probably found her in some cheap lap dance bar. Never eats nothing but fries, poutine, and *pâté chinois*... no teeth probably since the age of 16, all the better to suck on Mr. High and Mighty's poor excuse for a prick.... So then I says to him, take your slut and have her.... I'm gonna get me a *goyim....*"

The ex-Mrs. Mendelbaum laughed as she picked up her order, looked me square in the eye: "Yeah, some handsome young goy with a nice hard *karnotzle....* here, that's for you, go spend it tonight on some nice *medeleh...*"

She tipped me fifty cents, took her sandwich and Danish and went off with her friend, Sonia, back to Accounting.

After the lunch rush, we cleaned up and while Frau Schoendorf made the salads for the next day, her husband and I watched *The Flintstones* while we waited for the phone orders and afternoon snack deliveries. Herr Schoendorf loved *The Flintstones.* His favourite character was Barney, and he tried to laugh just like him. Often, too often. It annoyed me to no end. I used to fantasize about hitting him with a hot spatula from the grill, about pouring the hot fat from the fry pans on the Nazi bastard's head, about having him as some character in the show, a cartoonesque intruder that Dino bites in the ass and chases down the streets of Bedrock.

In four months, I had become Herr Shoendorf's understudy, part of his new *Hitler Jugend.* It wasn't hard to become anti-Semitic, especially at his prompting. I too had an unfortunately long history of it in my family: Hungarian aristocrats who still remembered what had happened during the first revolution of 1919, an uncle who had been a card–carrying member while he served in the army, the festering Eastern European hatred of Jews.

And there were the peddlers, who treated me like shit every day, their own hatred of gentiles apparent, though perhaps more forgivable since many of them were first generation survivors.

I finally left Brown's on a Friday afternoon, just hours before the start of the Sabbath. The peddlers would wrap up their business usually by lunchtime on Friday, and they would spend the hours before going home to their families gambling at cards in the back room just off the cafeteria where I was working. It was my job to go in every twenty minutes or so to take their orders. Herr Schoendorf made sure that I took everything on paper plates and cups since fights often broke out over accusations of cheating.

That Friday, I went in to the back room to get their orders for coffee. There were about six of them there, playing poker, most of them sitting on their money to prevent others from grabbing it, all of them smoking huge cigars and yelling.

"Hey, *goy,*" they would call, and give their order.

That day, Frankie Schoenberg was winning big, and Jakob Lindemann, who was losing to him, was getting redder and more furious by the minute. It did not help that Frankie was taunting him whenever he had the chance. I knew some German, and it had been easy for me to pick up their colorful Yiddish expressions, so that I came to know most of what they were saying to each other or to me.

Frankie was saying: "So Jakob, you still think you are such a *Gantseh Macher?* You lose again. . . ."

Jakob Lindemann was turning purple with each insult. "*Kush in toches arein–!*"

"Hey, Frankie, and you know he has a *tuches un a halb,*" from Moishe Landauer, who was still in the game. They all laughed at this, except, Jakob.

"Hey, Frankie, is it true that you told Jakob he had a small *petseleh* when you were taking a shower after your *schvitz* last Tuesday?"

"No, I told him it was probably only a *farshlepteh krenk. . . .*" They all guffawed at this, as I stood to the side trying to get their attention.

"Hey, *goyim. Gibt mir* a coffee *mit* a Danish. I've had it with the *chazzerei* you serve in that restaurant of yours. Move it, and stop staring with your *ferprishte punim.*"

I knew that he was commenting on my pimples, but it was my job to be pleasant, no matter what. I took their orders and went back to the counter to make up the sandwiches, coffees, and Danishes they had ordered.

When I returned, Jakob was yelling at Frankie, calling him a cheat and a liar. Two of the others were holding him back, and Frankie was putting the money in his pocket, while shaking his fist in Jakob's direction.

"You're *meshuggeneh,* that's what you are. . . ."

"Your coffee's here," I said, in the momentary lull. Jakob looked at me, and told me to put everything down. Then he told me to leave, and quickly. I didn't move, waiting for him to pay me. I knew that at least once a week they tried to stiff me for any amount they could. Tipping was out of the question. Then, Jakob looked at me:

"And you, you're waiting for something maybe?"

"Yes, that will be seventy-five cents." The others had all paid their tabs.

"Seventy-five cents for something that tastes like dish water?" Jakob answered. "I told you I wanted my coffee in a real cup, not this paper stuff."

"Sorry, but my boss says no porcelain in the back room, only in the cafeteria."

"GET ME COFFEE IN A REAL CUP!" Jakob screamed.

One of the peddlers said: "Leave the kid, already. He's just trying to make a living, like all of us."

"*Oych mir a leben?*" Jakob scoffed in my direction. "Now get me a real coffee like I said."

"No, sorry."

"No, here's a 'no' for you!" At this, Jakob, furious now, flung the hot coffee in my face, landing half of it on my shirt.

I totally lost control and jumped at him, calling him every name I could think of while wrestling him to the floor as the others leaped on me and peeled me off.

"And here's one other thing for you to remember: *a chazer bleibt a chazer*... A pig remains a pig. Try that on for your Joy of Yiddish, you rotten bastard." I spat this at him as I ran, dripping with coffee and sweat, back to the kitchen.

Herr Schoendorf had no choice but to fire me, though I think he secretly relished what I had done, but business was business. It took me a week to calm down, and longer to forgive.

Walking along St. Laurent, I see that Brown's is long gone, replaced by trendy boutiques, restos, and Lebanese take-out joints. The peddlers are also long gone from this street, resurrected only as a memory. I think that I will look on my shelves when I go home and read a few pages of Wiesel's *Night* or some Primo Levi, remembering that living and forgiveness must be forever joined.

CHAPTER 15

I walk down the corridors of my past, walk along Mont Royal Avenue and turn left south onto St. Urbain until I come to the gaudy Portuguese church at the corner of Rachel with its lights and kitschy decorations. I look across at the balcony on the corner leading toward Esplanade, a place I knew so well, and think of Catherine.

Catherine, who liked to talk about her past lovers and about the quixotic nature of love. She once told me about one lover, a judge, Sydney was his name. From Winnipeg. A circuit court judge, no less. She said he was normally a slow, considerate lover, but once she had tried talking dirty to him while they were making love, which had so shocked and excited him that he came immediately. I asked her if he had yelled at this point: "Here comes the Judge!" She was not amused.

Then there was Sacha, the Romanian. Catherine said that making love with him was a bit like doing gymnastics. It was never ordinary or straightforward man-on-top-finish-roll over and sleep, but had to be a performance. Sacha felt that he had failed if she didn't have an orgasm—he wanted histrionics, bells, whistles, and the curtain to rise and fall and the audience to clap for the main actor, which was always he. She told me Sacha liked to have his prostate massaged while he was making love. Sometimes she even had to shove a string of Buddhist meditation beads up his ass and draw them out slowly when he came to enhance the pleasure. I wanted to ask her if he had moaned *OM* at that point, but I knew better.

There were others, many others. Jean-Marc, the Professor of Comparative Literature, who made her dress up like a French maid from *The Story of O*. Simon, whose wife Miriam was her best friend, and with whom she had slept on Simon's first wedding anniversary when he came to drop off something from Miriam. Catherine told me she had come out from the bathroom stark naked except for a red garter belt, and Simon had missed meeting his wife for supper because he had become so inflamed by her charms.

"But you," she told me, "are my friend. I can tell you all of these things because you really listen and understand me and don't judge. I have no desire to please you since I can be myself." I was flattered, sure, although I wasn't certain that I liked the last thing she had said. I even nodded sagely a few times. I also wanted her but didn't know how to say it.

Catherine was a student of Opera and Lieder. We had met at the Montreal General Hospital where we both had summer jobs, and she learned that my German was good, even better than hers. I also knew the poetry of Schiller and Rilke and knew who Dietrich Fischer-Dieskau was. I was a failed poet, but a terrific hospital orderly. I could shave a cock and a pair of balls in under ten minutes without even a nick. Writing poems was another matter. Maybe I had held one too many limp cocks in my hand.

I offered to help her with the pronunciation of her part in the *Tales of Hoffmann*. I became fascinated by her lips. They were thick, sensuous, bee-stung, almost obscene...I would watch them, entranced, as she formed the high umlauts in *"schön"*—sometimes I would sit with the libretto on my lap hiding a hard-on. I think she knew this. She would eat fruit after—cherries, kiwi, bananas (they were good for the vocal cords, she claimed)—all of these passing through those lips.

It was 1976, Montreal's Olympic year and the city was alive with tourists. I was alone again. Maria, with whom I had been living, had gone back to the U.S., to play the dutiful daughter to her rich parents who paid for her stay at McGill and indulged her habits. She liked butter-rum ice cream, which she ate by the quart. Also, pesto sauce on pasta, iceberg lettuce, mushrooms of any kind, and stray cats. I had been one of her habits for a half a year. She told me that she had taken me in because I reminded her of a stray tabby with no place to go. Maria also had the habit of peeling the skin off her foot and eating it. The soles of her feet felt like sharp thumbtacks. I'd rub her feet each night with Johnson's Baby Oil and plead for her to stop the mutilation. I think she had some issues.

This was soon after the wild lovemaking had ceased, about three months after I had moved in. I still was in the habit of sleeping naked, while she wore a nightgown that I would spend the half of each night rolling up past her waist until the round, white orbs of her ass were in full view. I'd then inch my hard penis between her cheeks looking for a "dream fuck," for some sign of wetness that I tried to will from her. Sadly, it never happened. The best I got was one of her juicy thighs, thrown over my leg and slightly opened. I would stroke her cunt slowly, sometimes for more than forty-five minutes—I could tell this by the number of hard-ons I raised and lost during that time. Often, my balls were so swollen that I wanted to scream from these half-ejaculations.

Anyway, Maria would eventually get wet. But even then, it was a no go. All she wanted was for me to stroke her clitoris with my finger while my wet cock brushed against her *mons veneris*. At the same time, she let me lift her gown up over her large breasts. I would bend over, my neck straining, the fifth vertebra in my cervical spine bulging, my right arm numb from cupping her ass and trying to insert a finger into her (to no avail!), while slowly lapping at one never quite turgid nipple until she finally shuddered and came. After months of this, she finally let me slip into her the night before she was to leave for the summer. I came violently and immediately.

This last indignity drove Maria back to her habit. The next morning, I woke up to find her packed and gone on the early flight. On the bedside table was the entire outline of her foot, with only the skin perfectly peeled off. I never knew why she did this. Was it a last reminder of what I had lost, or a snake shedding its skin to begin a new life? Maria was gone, even the rank smell of her (she never liked to bathe much) just a memory—all that was left was a perfect fit for a shoe! And on the kitchen table a note:

Don't forget to feed the cats. I'll be back in September. You can stay all summer and even later if you really want to. By the way, I have been seeing Ruben (her lab partner). He is in Israel now, but will be back in September. I'm sorry. I should have told you sooner. You were always my favourite stray cat.

Maria.

It was a beautiful, warm summer day in Montreal. I had two cats to look after (three, if I counted myself and if she could be believed), a free apartment for the next two months, and the imprint (in skin!) of her right foot. I also had a summer job shaving old men's balls at the Montreal General Hospital. It was only 9:30 a.m. I had a whole morning and early afternoon before my shift started. After dozing, I awoke to the warm sun through the half-parted curtains and a hard-on. Reaching over to the bedside table, I took Maria's last token and wrapped it around my penis and slowly started stroking. The skin of her foot chaffed and bit the head like nails. I threw the skin into the garbage can next to the bed. My penis shrank, and nestled sadly on my thigh. I slept.

And so, Catherine. We worked on the same ward that summer, 15 West, Surgery. My German coaching and pronunciation lessons turned into dinners and talk on our days off. I told her stories about my days in Innsbruck, Paris, Firenze, Budapest, and Ibiza. I told her how we had run hashish from the Rif Mountains of Morocco to Munich's Schwabing district, passing through four borders with twenty-five kilos soldered into the bottom of our VW van. About Karl Heinz, our connection, who paid us in fake Deutsch Marks so that we were stranded with no money, having to sleep in the English Gardens and steal remnants of croissants and *kaffee mit schlag* from the café tables.

I spoke about Keats' "Ode to Melancholy" and the saddest lines of poetry ever written in English, of my favourite novel, *The Recognitions*, of Marvell's plea to his lover, and Donne's "Holy Sonnets." I read to her poetry, the "Duino Elegies" (in German) and Rimbaud in stilted French. I even read her a poem I had written, which went something like this:

The art of hiding in trees
Is the memory of your body
Rough like tree scruff;
It is two little girls
Climbing and me staring
Up their dresses
And them laughing
So hard in the trees
That one started to pee
So that the pee
Ran down the tree
Onto my face
That wrinkled, then,
Only into smiles.

Like I said, I was a failed poet, but these lines touched her, she said. She thought they were about the loss of youth and innocence (they weren't). I wanted to say that they were really about looking up girls' dresses, but I didn't. She kissed me gently, then more fiercely, and gave me her tongue. I feasted on those lips and stroked her body and cupped her ass in my hands.

"Wait," she whispered. "Soon. It will be better. You can cook me dinner and give me wine and tell me more stories. Then, we will walk by the mountain and make love, hearing the noise of St. Urbain Street outside my windows." All this poetry bullshit had probably ruined her, but I was too filled with desire. I looked at those full lips and weakly nodded assent.

I met my friend, Greg, at our night class at Sir George Williams University a few days before Catherine had promised to have dinner with me, and more. Greg and I were both mature students taking *Introduction to Poetry.* Our professor was a Harvard grad, a student of the Americanist, Bercovitch. In addition, he claimed to be a Buddhist and told us that he played a hand-carved flute he had acquired in Nepal. He wrote poetry and meditated on the meaning of life in the Eastern Townships. A dead-ringer for Gary Snyder, he had published one book of poetry called something like *Left-Hand Job,* all about "touching the Silence." Indeed.

After class, Greg and I strolled to Toe Blake's on Guy and Ste. Catherine. We ate pig's knuckles and sauerkraut with hot Dijon mustard and washed it down with pints of draft. Each time we ordered two more, Henri, our waiter, would sashay over, twitching his ass that seemed to be poured into his jeans. Henri liked Greg's rugged maleness and did everything to get his attention. I didn't rate. If only Henri had known how much I understood gay culture and that I was a poet (albeit failed)! After all, I had read all of Wilde, and Allen Ginsberg had pinched my ass at a party when I was eighteen.

Greg loved to talk about the women he had slept with. He had designed his own fuck-pad. Good at electrical work, he had wired his apartment so that the lights dimmed and the music would start to play as if by magic with just one clap of his hand. Greg practically lived on Crescent Street from Thursday to Saturday nights.

He told me that during one of his many appointments in the Department of Urology, undoubtedly being checked out for STDs, he had stolen a tube of xylocaine, which the doctors used to coat a catheter that would be inserted into a patient's penis prior to a cystoscopy. Xylocaine was like Novocaine and would numb any sensation so the catheter wouldn't hurt. Greg said that he would put a tiny bit of it on the head of his penis before fucking a new girl he had picked up. This would numb him so that he could last longer. The word was out about Greg and his staying power on Crescent, or so he led me to believe.

"You have to be careful," he warned me," to make sure you don't use too much, or you won't feel anything at all and stay totally limp." He grinned, and passed me a small tube. "After a night of this, even Catherine of Siena would give up her vow of chastity."

Saturday night finally arrived, and Catherine. I cooked her a meal of *Wiener schnitzel* with wild rice, mushroom sauce, and asparagus. I had even bought raw oysters to go with the first bottle of Chablis Thorin. We listened to some Chick Corea, and Miles' *Kind of Blue.* Then, I served up my trump card: two tickets to a performance by Oscar Peterson with Joe Pass at the Queen E. Ballroom. We had great seats. Oscar appeared decked out with a fake Olympic gold medal over his tux; even Joe Pass seemed not too stoned for some mean licks on "Ain't Misbehavin'." A man next to us, an Italian tourist, shouted out at one point of the performance:

"Oscar, playa "*Laura*" for me, *per favore!*"

Peterson looked up disdainfully from the piano: "I didn't see you pay more than the $25.00 entry, chump."

The man sat backed, crushed. Catherine, quite drunk by now, leaned over to placate him in her best *Rigoletto* Italian, and as she did so, she knocked over three quarters of a $45.00 bottle of Chablis I had ordered that had been sitting on ice in a bucket by our table. After, we laughed and staggered up McGill College to the campus, and she straddled me on one of the benches by the Stephen Leacock Building and kissed my deeply.

"Now take me home," she said, just before she vomited up her *Wiener schnitzel,* asparagus, oysters and about $30.00 worth of Chablis all over my only summer suit.

I thought of Homer and those lines from *Ulysses* about how poets have to listen to the song of the sirens. Catherine, my siren, my inspiration, lay in bed next to me, naked, sleeping. And snoring. This was her song, and I was Odysseus roped to the stake of my own desire, screaming to the waxy-eared mariners. I must have watched her for a good part of the night as she slept, oblivious to the world and to me, until I finally dozed off in the muggy July dawn. I awoke some hours later with the sun warming me through the windows and the noise of St. Urbain Street's late morning bustle. And Catherine. She had flung her leg over mine, her tousled hair and her nakedness, her semi-sour Chablis breath warming my chest. Slowly, I disengaged myself from her embrace while she groaned (or was it moaned?) softly in her half-sleep. I went to the living room sporting a serious erection. I found my pants, flung there the night before, and extracted the small tube from my pocket.

When applied, the xylocaine felt warm and tingly and seemed to send waves of electric pleasure over the head of my penis. It made me even harder as I climbed back into bed with my sleeping goddess. Slowly, ever so slowly, I began to caress her until she let out a soft moan. I could feel her opening up to me like a flower, her eyes looking at me still unfocused in her half-sleep. Finally, I rolled over and prepared to enter her, and in that moment felt all my longing, desire, and imagined triumphs cohere. And then I felt it.

Or, more precisely, didn't. I looked down at where my erection had been, wondering even if my penis was still there, feeling nothing, only numbness.

Meanwhile, Catherine was now truly awake and moving her hips slowly under me in anticipation. She locked her lips to mine, fiercely:

"Come on. Now. Take me," she moaned.

I was frantic. My groin had disappeared, only a hollow numbness remaining where my desire had so firmly been. I tried to stall for time. I bit the inside of her thighs, caressing her wetness with my tongue. Catherine bucked, moaned and shuddered from all my attention. Then, she reached down, seizing my limpness and tried rubbing some life into it.

"What's wrong? What's happened?" she panted.

What was there to say? I racked my brains for something, anything. Meanwhile, I tried to will back desire into my frozen loins, to no avail. It found its place in the head, in the imagination, and refused to translate into the more immediate physical realm. Catherine smiled and kissed me tenderly.

"It's OK," she whispered. "Lie back and relax."

Catherine kissed her way slowly down my stomach to my groin. Adroitly, she took me in her mouth and worked it with greater and greater passion and intensity. I could see that she was an expert, that I was being swallowed by one of the best, but all to no avail. Then, she stopped, looking up at me with a mixture of anger and worry on her face.

"What's wrong?" is what I'm sure she wanted to say, but it came out as something entirely different. It was more of a gurgle, a rasp, a gasp, something mumbled. Catherine looked at me in panic.

"'Elp 'ee; 'elp 'ee...!" She gestured frantically toward the bedside table. I flung open the drawer and found an EpiPen. She signaled me, miming for me to inject her, all the while grasping her throat with both hands.

And then I understood. Catherine had told me some time ago that she had had an allergic reaction to medication, probably penicillin, so she always kept epinephrine handy. Now, she thought that she was experiencing anaphylactic shock and wanted me to give her an injection. How was I to tell her that it was the xylocaine from my penis that had numbed her throat, leading her to think that it was swelling up? And speaking of swelling up, something strange had occurred. Catherine's caresses had revived my own frozen member, so that I stood bold and erect before Catherine's horrified gaze.

I had no choice. It was the honest, gentlemanly thing to do. I held her and confessed. Catherine lost that horrified, panicked expression; it turned to anger and fury.

"Why, you bastard, why did you do this? Didn't you think you could satisfy me as yourself?" She had found her voice again, and it was shrill.

This was not a question I cared to answer truthfully, so I replied:

"I was in awe of you... I thought I wanted to please you above all else." I knew it sounded lame the moment it came out of my mouth. She glared at me.

"I want you to leave. Now. Goodbye. That's all. Now. Please."

That was it. I put on my clothes and walked into the sad July afternoon with my no longer limp but unrequited cock. What had one of Kosinski's female characters said? Something about being wary of men with imagination, I think.

Thus, it was with Catherine. I did see her again when she had her graduation solo Lieder recital. We even spoke briefly. She told me that she was now with someone who "specialized" in singers, whatever that meant, as she gave me a frozen smile. That night, I sent her a bouquet of roses with a card that read: "*Wunderbar.* A truly amazing performance. You are a real, future diva. *Ausgezeichnet.*" I signed it Rudolf Bing, conductor of the Berlin Opera Company.

And then I sat down to wait beside the black telephone.

And suddenly, there in the middle of rue St. Urbain, I remember the first phone message on the day I was discharged. The woman's voice that had sounded so familiar and the Lieder music in the background.

CHAPTER 16

Why would Catherine be calling after all these years? She was living in Toronto, the last I remembered, though the number that had shown up on my phone was local. I vaguely wonder how she looks after all these years. Older than me by a year or two, she would be in her early sixties.

When I arrive back at my apartment, I go to my computer and Google her name, but only get two hits that are vaguely promising. When I follow a link, I don't learn much, except that she's apparently teaching at the music conservatory of some college in Toronto and that she still runs a voice studio. Yet that brief ghost of a voice on my answering machine. I still have the saved message, and listen to it again, then check the phone number. It is a 514 exchange, so I know it is somewhere in the city.

I call the number, and a male voice, shaky and weary, answers on the seventh ring, just when I have decided to hang up, feeling like a young boy trying for his first date.

"Yes?"

"Hello, I am calling because I received a call from this number a few days ago?"

"It is possible." There is a strong hint of an eastern European accent, despite the impeccable French. And suddenly I remember, but it seems unlikely after all of these years. Paul.

"Paul, is that you?" I have switched to German, and there is a long pause.

"*Ja, und wer sind Sie?*"

I tell him my name, but he doesn't remember when we met over dinner with Catherine more than twenty years ago, just before she was to leave for Germany to study singing. We had gathered at

Carmen's on Stanley Street. Paul was an immaculately attired man, then in his sixties, Romanian, a poet and professor of linguistics. He was faultlessly polite, but kept stealing glances at me as I spoke to Catherine. Paul was most attentive to her, filling her wine glass, rising when she went to the washroom, and holding her chair for her when she sat down.

I later learned from Catherine's roommate that Paul had paid for her ticket to Germany; in fact, he had paid perhaps for much more, not just to finance her studies, but had supported her even during her studies in Montreal. I wondered in return for what.

"Paul," I tell him. "I am an old friend of Catherine's. The last I heard from her was several decades ago, but last week there was a message on my machine and a voice that sounded familiar. There was Schubert playing in the background, one of her favourite songs, I remember."

"Yes, it was her. I know she wanted to call you, to talk."

"Has she returned to Toronto? Is that where she is still working?"

Paul hesitates. Then, he finally speaks: "No, she is here in town for a time. She is staying with me for the moment." There is a long silence.

"Is she there now? May I speak to her?"

"She can't come to the phone, but I will tell her you called." More silence.

Then: "She's dying, you know. Cancer. Breast."

I pause, unable to speak, shaken. Catherine, dying! The same cancer that had taken my mother, and now her. I swallow hard, unable to think of anything appropriate to say and finally respond, lamely:

"How long has she been in town?" Paul waits a long time before answering:

"Most of the winter. She has had the full course of treatments. Now, there is nothing more to be done. Palliation is all."

"And how can you look after her yourself? You must be in your eighties, no?"

"We manage, we always have," he sighs heavily. "I must go now."

"Please tell her I called," I reiterate before hanging up. I try to recall what Catherine had looked like over the distance of the years. She was blond, of Nordic origin, not conventionally attractive, with large, almost too full lips, and tall. Elizabeth found it hard to understand why I had been attracted to her, and in retrospect I see now that it was the desire to be in love, coming so soon after my split with Maria.

Catherine and I had rekindled our friendship and became lovers again briefly, faring much better than during the xylocaine fiasco. We had corresponded while she was studying in Europe. Shortly after her return to Canada, she had moved to the West Coast where she spent over a decade. We had lost touch during that time, as it often happens. We had not communicated in more than two decades.

I try to imagine how Catherine might look now, gaunt, emaciated from the cancer, probably bald from the chemotherapy, the radiation marks etched onto her pale skin. Catherine, who had always taken pride in her appearance, her allure. How could someone like her be left a broken shell? The awfulness of it all! I wonder if she would be spending her last days at the very hospital where we had met years ago, I as an orderly and she as a ward clerk.

I remember one time while we were lovers again after reuniting when I was working the night shift and she the afternoons, so that I would come home in the early hours of the morning and sometimes find her in my bed, in those days when I felt my life was filled with adventure, possibility, and grace.

There is one evening that comes back to me. It was nearly 3:00 a.m. as I passed down the long hospital corridor toward the sunroom. The passage was in almost total darkness except for the dim night-light near the door to the patients' rooms, the only real light coming from the Nurses' Station at the entrance to the ward. I could hear the muffled breathing of the sick and the sounds of restless tossing from the more active. There was an hour free to rest before the early morning work began again prior to the start of the day shift.

We had just finished the hourly rounds, me and the night duty nurse, Marie-Claude, a young woman of twenty-two, seven months out of nursing school. Each hour, we went with our flashlights to check on the patients, to turn the bedridden onto another side in order to prevent bedsores, to check on the living and the dying. Although this was the routine, each time we entered a room, our hands cupped around the tiny beam of light to avoid waking anyone, there was always a tension waiting for the next intake of breath to see if it did come, to make sure it did. Sometimes it was almost comical. We would wait, seemingly forever, for the man or woman in the bed to breathe, and when the breath announced itself in a loud snore or gasp, we were always shocked by our relief. This created a nervous bond, a timid intimacy between us.

The sunroom was also in darkness. There were comfortable chairs to sleep on and large windows with shades that could be drawn overlooking the city. But as I sat that night, I decided to open them, to look at the perpetual lights from the large downtown high rises and the occasional car passing over the Champlain Bridge. Below, I saw the river and the bridges that led off the island. To the left, there was the mountain with the solitary cross illuminated at the top. Down near the waterfront was the steel mill with its lit sign, DOM-O, flashing with its missing "C" that had not been replaced in at least the three years since I had first observed it. That night it struck me as amusing, the cross and the unintended pun of the flashing sign. With some imagination you had "Dominus." *Dominus vobiscum,* from my youth, listening to the Latin of the High Mass, before it became less of a mystery through the vernacular. *Et cum spiritu tuo.* There were worse things one could think about.

I had always loved the city at this time of the morning. It was too late for most people and too early for the dawn light. Everything seemed peaceful. The night was soothing, an easy handle for thoughts to take their luxurious shapes and to daydream close to the reality of the job. I had been working as an orderly for some time at the hospital, often hating the mess and the dirt of the work, but other times finding both a joy and humour amidst the grimness of the pain and death that, after a while, took their place in the normal scheme of the world. I sensed an obscure truth in the work I did, the care of the sick and the dying, a reality that had to do with people at their most vulnerable, their most human, where the best and worst was brought out in them, and this somehow redeemed the tedium of the job.

The night usually passed slowly. You became almost painfully aware of time and how some people had too much of it and others, near their end, not enough. That night, I had stayed longer than usual, perhaps longer than necessary, in room 1729 where an elderly man lay dying of cancer. He had been on the ward for over three weeks now, diagnosed as terminal, DNR, and was waiting to die. For the last ten days, he had been on morphine, yet had always managed to retain some lucidity and offer a smile, or mumble his appreciation for anything we did to ease his discomfort. He had taken a turn for the worse and his wife was with him, maybe for the last time. I had gone in to position him and the man barely recognized me through the pain, while his wife sat holding his hand, past tears, exhausted. I had lingered, even though it seemed like a travesty to be there, but something made me want to be part of the final intimacy even though the unspoken rule seemed to be to avoid the dying in their final moments.

DOM-O flickered below, a blind, red eye blinking in the darkness. I thought of the dying man and his wife with him and wondered about the life they had lived together. I had felt like a stranger being with them earlier in the room; she seemed so enclosed in her grief, and he in his struggle to gain release. My inexplicable longing was a form of love. This couple was a mystery to me, just as my own life with Catherine, with women, remained a perpetual mystery. I wondered if they had loved one another. If they had known in better times what it was to be apart and singular and to accept that you could never really know the other except in what they cared to be for you. Whether they had kept many secrets and lived part of their lives withdrawn, hidden from each other. The truth remained as well in what one didn't care to know.

Between 3:00 a.m. and 6 were the most difficult hours to stay awake. Even though you may have slept eight hours or more the previous day, it was barely possible to keep the eyelids open. I caught myself dozing and woke with a start. The passageway was quiet and the illuminated dials on the hand of my watch showed 3:42. I still had over a quarter of an hour before making the next rounds. Nestling in the large easy chair, I shivered slightly. I thought of the woman with her dying husband, remembered her face and the emptiness in it that was almost like mute anger. Was it at me for lingering in the doorway? I didn't think so.

I had always been a secret voyeur, even in my own life with Catherine. She'd be asleep because I had nocturnal habits, I'd watch her, sometimes for long minutes, wanting to understand some question that I couldn't even voice to myself. I often marveled at her grace in sleep and felt that it was her beauty and the hidden mystery of her that I could never fathom. I would watch her, almost angry with her for being so self-contained, so withdrawn from my own impatience or need, a need to say something, to do something, *now,* as if waiting until she awoke would be too late and the instant would be lost.

I'd often think about Catherine and wonder why, after the ease of being with her, there was still a need for words. What I wanted to say to her would be nothing more than a catch in my throat. Finally, I always wondered what new things I could think to say, some feeling beyond knowing, some moment as simple as returning to my first attraction, which still eluded me.

She said my hands had first caught her attention because they held some knowledge of a woman's body: hands that were soft, unlike most men's hands. I loved her for saying that, lying together easily after making love. The single light came from the last crescent of the month-old moon. At least I wanted to remember it that way.

I was sound asleep in the easy chair when Marie-Claude shook me by the shoulders.

"Stephen, *viens vite*... quick... I need you."

Confused, half asleep, I got up to follow her, noting the alarm in her voice.

"What is it?" My watch showed 4:36. I had overslept, sure, but that didn't seem to be it.

"Monsieur Ramsey, in 1729. He's really bad. I phone the doctor but he say there was nothing they could do. Just to give the meds for the pain. He's gonna die, I just know it."

Together we entered the room, closing the door carefully. The old man, his jaundiced face above the white sheets, lay on his back, his breath coming in laboured gasps. His wife kneaded the sheets in her fist, weeping silently.

"Marie-Claude," I offered, "take Mrs. Ramsey to the nursing station for a cup of coffee. I'll stay here for a while."

Gratefully, she left, her arms around the shaking shoulders of the man's wife. Left alone with the dying man, I stared at the glazed eyes and watched the body fighting to survive. Half terrified, half fascinated I sat wanting to see it, to understand the finality, to see a graceful departure from the husk of the disease-wracked body, but the man in the bed was stubborn and continued to wheeze and gasp.

After a while, Marie-Claude came back into the room. She was pale, and I could see that she had been crying. She had a needle with the morphine in her hand. It was time for the q4h injection.

"How is she?" I asked.

"*Elle pleure.* Crying." She didn't want to talk. Almost perfunctorily, she attached the blood-pressure cuff to the patient's wizened arm. The man gave a loud gasp and she recoiled, but continued to watch the gauge.

"*C'est trop bas.* The morphine gonna kill him for sure."

"Then give it to him."

"I can't. He will die. I never seen it before. *Chui pas capable.*" Her voice was tense, a hysterical whisper.

"Marie-Claude, *écoute–moi*! It's time. Even the doctor ordered it for the pain. Show some humanity, for Christ's sake. He's suffering too much. It will be an easy death."

"*Tu comprends rien....* I can't."

I looked at her. The tears came freely down her cheeks. She looked at me, hating me, hating the moment.

"It's all right," I told her, putting a hand on her arm. "Go see Mrs. Ramsey. I'll stay."

Her eyes blank, the tears drying on her face, she left the room, softly closing the door without looking back. The needle remained on the bedside table.

I took the needle carefully and inserted it into the soluset connecting the IV bottle to the man's arm. Depressing the plunger,

I squeezed the morphine into the saline solution that was dripping from the bottle at a slow rate. Then, I opened the clamp all the way to facilitate a rapid drip and sat back, waiting. Within minutes the soluset discharged its content into the arm. Almost immediately the man's breathing became shallower and less laboured. He breathed once like someone stopping to think of something for an instant, and died.

I sat watching for a few moments. It was never like I expected it, yet I did not feel cheated by the moment. I noticed only my own steady breathing in the silence of the room. Extending my hand, I touched the still warm body and searched for a pulse. It was gone. It had vanished as quietly, as suddenly as the silence had descended upon the room. Gently, I drew the eyelids closed, then left.

My watch told me that it was after 5:30. I went to the nursing station and looked at Marie-Claude and nodded. She cast her eyes down and continued with her charting.

I noticed Mrs. Ramsey sitting in the nursing station, numb, distant. She did not see me, and she held her face in both hands.

I went through my usual work routine for the rest of the shift. Some of the patients were waking up and asking for the nurse. When I finally left at 7:30 the door to room 1729 was still closed.

The morning, as I walked home on Pine Avenue by the side of the mountain, was fresh and sunny. Cars passed by with increasing frequency; other people on their way to work, beginning their day. The lights on the huge cross on the mountain had automatically turned off. Through the trees I could see DOM-O continue to flash, its red lights illuminated now in honour of another working day.

When I walked into the bedroom of my flat, Catherine was there, asleep. I looked at her for a while, thinking how beautiful she was and how she too slept in her own state of grace. I drew back the curtains and the morning sun entered the room. Catherine opened her eyes, startled by the brightness, her hair tousled by sleep. Then, she smiled up at me.

"Hello, sleepy-head, "I said gently.

"Ugh," she grunted, then turned away from the light and drew the blanket around her head. I pulled it back, kissing her naked back, inhaling Catherine's warmth. She nestled against me, her eyes closed, silent.

"Last night…" I began, then stopped, stroking her face.

"What?"

"Nothing… nothing at all. Go back to sleep. I'll join you after my shower."

I stopped by the window, looking outside at the life on the street below, then back at Catherine, half-asleep in the bed, remembering her warm breath on my arm, her soft body. I could feel the heat of the sun through the windowpane. It was the same sun that had shone long before for others, and would shine for all the others to come as it did now on the awakening city.

So, I remember Catherine and imagine her lying in her bed, Paul attending to her, perhaps passing a cold cloth over her forehead, playing her favourite music, being there for her beyond all the lovers, the betrayals, his own ageing frame, stooped in love, offering her final comfort. How many of us would ever be that fortunate? It is growing dark. Cicadas hum in the beech tree outside my back balcony, a faint quarter moon lighting up the back lane. Thoughts of our mortality: the truth that makes all men miserable, terrifies us, and keeps us from living.

CHAPTER 17

After I have hung up the phone, I sit and watch the evening settle, thinking about food for the first time in a while. The medication has taken away my appetite, so that I eat sporadically at best. Yet today, for some reason, I feel hungry, perhaps not enough to actually cook, but hungry for the flavours and spices that I grew up learning to love.

When I was in my early teens, my father had taught me to cook seven basic meals, survival meals, as he had called them. I used to watch him cooking in the kitchen every evening and would always wonder what pleasure he derived from it. Yet over the years we spent together, after my sister had left for college, I had learned to relish the smells and spices of the dishes he discovered as he became a better and better cook in his old age. The smells of frying bacon, paprika, and garlic always filled our flat, and he taught me to more than just to survive over the years. When Elizabeth and I first started dating, she was always taken by the meals I made for her, since she, at that time, never cooked. I also taught Nico some basic dishes before he moved out, though for him eating was simply a necessity and a nuisance, and I suspect he never related to it the way we had done because of our Eastern European upbringing.

As a child in Hungary, especially in the early 1950s, there was always a shortage of food. My father would take me with him after we had received our food rations, and we'd wait for hours in long lines of people. By the time our turn came, they often ran out of the basics and we'd return home with barely anything to eat. Mostly, we got bread, a few potatoes, the odd onion, a bit of lard or bacon, or even an egg, and maybe a small gristle of meat, usually horse, but rarely, pork. My father was once able to get hold of crackling, from a goose, I guess it was. My mother fried it up and set it on the table to cool in preparation for our supper, which was noodles covered with a bit of sour cream and cottage cheese to be topped by the crackling. However, I was starving by the late afternoon so I went to the bowl and kept helping myself, relishing the salty flavour, and sucking on the grease that dribbled down my chin. I ate so much I became sick and threw up, and it was then my mother discovered I had eaten our supper. I received a half-hearted beating, but from that moment on, food became a kind of obsession and security.

I flip through the old photo album, and there is this picture, black and white, faded, of my father, my grandmother, and my older brother in the Hungarian countryside, all formally posed on what seems like a balmy autumn day. My father is attired in a three-piece suit, a starched collar holding in place the impeccably knotted tie, a bowler hat perched on his head, as he stares into the camera, blindly. My grandmother is wearing somber colours with a black lace veil covering her face, holding an umbrella in her hand. My brother is the only one smiling through large owl-like glasses, a child of five or six in a Lord Fauntleroy coat, cap, shorts, and leggings. The picture was taken before the War; my sister and I hadn't been born. At their feet is a gurney on which a huge dead pig is lying, its bulk barely contained on the slab, the snout curled into a half-smile like some terrifying Lord of the Flies they had all come to praise.

I learned early the importance of pork in the Hungarian diet, especially during the times of deprivation before and after the Revolution of 1956. That picture was probably taken during the ritual pig slaughter in the country, usually at the end of October in the early hours of the morning. My father told me they'd be awakened by the screaming of the pig as the knife slit its throat, and after, the women would drain the blood, singe the hair off the hide, put aside the fat for lard, and make the different sausages for the celebratory meal. Every part of the pig would be used, even the snout and ears for headcheese. The priest would come to bless the house and join the feast, a ritual he repeated several times that day as he went from homestead to homestead. Several priests, my father said, died each year from trichinosis, contracted in those households that didn't observe the proper sanitary practices or undercooked the sausages.

I look at my father's face as a young man in the picture and try to imagine what he must have been thinking before the tragedy of the war, the death of my mother, and the collapse of his world. Dr. Rheinblatt has told me that my sense of order and neurotic ritual is probably derived from what I learned from him, but he may not realize that is precisely how my father was able to survive. The memories I have of him are always as an older man (he was forty-four when I was born), immaculately dressed, trying to retain the last vestige of dignity as his life spiraled more and more out of his control.

My father would always wake at 5:00 a.m. or even before to begin his day. Usually while standing, he would pour out a measured bowl of "Special K" cereal and drown it in weak chamomile tea, replacing skim milk. Since the second operation, he had developed lactose intolerance, so he played it safe. By 5:20 he was finished. He'd run a bath, spending no more than fifteen minutes in the tub, and after, his hair slicked back from the water, he'd apply Johnson's Baby Oil to his scalp and all over his body. To finish, he would half squat, one foot perched precariously on the toilet seat, and squirt some Preparation "H" into an orifice.

After dressing carefully in a shirt and tie, sometimes even a suit jacket instead of a cardigan, he'd sit by the window and watch the emerging light over the great spread of conifers rising like green bristles over Baker Mountain in the distance. Sometimes he would read his Bible for a long time, but he habitually spent at least twenty minutes of each morning writing in his journal, of which more than ten volumes rested next to each other, neatly aligned on the very top of the bookshelf.

Every time I visited, the smell of cooking food would awaken me in the morning. The cooking of the day's meal was akin to a sacred ritual for my father, and my rare visits always necessitated the preparation of various delicacies. I remember one particular time not long before his illness became full blown when I had arrived by the one bus that always took over three hours from Montreal, nauseous from having been tossed through the forty-three turns of the Wilmington Notch, or Kidney Buster Pass, as I had come to call it. I had dreaded the trip by bus, but Elizabeth had to use the car that weekend, so I had little choice. My father had prepared plates of hors d'oeuvres: Ritz crackers thickly buttered, topped with salty anchovies, salami slices, ham, and sausage, or spread with *körözöt,* the tangy Hungarian cheese made with paprika and caraway seeds. And there was always plenty of beer, and his homemade pastries, the chocolate squares and two kinds of strudel: apple and the sweet raspberry with powdered confectionary sugar sprinkled on top.

"Eat, drink, smoke if you want to," he told me. "You're too thin, and you really should get a haircut. Doesn't it bother you, all that hair riding up your collar?"

"No, it's fine," I answered. "I like it long." And then, "No thanks," after my father offered me another bottle of Heineken.

"So, go ahead and tell me about everything. It's been so long since you were here, so long since it's been just the two of us talking."

His hands were slightly trembling, more noticeably than they had been the last time I had seen him.

"How is Elizabeth? And your own work, your teaching?" I didn't answer. I knew that my father was wary of Elizabeth, though he liked and respected her, and she, for her part, was always nice to him during his stays with us when he came to Montreal for his ongoing treatments.

My father had accepted and approved of our union, but I still think he preferred Maria, on whom, when she had visited that one time some years ago, he had turned the full power of his European-gentleman's persona, and Maria had pronounced him "charming," to my snort of derision. Elizabeth knew better, and never fell for his ruse, maintaining a polite, albeit distant respect for him, though I now know how much his presence in our household wore on her, especially as his visits became more frequent and longer in duration due to the deterioration of his health.

After Maria and I had split up, the first thing my father did was contact her and ask her to come for a visit. Some European gentleman, he was; better to call him out for his real intentions. I found that this rankled me still, and as I thought back on Maria bitterly, something compelled me to ask:

"Does that woman, I forget her name, the Ugandan student, still come by to clean for you? Are you still sucking on her tits for that extra twenty dollars you slip her beyond her hourly?"

My father frowned at me.

"A real gentleman never tells, especially about affairs of the heart. Besides, she lets me do it for free now—these old lips, you know...."

We both laughed, me in spite of myself.

"*Apu* (this was the name I always used), what was it like after the war, when mother came back from Holland and you returned from the Russian prison camp after fourteen months away? You told me that you had boils all over your body, that when you were released and coming back by train in the cattle cars, the women in the villages near Temesvár, the Hungarian part of Romania, gave you soldiers home-spun Baltic yogurt with black rye, still warm from the oven; that once, when the cars that transported the released prisoners stopped by a field of plum trees, you all lay down on the ground and gorged yourselves with plums, not having tasted any fruit for two years, your gums bleeding, your teeth loose like piano keys. And after eating, one of your company, a young, sickly boy had such a bad case of the dysentery from the fruit that you and another soldier had to hold him out the door of the boxcar while he shat his guts out, and when you came to a village you asked one of the women for used coffee grounds which you fed to him with the last of the morphine capsules you'd hidden in the lining of your pants. That saved him, so that when your train pulled in at the Keleti in Budapest, he was sleeping like a baby, his head cradled on your lap...."

"How do you remember all of these stories?" he had asked.

But by then, I was unable to stop.

"And what about when you and the three younger soldiers you shared your tent with...you know, the ones who asked you to read to them every night (you had a tattered copy of the New Testament in your pack, the other sheets used for toilet paper, but you had refused to desecrate the Word in that way)? And you teaching them to wash with their own urine, and standing in line for your daily glass of water, a rind of stale bread, some soup that looked and tasted like dirty dishwater, wolfing down everything in under a minute, then lying in the tent, crazy from hunger and thirst under the hot summer sun. And when the rain finally came, how you all stripped down and watched the rivulets of dirt running down your bodies, your faces lifted to the heavens, finally drinking, drinking the rain, finer than any drink you had ever had...?"

"I forget all that. That was a long time ago–a world away," my father had answered, his shoulders stooped as he shuffled to the kitchen. "I have to check the dinner. The veal shanks with the stuffed garlic buds take six hours at slow simmer, but I have to make sure the garlic doesn't turn brown too soon or it will become too bitter. I also have to make potatoes and sauté the breaded mushrooms. Do you want wine with the meal, or more beer?"

I stared after him, hearing this last part from the kitchen, hearing the clanging of the pots and pans and utensils. I sighed and sat in the chair next to the old photo album and started going through it, abstracted, page by page, seeing all the faces from the past and of all the dead. Finally, my father called me.

"Set the table, will you–and don't forget the gravy boat. The new corkscrew is on the sideboard. See if you can open that bottle of Merlot. I bought it because I knew you were coming."

Dinner was long over, and it had turned into late afternoon. Shadows of the clouds slid down the mountains and the autumn day seemed to be in a half-light. I heard my father groan in the bathroom, the sound of diarrhea, and then the toilet flushing. He had eaten too quickly again. Through the divide into the kitchen I had seen him furtively holding a large bowl of the remaining potatoes and fried mushrooms, drinking the greasy leftovers hungrily even after he had gorged himself on the one meal of the day he allowed himself.

"Are you alright?" I tapped on the door of the bathroom.

"Yes, I'm fine. Just the usual." We were both silent for a while until he emerged from the bathroom.

"*Apu,*" I began, and then stopped until, finally, I said: "The meal was delicious. You really outdid yourself. I forget how much I miss veal sometimes–Hungarian cooking in general."

"Yes, a man has to know how to cook. I think I taught you that. That's one skill you'll have for the rest of your life."

Then, he continued: "Now if you could clean up in the kitchen, I think I'll read a bit and nap for an hour."

There were many dishes, most of them covered in grease so that I had to empty the sink twice and refill it with fresh detergent. It had gotten almost dark now. I remember noting that the days seemed shorter in the mountains. I felt tired, drained, and I yawned, wondering if it was the heavy food or the mountain air that always made me so drowsy.

I looked into the living room and saw my father asleep in his La–Z-boy chair. He was snoring loudly, something that had always annoyed me, but today his breathing seemed laboured and noisier than usual. I noticed that there was a line of spittle fallen onto his chin and onto the impeccably knotted tie, and his glasses threatened to slip off his nose.

I walked quietly up to my father, gently removed the book he was holding that had slipped into his lap, and went to replace it on the shelf. There was a space next to the line of journals, and I took the one closest to the end from the shelf furtively and began to page through the parts most recently filled with his meticulous script. I had always wondered what the journals contained, maybe all the stories of my father's past, his secret life, perhaps ideas, wisdom, notes for a novel. I had often thought about this, every time I had observed his rituals in the early morning during my visits.

I began to read hungrily. I read each page at first, and then more, faster, finally skimming the pages, my astonishment growing with each sentence. Each diary began the same way. First, my father recorded the day's temperature and then wrote a brief comment about the weather forecast. He described his rituals, his breakfast, his bath, how he had dressed, what he wore. All of this was followed by a single quote from the Bible–nothing more, just a cited passage. Finally, he recorded the number of pills he had taken and how many bowel movements, everything that has passed for action during each day.

The one time that I had stopped to read in more detail was the entry from six weeks before, the last time he had come up to Montreal for his appointment. Halfway through it I read: "Dr. Salley said there is a recurrence, sooner this time than the last one. They cannot operate at this time." There was also a quote from Timothy 2, Chapter 4, verse 1: "I charge thee therefore before God, and the Lord Jesus Christ, who shall judge the quick and the dead at His appearing and His kingdom." The page finished with a detailed description of the evening's meal Elizabeth had cooked–filet of sole basted in flour, egg, and batter.

Almost guiltily, I replaced the journal in its row, straightening its spine to align with the others precisely as my father liked them. I looked over at him, at his hands with the liver spots, the few remaining tufts of curled hair, the mole on the right thumb, the hands, seemingly trembling even in sleep. I thought of my father's other life, the one he never spoke about anymore, of how he must have had to fight back the horror of that camp every day. In his old face, I saw how he must have looked as a younger man, face upturned to the falling rain that had finally come, huddling naked in half dance, half supplication, perhaps even laughing, bathed by the healing rain.

My father, sleeping in his chair in the half-light of early evening, now grown sick, so old.

I close the pages of the album, caught in the ache of memories, and decide to go out to eat. I walk along Sherbrooke until I come to a café across from the park at the corner of Girouard next to the old Cinema V, all boarded up, that too all but forgotten. Inside,

I order a soup and a sandwich, smelling the aroma of tea, spices, and strong coffee. When the food is served, I recall the short grace in Magyar my father had taught us, his children, something we would always say before our meals. It is a simple child's rhyme, and I whisper it silently before I begin to eat.

CHAPTER 18

There are forty-three curves along the stretch of twenty-some kilometers of what locals call The Notch between Lake Placid and Wilmington, New York, the small village at the foot of Whiteface Mountain, the second highest peak in the Adirondacks with its barren top of granite rock that from a distance appears as a patch of snow. It was early fall, I remember, and the leaves had just started to turn into their patchwork of brilliance.

It must have been just after dawn, and I was alternating between speeds of seventy-five and one hundred kilometers, which was much faster than I normally should have gone, having driven this road so often. The familiar rocky shores of the Ausable River went by like a blur on the left. Usually, several fly fishermen in hip waders would be casting into the dark pools where the rushing water gathered among the larger rocks, but the trout season was long over and the river was empty of life.

There was no oncoming traffic as I accelerated along the final two kilometer stretch of road, just past the turnoff to the chair lifts leading to Little Whiteface, past the Hungry Trout restaurant where I had worked decades ago doing kitchen prep and washing dishes. I thought back on the phone call in my hotel room just after four that morning.

Elizabeth had phoned saying:

"The hospital just called. Your father's in a bad way. They say to come right away, as quickly as possible." She had hesitated for some time, then, finally: "I'm sorry...are you ok?"

"Thanks for letting me know," I remember answering her blankly. I started to say: "How's Nico?" but she had already hung up, so

I placed the phone back on its cradle and started to throw my things into the overnight bag before setting out.

I thought of my father lying on his sickbed on 10 East, the ward for terminal patients. I had been to visit him just before setting out to settle his affairs in the small Adirondack town of Saranac Lake, a two-and-a half hour drive from Montreal. He had lost a lot of weight during the last months of his stay and looked gaunt and grey. The bowel cancer, which had been under control for over a decade, had metastasized and found a new site in the bladder and lungs. The staff said it was only a matter of time, and that they would keep him as comfortable as possible with morphine and oxygen.

He had tried to sit up when he noticed me and waved his arms weakly, signaling me to approach. He was an old man in his early eighties with closely cropped white hair and a thick, trimmed military mustache, long pointed ears that had struck me that day as being almost absurdly genie-like. I leaned over to kiss him on both cheeks in the formal European manner, and he grasped my hand fiercely, determined, so that I had to finally pry his fingers loose.

As I was driving, this image came back to me as I picked up the coffee from the cup holder next to the gearbox. The remnants of a breakfast sandwich I bought at the twenty-four–hour diner in Placid sat on the passenger's seat in its greasy wrapping.

My father had loved to eat and hated fast food. Civilization, he once said, had come to an end in that vast expanse of raped nature, rutted by the bulldozers and turned into concrete malls and fast-food restaurants sprawling over most of North America. He had loved good food, loved cooking it, looking at it, talking about it, but most of all eating it. In my mind's eye I see him standing in front of the marzipan genie in the display window of Demel's pastry shop in Vienna in his Pichler hat and Loden coat, his silver-tipped walking cane glittering in the sun, savouring the moment in the crisp autumn air before entering the world of confectionary smells and strong espresso. He'd sit and order the chestnut cake with *schlag,* the heavy whipped cream, and a coffee with *schlagober.*

Or I can envision him on the terrace of the Café New York in Budapest over a glass of *Tokay Aszu,* perhaps at the same table where Karinthy had sat when he wrote about the death of the Hapsburg Empire. My father sitting there, lamenting the chipped marble on the table, the dust on the chandeliers, Stalin and the Russians, the death of his world, that so familiar city, himself a stranger now, dying, in a land eight thousand kilometers away in a country whose language he had never quite mastered, soon to be scattered dust.

I remembered the last time he sat in our kitchen, watching me make chicken paprika the way he had taught me. But not quite. Instead of lard, I had used olive oil, my own concession to health and diet. *Never the same,* he had said. *You must use lard for the flavour.* My greatest betrayal was while he was visiting with us that summer before his final admission into the hospital. Even though he was already weak, ill and tired, he had sat on a chair watching me cook, going through the ingredients, giving directions: *Now, slowly stir in the sour cream... no, don't let the sauce boil, or it will curdle...*

But I had betrayed him that day. Instead of the lard, I had sneaked in the oil. Yet after we had eaten, he had pronounced the meal "excellent."

Approaching the turnoff to the gravel road that led down to the Fish 'n Game Club down by the shore of the Ausable River, I saw a sudden blur of brown and a powerful jolt along the hood of the car sent me careening into the field by the side of the road, and stopping just before smashing into a large spruce. In my confused and dazed state, everything unfolded in slow motion: the animal bolting out of the woods from across the highway: my inability to veer away or stop because of the speed at which I was travelling:

the loud thud of the deer's body hitting the windshield and rolling off the hood: splayed hooves shattering the glass on the passenger's side, followed by the car's wild slide across the gravel, ditch, and into the field.

Trembling, I unbuckled the seat belt, opened the door and gingerly stepped out of the car to survey the damages. There was a dent in the grill and the windshield was partly shattered with a long hairline crack that covered one side leading to just above the steering wheel. Some blood splattered part of the glass. The car sat at an awkward angle, its nose pushed into the slump of the field that declined down to the tree, a swath of tire marks cutting jaggedly into the grass.

Beginning the slow trek back to the road, I noticed an almost imperceptible movement in the copse of trees to my left. As I approached, the back hooves of the deer were spasmodically kicking at the ground, trying to right itself. I came closer. The animal, a three-pronged buck, lay among the gravel, shuddering, its breath coming in short gasps. Its mouth was partly opened, the flat teeth bared, and white foam flecked with blood pumped out of its nose.

I had to do something, so I searched nearby hoping to find a stick or a rock and found a large piece of granite, almost too heavy to carry to the deer struggling to breathe. I walked up to the deer's head and lifted the rock with both hands, hesitating for a moment, uncertain. Pain and terror in the animal's eyes, brown pools of liquid, followed my every move. I finally brought the rock down with all of my force on the deer's skull and jumped back, panting. The deer jerked, its body convulsing, its legs kicking out in the air. Sickened by the sight, I reached for the granite now lodged against the animal's nose and felt the coarse bristle of its coat brush my hand as I grasped the rock. Raising it high, I brought it down with full force onto the deer's skull again and again until the animal gave a final spasm and became still.

I stood there, trembling, knowing it was finally dead, no longer in agony, then turned back to the highway, my face wet from sweat and tears, walking as if drunk, the dizziness in my head, a dull, numb humming.

A tow truck had come at last and pulled my car out of the ditch to take it to the garage in Lake Placid. I rode in the front with the driver and mentioned the dead deer, but he told me not to give it another thought since this was a common occurrence in these parts. I needed to explain to him what it was like smashing the granite down on the animal's head, shock reverberating through my arms as the rock had met the hard yield of the animal's skull. Above all, I thought of the moment when the light went out of the animal's eyes and my own trembling memory of this, but the driver was a silent type, smoking, undoubtedly thinking about tourists and drivers in his part of the world. When we arrived in Lake Placid, I was lucky to find a rental car, which I drove more slowly and carefully despite the urgency to get to the hospital, arriving there only in the late evening.

I remember approaching the bed where my father lay gasping for breath despite the flow of oxygen through the mask affixed to his face. A catheter bag was attached to the bedside railing, its content filled with urine, sludge, and blood. I stood looking down at him, whose vacant, glazed eyes seemed to focus at some spot above my head. His rate of breathing increased over the next hour and I reached out to grasp his hand, but then hesitated, withdrawing, watching, both hands clenched into fists by my side.

At some point, I must have drifted off into a deep sleep, exhausted from the events of the day, and it was still dark when I awoke to the loud gasps of strained breathing coming from the bed. In the dim glow of the bedside light my father seemed to be shuddering and the oxygen mask had slipped off his nose, resting by the side of his face. As I reached over to adjust it, the rate of his breathing seemed to increase, and then it paused for a tense moment as he mouthed a wordless *OW*, his face contorting into a grimace before freezing into immobility.

I stood there staring down at what had been my father, and then slowly drew the curtains around the bed and went to the nursing station. A young Haitian nurse accompanied me back to the room and checked my father's vital signs, then unceremoniously cut the rubber balloon attachment of the catheter, grasping my father's shriveled penis and withdrew its bloodied length in front of me. She looked at me perfunctorily and asked if I wanted to wait outside while the Resident on duty came by to call the time of death. I continued sitting, not answering her, and she eventually returned with what I knew was the hospital shroud kit, followed shortly by the young doctor. The Resident spoke sharply to the young nurse, asking her in French if she couldn't have waited until the "family" had departed. Then, he wrote something on the bedside chart and asked me to accompany him.

In the room next to the nursing station, the doctor appeared uncomfortable, telling me that my father had suffered cardiac arrest, that it had been swift, that he was out of his misery. He spoke quickly, mouthing empty words, almost desperately anxious to get back to his other duties among the living. I thanked him numbly and returned to the room, and when I parted the curtains around his bed, I saw the shroud kit lying on the table as I looked at my father's face one last time, now motionless and grey, one eye partly open staring off into nothingness.

I walked past the nursing station and glared at the young nurse who avoided my eyes, continuing her charting. I took out my cell phone and dialed. Elizabeth picked up the phone at her end almost immediately, and I told her softly:

"It's over. He died about twenty minutes ago." I then hesitated and continued, "It was quick. I don't think he suffered much," though I could still see in my mind's eye my father's final wordless utterance of pain.

"I'm sorry," she replied, after a long pause. "I really am. How are you?"

"Alright... managing."

"Stephen," she said, "I am so sorry... for everything. Please know that."

"Yes," I replied. "I do know it." And then almost formally in a monotone I told her about my accident, the car, and how I needed to go back to Lake Placid and would probably be away for at least another night. I had shut down, as was my habit.

"My God," Elizabeth cried. "Why didn't you let me know? Almost an entire day has gone by without me knowing anything. What's wrong with you? Why do you have to lock everything inside?" But then she stopped and was silent.

I walked back to the parking lot and found the rental car and drove south onto the 15 over the bridge toward the border. Exhausted and somewhat disoriented, I joined the flow of early commuter traffic heading toward the South Shore.

It was close to noon as I entered the first curve of the Notch slowing down, approaching it warily. After the interminable twists and turns, I finally arrived in Lake Placid and drove around, looking for a motel to spend the night, hoping that the garage where my car had been towed had begun working on it so that I could leave to go back to Montreal the next morning, though I also was in no real hurry to return.

It promised to be a beautiful afternoon with the sun shimmering on the vast lake, a hint of seasonal change in the wind that tossed my hair and cooled the sweat on the back of my neck. I walked onto the main drag, wanting to be swallowed up in the flow of pedestrians and tourists ambling along the street, who stopped frequently to look into the windows of the many stores and boutiques, oblivious to each other, of other lives, caught up in the rhythm of their days. The routine activities that one could control, those things that guided one's daily life made it all seem secure, safe, and the whole lot almost possible.

Images of everything that had happened in the short space of a few hours assailed me, a distorted kaleidoscope that pressed in so much that I needed to break away from the crowd of tourists hogging the main street. I experienced a moment of disquiet and light–headedness, so much so that I had to stop and grasp the wooden railing that separated the human traffic from the drop that led down to the water. Then, I quickly thought of other things: the car, the length of time it would take to repair it, the cost and how to spend the next few hours, waiting. Despite everything, the damage was most likely minor, and people here were probably used to such incidents happening all the time.

CHAPTER 19

"Tell me about the day it happened," Dr. Rheinblatt says. For a moment I think he is asking me about the deer, my father's last moments, but then realize we are back to the inexhaustible theme of my suicide attempt.

"Again, the euphemisms?"

He ignores this and continues: "You were teaching that day, no?"

"Yes, it was near the end of term. The Christmas break was looming."

"And your wife? Where was she at that time?"

"We had split by then. I had been more than a year on my own. Nico was away at graduate school. We had sold our house and split the profit. I was in the place where I am living now."

"What can you remember about that day?"

"Remember? I remember that I was teaching my last class of the day on the Metaphysical poets. 2:55 on a Friday is always a particularly challenging time. Those students who did attend the class had settled into that resigned state of waiting out the hour and fifteen minutes, hoping that their presence would be remembered in my final evaluation. Many of the others stayed away every Friday, and even though the course outline ominously warned that 'Attendance Is Mandatory.' My students had long ago called my bluff and knew that I was a soft touch."

"Go on."

"So, it was particularly surprising when this blond with the swan's neck walked into class five minutes late. She was all long, bewitching legs, hair, the model's slump, cool dismissive gaze, and that long, graceful neck. She walked in, and the class froze; the other girls stared at her thinking their own thoughts, the boys thinking theirs, and she coolly looked back at them, acknowledging them, dismissing them, then sat in her usual seat (always magically never taken) and proceeded to file her nails."

"And you, what were you thinking?"

"Of her? She was attractive, sure. But for Christ's sake, she was only eighteen. I was thinking more about the irony of the situation. Here she was, someone who hardly ever showed up, and when she did, she totally took over the class."

"Took over? How so?"

"Well, I looked at her and at the class and knew that I had lost them, no longer to just their weekend thoughts and boredom, but to her, to the IT of her presence."

"What do you mean by that?"

"Her youth, beauty, sexuality. Here I was talking about poetry, about 17th century metaphysical verse, and here were my students actively living out their fantasies. I had no chance."

"What happened then?"

"Forcing a measure of enthusiasm into my voice, I continued my lecture. If you care to hear it, it went something like this:

"'Now, you may remember from our last class that we had talked about the beginning of Marvell's argument to his mistress where he sets up a hypothetical world of Arcadian delights. Can anyone tell me how the poet uses irony in the depiction of his slowly rousing passion toward the object of his love?'

"This was followed by silence. Not unused to this, I continued, prompting: 'Now, surely you remember what I said a conceit was?' More silence. Students looked down at their desks, avoiding my eyes, or drawing pictures (of me? I wondered) in their notebooks. She of the swan's neck continued filing her nails–a Dickensian woman for whom I could all too easily have substituted the nail file for knitting needles."

Dr. Rheinblatt does not acknowledge the reference.

"Go on," he says. I notice him stealing a glance at the clock artfully concealed from my view.

"More silence followed, so, finally, I sighed and fell back into my safety net and asked: 'What do you make of this issue of irony in the first part of the argument, Linda?'

This was addressed to my ninety plus student who always knew the answers, but saved my dignity by refraining to comment until called upon, who was a Future English Major, perhaps someone who would stand one day where I stood, who would one day learn (too late!) what it was to Suffer, not as idea or literary theme, but as a real, integral part of life. Titters of laughter ran through the classroom.

"'Yes, Linda?' I prompted.

"More laughter followed. She was absent, for the first time all semester; she had also failed me, gone perhaps to her own weekend dreams. They knew, my students. Oh, they knew. The class snickered and checked the time, freedom just a short stretch away. Perhaps they were glad, not that I had been embarrassed so much, but that they had been vindicated because Linda, whose powerful insights had made them squirm and excluded them from the dialogue, had left for parts unknown."

"And how did this make you feel?"

"Furious, for some reason. I took this somehow as a personal slight. Strange, given that I am a seasoned teacher, and had long ago become a cynic about the worth of what I was teaching. Anyway, their laughter, which I normally would have shared, for I always had the ability to laugh at myself, turned into anger. Even though I knew why and also knew it was unreasonable, I couldn't stop myself."

"What were you angry about?"

"That's it. There's the rub, as the bard says. Angrier at myself for wanting them to care about what I was teaching, I suppose. Or angry at myself for caring about the tragedy of it all."

"What tragedy do you mean?"

"The usual refrain. My stale metaphor about the fall of Icarus. The Bruegel picture I'm always telling you about. The boy disappearing in the waves and the merchant ship sailing calmly by. Most of my students are studying either commerce or science, I don't need to tell you. For them, poetry, literature, things of the spirit hardly matter. But I digress."

"Indeed. Then what happened?"

"Well, I picked on the immediate culprit, the outlet for my frustration. The babe with the swan neck. 'So, Ms.….' I remember saying. Here I had to pause and check the class list. There it was…Cheryl Fine. After thirteen weeks.

"'Yes, you, Ms. Fine,' I said. 'It does help if we bring our books, even better, if we read the material. Anyway, never mind. All right then. Do you have a book now? Goood. So. What about the next passage, right after where we stopped on Wednesday? What do you think the poet means by the line: '*My vegetable love will grow*?' There was no answer.

"'Yes, Ms. Fine?'

"'Maybe he's talking about growing a cucumber.'

"A miracle. These were the first words she had spoken in my class the entire semester. Lucky for her there was a 5% mark for class participation. But that day, for some reason, I could not let it go, as I knew I should have done.

"'And why, pray tell, that noble vegetable, Ms. Fine?'

"No reply. She was truly embarrassed now, her cool and composure gone. She turned to the boy next to her, Jason, a B student, he of the flaming zits, and whispered something rapidly to him. Jason blushed, redder than marinara sauce.

"'Actually, Ms. Fine, you have made a most astute observation. *Vegetable love* implies fertility, ergo sexuality.' I then turned to the entire class. 'A cucumber, as your sensitive peer so accurately pointed out, is the most phallic of vegetables. It grows and grows like other things we know and cherish. Still confused? Then how about this one: you have probably all heard from your parents or grandparents Mae West's famous line? No? Well, let's rewrite it from the metaphysical perspective: "Is that a cucumber in your pocket, big boy, or are you just happy to see me?" And that, ladies and gentlemen is what is known in poetry as an extended conceit. Thank you.'

"She rose, glaring at me, grabbed her purse, and walked quickly out the door slamming it. Twenty pairs of eyes followed her, seven of them, at least, lovelorn, one pair particularly so (Jason would always remember that day, for she had spoken to him! The evening scrubbing with the Clearasil would take on a special poignancy henceforth!) Twenty pairs of eyes avoided mine as I stared after her."

Dr. Rheinblatt is silent for some time, writing on his pad.

"And why do you think you humiliated your student?"

"Humiliated?"

"Yes. What were you feeling angry about?"

"Well, many things. Her contempt of what matters to me. Literature. Art. Things of the spirit."

"Enough to make you lash out?"

"Yes, I suppose."

"And what did you do after?"

"Well, that class finally came mercifully to an end. We had stopped at the crucial point of the second part of the poet's argument to his mistress, the part where he threatens her with the tomb. It's one of my favourite lines:

"'*And worms shall try thy long-preserved virginity.*' One of my students had actually gasped as I read it out to the class that day. 'Gross,' I heard her say. The students filed out, chattering to each other amiably, off to their dreams and the weekend. No one bothered to say goodbye."

"So, you felt a bit sorry for yourself, for the fact that nobody understood you, or felt about things the same way as you?" Dr. Rheinblatt asks.

"Yes, I suppose so."

"And what happened then?"

"I wanted to tell them the point of it all, but they didn't get it."

"The point being?"

"The point of it all, I wanted to tell my class, was passion. Youth. And Death. There was, of course, Death, which gave flavour to it all. Marvell was a young man in the prime of life who knew the poignancy of '*Time's winged chariot.*' Above all, he was someone who, purely and simply, wanted to get laid but knew the secret of making lust poetic under the rubric of love. Of course, the poem had humour, and my students laughed when I pointed out the obvious lines. It didn't really matter if the intention was purely rhetorical, for by the time you finished the poem, it had all gone beyond the loss and even transcended the mistress herself, leaving only the magnificent words to do battle with the forces of Time."

"Do you envy your students' youth?" Dr. Rheinblatt asks.

"Yes, I suppose I do. That day was some kind of an epiphany for me. My own face mirrored in the window, reflected back, waking from the reverie of sitting in a dark classroom, long after all my students had left. Jesus. I saw my own image in the glass, grey hair, lined face and all. There was the start of a middle-aged spread. Dandruff. More."

"And that made it bitter for you?"

"Yes, the poignant realization of mortality, not the fright I had felt as a young man, waking in the middle of the night... the Kierkegaardian fear, sickness, and trembling, but something more tangible. The palpable sense of my own age."

"And what did you think about at that stage?" Dr. Rheinblatt's voice is almost gentle.

"About what I had said to them earlier, my students. '*Carpe diem.*' Seize the day."

There is a long silence, as Dr. Rheinblatt looks at me, waiting for me to speak.

"And you know something? They had, my students. Gone to their weekends, leaving me to my thoughts, to languish in the slow-chapped power of memories."

Against my better judgment and purpose, my eyes suddenly fill with tears that come freely, and I do nothing to hide it from Dr. Rheinblatt, who leans forward toward me and folds his hands, for once, almost benignly.

CHAPTER 20

How had it happened, he wanted to know? It is not so much the "how" but more the "why" that still interests me. The "how" is all too mundane. A bottle of pills imbibed with several shots of Chivas Regal and a beer chaser. Even then I hated the taste of the raw Scotch, so I suppose the concession to beer was a testament to my desire to live, as Dr. Rheinblatt will probably tell me during our next session. I sat down in my armchair, waiting for the end, wondering whose words I'd want to read preparing for the finality. I thought of Sylvia Plath, her suicide attempt as a grand "striptease" but realized the hyperbolic nature of that phrase. Perhaps someone milder, wiser; maybe Emily Dickinson, who was so intimately acquainted with Death. I took down her collected works, opened randomly, and read one of the passages equating death with desire.

No, not quite right. I did not want to make the Last Exit not fully understanding what the poet meant by that. Was it the mystery of Death, of Life, of Divine Love? I truly didn't know. My eyesight started to get a bit fuzzy and a tremendous heat coursed through my body. I felt weakness, some melancholy, but no real panic. Arrangements had been made. I had laid out my last will and testament, leaving everything to Nico. The hardest had been the letter to write to him: my apology. And the other letter to Elizabeth saying finally all the things I had left unsaid. What book did I want to leave lying in my hand? Nico understood symbols and metaphors, so I wanted to leave him some clue, some hint, some hope so that he wouldn't spend his life bothered by the reasons why. I had laid the pages of my finally finished manuscript totaling over 400 pages next to the other documents. Nico would know what to do with that: read it, and then burn it as per my request, written on the final page, if he even decided to read that far.

As I looked at the manuscript through the film of the drugs I had consumed and my own despair, I suddenly remembered Camus' words about a modernist writer who had committed suicide to bring attention to his work. Ironically, his work was judged as less than mediocre, despite all of the attention it garnered. I started to laugh then, laughing until the tears began to flow. In that moment, I understood that my moment of existential authenticity was nothing more than the pitiful desire for recognition and sympathy. Was it too late, I wondered? For what? My eyesight was starting to fail; so, it was true then after all what Miss D. had written: the failure to really *see* just as our sight is failing?

Clutching her *Collected Poems,* I opened my apartment door and stumbled down the hallway toward the building's entrance, only to encounter the three elderly Scottish ladies who shared the flat next to mine. They were called, as their mailbox affirmed, the Misses Mousley, tiny creatures straight out of some Beatrix Potter story with curled perms and pussycat glasses from the 50s, dressed uniformly in tartan. The eldest, I believe, was ninety-three years old, and it was she who addressed me as I felt myself slipping to the ground before them.

"Why, whatever is wrong, Professor?" (They were impressed that I was a "literary scholar," as they liked to call me. I had known them for some months, ever since I had gone off on my own after Elizabeth, and had had them over once for sherry as they murmured among themselves, admiring my rows of books while we listened to Glenn Gould's version of *The Goldberg Variations*). The last I remembered was one of them saying "Oh dear, oh dear, whatever shall we do?" And then the *Collected Poems* slipped out of my grasp and I knew nothing.

When I awoke, coughing, as they withdrew the airway from my throat, tasting the raw charcoal and hearing the insistent "blip" of the monitors, I tried to touch something, but felt the tug of the restraints on my hands though I did see the *Collected Poems* on the night table beside me. During the next few weeks in the institute I wandered along the hallways gripping the railing to steady myself from the effects of the Largactil, searching for my Carl Solomon, encountering instead boring, self-absorbed people, some truly troubled, some plain messed up. One day, I opened up the book of poems and found a note written in dainty cursive that read:

"Dear Professor. We hope you are recovering nicely from the strain on your nerves. We wanted to make sure you had this book in your hour of darkness to offer you some small solace. Miss Dickinson was surely a fine poet, such a purveyor of Truth, don't you think, perhaps a tad obsessed with the Great Beyond, though she surely did affirm the glory and grandeur of God in every turn of phrase? Be well, dear heart."

It was signed "The Misses Mousley." I smiled for the first time since I could remember.

During my two months on the ward, I went through the different Phases until I arrived at Number Four when you were given the privilege of going off the ward out into the city, after having signed out and having given your destination and estimated time of return. At first, I made tentative forays into the downtown, walking the stretch between Peel and Atwater along Ste–Catherine, judiciously avoiding the bookstores since the young resident, a student of Dr. Rheinblatt, believed that it was the intellectual fatigue of my work that had driven me to the Act.

Which was what they called it, even among themselves, I later learned. I wondered if any of them knew the *New Testament* or read the "Acts of the Apostles" as some kind of suicide mission, though I guess in the case of St. Paul it was of sorts, albeit in his eyes a transcendent one.

Walking back along Ste–Catherine I wandered as far as Philips Square and then down to René-Levesque to the Cathédrale Marie-Reine-du-Monde and entered. I remember having gone there several times during my years in graduate school, not for solace but for the weekly mass said in Latin. I had studied Latin in high school and university, and the formality and grandeur of the High Mass spoke to me, though I never fully understood why. I still knew all the responses from my youth, having been forced to attend a Catholic school that demanded daily attendance at church.

Entering the cathedral, it struck me how austere it is on the inside, how devoid of the grandeur of the European cathedrals I had visited so often in my youth while travelling in Europe. Unlike the Duomo in Firenze and St. Peter's in Rome, all this had going for it was the outside architecture. The inside was drab, and even the paintings on the ceiling were faded and of poor quality. Brown empty pews stretched the length of a football field with no more than twenty souls, some praying, most just sitting forward and obstinately gazing toward the altar where a woman's voice was droning in French and her students, obviously from a Catholic school, were repeating their rote responses.

The figure of an old woman sitting in a pew near the sanctuary of one of the rooms, which housed the corpse of a bishop and was locked to the public, caught my attention. She was in ragged clothes, a shopping cart with a worn cloth cover standing next to her in the aisle. Plastic bags abounded, and what looked like some dirty clothes had spilled over onto the pew. She was clutching them and sleeping deeply, her snoring reverberated in contrapuntal rhythm to the droning voice of the woman and the children in front of the altar. She had found a haven, a sanctuary from the noise and chaos of the city where the cars went roaring by outside.

I remember how different walking through St. Peter's in Rome was back over thirty years ago when I had travelled there. What struck me about the Italian churches was how utilitarian they are, there for the general public. I remember attending a mass one Sunday and watching the Italian families with their *bambini,* who ran around and played during the service. One family had even bought a basket with food, and the *Nonna,* a woman in her late seventies, sat half listening to the priest while slicing salami and putting it onto pieces on bread, feeding it to the grandchildren who came to her between playing. It had struck me the caring and love she showed them: no attempt to curb their youthful exuberance, so that it seemed that religion was truly part of the ritual of everyday life.

And I also remember another time in Paris. I had just come back from Sunday morning tea at *Shakespeare and Company* (George Whitman, the owner, was still alive back then, a formidable man, a Marxist and socialist who practiced generosity more than most by offering his store as a haven for the poor poets and artists who walked through his doors, offering them a chance to congregate and read their work). After the morning gathering, I walked across the Seine and almost immediately came to Notre Dame, that great medieval cathedral with its flying buttresses and spires pointing toward an empty heaven. Once inside, it struck me how quiet it was and, above all, how dark. The only light emanated from the stain glass window in the ceiling above the altar, high, high up. I remembered what I had learned about the Middle Ages, about the concept of "other-worldliness." The cathedral was a testament to this belief: the lot of Man being sorry, Man who lived in the constant darkness of the material world. The only thing to aspire to was the Light that came from above, from what they had conceived of as heaven, symbolized by the stained-glass windows.

Votive candles illuminated the dark corners, and many suppliants fervently but silently prayed. They looked small and lost in this great structure, and as I looked around its poorer counterpart in Montreal, I noticed a few souls, head bowed, eyes tightly closed calling on their god to give solace to their lives. It somehow made me uncomfortable to watch them and perhaps to be watched by them, the perpetual voyeur of the suffering of others; someone who has his need as well, though with no place to find an outlet for it. I was moved then to see them, and to see how empty the church was, no doubt a reaction to the Duplessis years and the Quiet Revolution when the populace finally turned against the tyranny of the Church. Despite this, mystery imbued this sacred place and the need it has represented throughout the ages, so I slid into a pew and closed my eyes.

Perhaps the mystery of a place of worship is what Huxley meant when he wrote about the desire to transcend our self-consciousness. What are the deepest needs that religion tries to satisfy? A connection with nature? With others? A sense of belonging to the earth and the universe unlike the existential isolationism that was so much in vogue after the horrors of the Second World War? Huxley had written about this after his mescaline experience in his *Doors of Perception.* He talks about the mystic Meister Eckhart who first wrote about *Istigkeit*–"Is-ness." Huxley wonders if art is a kind of *ersatz*–an ultimate fabrication, if even the artists who saw the world most profoundly were actually presenting a false construct. This made me think of something Dr. Rheinblatt had said or perhaps uncovered in our discussions: my use of literature as the fabrication of an ideal that didn't exist and never could, a state of being that is desired but is ultimately life-negating. When talking about perceiving through the mescaline experience, Huxley had written that one should always see this way, but the irony of this is if we did, we wouldn't want to do anything else except remain high and stare at the world. Thus, while one would be delivered from the world of moral judgment and utilitarian concerns, overvalued words and religious ideals, it would also lead one to the devaluing of quotidian, ordinary relationships and ultimate estrangement from our place in the world.

This may have been what led Christian mystics to the idea of the denial of the senses and of sensual experience and to their embrace of the concept of "other-worldliness." St. Theresa had written that the transcendent, mystical experience occurred when *"the soul is fully awake to God... but wholly asleep as regards to things of this world."* Similarly, St. John of the Cross, denying the senses, wrote there could be *"no sensible representation of God,"* which, upon first glance, could mean that God could only be experienced through faith, but upon closer examination could mean that our sensory faculties were actually at odds with our experience of the Divine.

I remember the night when I first took peyote with a friend from university days. We had each ingested eight buttons and soon after had become sick, vomiting profusely. Almost immediately, I felt a tremendous pressure in my head, a pressure that seemed so great I thought to my horror that my head was about to burst and that I was on the verge of losing complete control of my physical being. This didn't last long, and a great calm seemed to descend, a kind of humming of the universe around me. I remembered John Cage's words about silence, that it was actually a composition of the noises of life. I became acutely aware of the intake of my breath, the beating of my heart, and the noises that my own organs made simply in being. I was filled with a great joy–a sense of wonder is how I can best describe it–and also a tremendous sense of peace.

I looked at my friend, who held his face in his hands and appeared to be weeping. Finally, he looked at me with tears in his eyes and smiled, saying simply: "Yes...this is it...yes!" I didn't have to know what he meant, but just nodded. We passed through many of the phases Huxley describes in his essay, listening to music that gave us both a deeply sensual pang, and gazing at objects that seemed to be alive and vibrating with their inner beauty and life force. While there was the visual enhancement of the sensory experiences, a profound awareness pervaded our experience, a sense that time had stopped, that we were fully living in the moment, and that the desire for empirical affirmation, as Keats had written in his letter on Negative Capability, was meaningless. Gone was the need to differentiate, the need for moral judgment, and the dichotomy of opposites. Gone also was the need for words; there was only the silence around us, the shapes of the night and the earth that seemed to rock us and whisper some cryptic message meant for us alone to decipher.

Some hours passed, and at what I now consider the height of the experience, we ended up outside, walking through a park. How long we did this, I can't remember, but at some point, we had walked among a thick copse of trees and arrived at a clearing that was on the crest of a small hill. It was a balmy summer night, the stars were out, and there was a breeze that made the leaves on the trees below us shimmer with an almost ethereal living motion. We lay down on the soft grass and looked up at the sky, speechless.

Slowly a feeling (how else to call it?) came upon me as I looked up at the heaven of stars above. Although I was gazing up from the earth, I was also floating in space. There was no longer any sense of what was up and what was down: I felt myself a part of the universe, a small speck of it, but a speck that was also as big as the heavens and both as far and as distant as the galaxies unfolding before my eyes. I experienced a profound loss of self, something that did not frighten me, but a sense that I was a *part* of it all, not apart or different. I felt that the earth was my home, that, by some hidden tentacles it held me rooted to it, and while I was a part of the earth, I was also the sky, the stars, and also the vastness that stretched as far as my sight could carry me.

That was the closest I have ever come to a feeling of religiosity, where my inner world merged with the outer, physical one. There was no sense of an outside force, a transcendent Being, except the sensation of containing everything in the universe within me. It must have been the same as the force of the Tao that the Chinese sages had felt, the great Void of Buddhism that was nothing yet everything, that profound connection to all of life. The only thing I could feel was gratitude and wonder. Like what the Christian mystics had asserted, I too became *fully awake,* but unlike them, the things of this world were just as alive, just as important as the perception of the Divine that had come with this insight. I felt acutely my own mortality, the human shell I was born to carry throughout my days, but also sensed that immortal part of my being that lived and connected at that moment with the heart of all life.

As I am remembering and thinking about it, I note how words are inadequate to render this experience, even though language is the only way to somehow guard the memory. I hold on to this experience, the wonder of it all. As Huxley asserted, whoever goes through this experience comes out different. Yet I also now know that to render this experience in words is useless since someone who is to experience something similar has to do it for herself or himself. Thus, it is with religion and faith: it comes to us only second hand through the rituals of religion and the edicts of dogma. Being there on that hill, stretching out to the heavens, feeling the thrill of my physical body on the grass, the points of light from the stars illuminating my being, I knew that I could never gain all of this by reading the words of others but that it had to be fully experiential and not rationalized, as Whitman wrote in *Song of Myself*:

You shall no longer take things at second or third hand, not look through the eyes of the dead, nor feed on the specters in books. You shall not look through my eyes either, nor take things from me, you shall listen to all sides and filter them from yourself.

Sitting in a pew of the cathedral, I thought of these things and made the effort to pray or at least an effort toward reverent contemplation in the silent echoes of the vast chamber, but no words came, and I knew then that I would never think of God in anyway except that pervasive Force that unfolds into the world, not as the God of Love and Forgiveness who died for the sins of mankind, but if there in fact is one, One who contemplates our actions and aspirations in ruthless silence. Ruthless because we cannot conceive that we are unimportant in the great scheme of things and that we are ultimately significant only with respect to how we accept or embrace our lives or how we refuse to do so.

These speculations eventually struck me as somewhat absurd, and I smiled to myself and for a moment almost started to laugh out loud. Why is one obliged to be so serious in a church? Why not, like in Rome be like the families who bring their many *bambini* to mass and slice salami to spread over thick bread? There is more a sense of life there, of living, not the pervasive aura of silent guilt, though always still perplexing. I thought of Larkin's great poem, *Church Going*, and what he wrote about the haunting mystery and paradox of faith.

As a young man of twenty I had travelled back to Budapest and had gone to St. István's Basilica. This was still under Communism, and while the church was open to tourists, locals were actively discouraged from attending the few services that were allowed throughout the day. Standing that day at the altar before a statue of St István carved out of Carrara marble with the archangel Gabriel holding the Holy Crown above his head, I heard a timid voice addressing me in Magyar, asking me if I spoke that language. When I replied in the affirmative, a pretty young woman in her early twenties linked her arms in mine, looked around her nervously, and asked if we could speak outside. At first, she asked me where I was from, and after replying from North America, she said:

"You do look Magyar, you know, but it is the jeans you are wearing that give you away. Nobody in Budapest wears Wranglers. It is a strictly western product, not allowed by the State. In fact, you could make some good money if you ever wanted to sell them."

This was true. I had heard stories from an acquaintance during my travels who had come to Budapest and had been asked by someone using mime and hand gestures to step behind some bushes and exchange his blue jeans with the buyer's pants for the equivalent of forty dollars, big money in those days when the value of the Forint was very low and life was cheap if you were a tourist.

"Please, young gentleman," she continued squeezing my arm tighter, "you have a foreign passport surely, probably from America? I need to ask a large favour of you. We will be having relatives in from Miskolc who have come for the big international football match, Hungary against Czechoslovakia. You know it is the qualifier for the Euro Cup perhaps? No? Anyway, tickets are not available for the regular citizens of Budapest. They are saved only for foreigners. It would mean the world for me if you could find it in your heart to try the ticket office to see if they will sell you four tickets. I will of course pay, and maybe in some small way repay you for your troubles."

By this time, we had come to Vörösmarty Square where the Ibusz office was located, the local agency run by the State that controlled entertainment venues as well as housing for tourists. At her urging, I entered and went up to one of the agents and asked in English (as per my friend's request) for tickets for Saturday's match. The agent looked at me suspiciously and blankly and addressed me in halting German. I replied in German and told him I wanted tickets, showing him my American passport. He examined it curiously, flipping through the different pages showing the many stamps from the countries I had visited and my resident's visa from Austria, where I was living and studying at the time.

"*Wir haben kein mehr. Alle karten sind verkauft.*"

He noted the obvious disappointment on my face, hesitated, and said:

"*Aber vieleicht kann ich etwas finden. . . .*"

I had come to understand from my friend that this was my cue, so I reached into my wallet and pulled out a U.S. ten-dollar bill and slid it across the counter. The agent looked around furtively, palmed the money, and asked:

"*Wie viel wollen Sie, noch ein mal?*"

I told him four, and he gave me the four tickets for an outrageous price, though this time in Forints.

I met my friend outside the entrance to Gerbaud, showed her the tickets as she thanked me profusely, telling me that God's grace had surely visited her today and how happy this would make everybody. She opened her purse carefully and counted out the amount for the tickets but was several thousand Forint short of what I had paid.

"Thank you," I told her. "That is more than enough, as I handed back a 500 Forint note to her. You keep this for yourself. Will you join me for a coffee?"

We walked into the late empire opulence of Gerbaud, perhaps Budapest's most famous café. I marveled at the mahogany woodwork, high ceilings and windows draped with heavy maroon velvet curtains trimmed with gold brocade, small round marble tables with elegant wrought iron chairs, and a long glass display case for the assortment of pastries and sandwiches. It was like walking into an older time, and you could almost imagine the poets who had sat there: Mikszáth, Karinthy, Füst, all those who had lingered there and written about the Hapsburg Empire and post-war Hungary and the advent of modern, more bitter times. There were a few customers only, most of them foreign looking, wealthier, not dressed drably like the average Hungarian, some of them lingering over espressos, reading *Die Zeit* or *The Paris Herald Tribune* attached to their wooden stands.

We were led to our table by a surly waiter who noted the cheap dress of my friend and my jeans and khaki jacket that made us stand out conspicuously in the solemn, airy room. The waiter asked me in German what I desired while ignoring my companion, who had meekly placed an order for seltzer water in Magyar. Finally, he condescended to look at her and spat out:

"The likes of you have no business here. This is an establishment of class." He had used the familiar "*tu*" form, reserved for intimate acquaintances. In this context, I knew that he was using it in its most derogatory fashion for someone of the lower class; in her case, probably assuming she was a prostitute.

I drew myself up and looked the waiter in the eye, telling him in my most correct Magyar: "The lady (and here my voice rose slightly) and I will each be having a glass of your best Tokay. You make sure it is at least 3 Putonos." I too had used the familiar form to address him, emphasizing the "*tu*". He turned a bright red and marched off to the service counter to place our order. My friend smiled at me in gratitude.

Her name was Aniko, and she spoke in a rapid, breathless Magyar, stopping often to ask me if I was following her discourse. I told her

I was and sat back, content to listen to her story punctuated with squeezes of my hand while leaning across the table and shaking her blond locks.

Aniko told me about herself, the sadness and struggles that were her life. Her father was a bus driver who worked the evening shift, and her mother had died when she was fifteen. They lived in a small flat on the Buda side near the old *Tabán,* close to where I had lived as a child. She knew my street and said our building was now a pension run by East Germans, catering primarily to their crowd and to Russian tourists. Aniko worked as an assistant pastry chef at the Budapest School of Tourism and Catering near the Kossuth Lajos Square, next to the Parliament. She was glad to have a steady job, but the money was not good, so she and her father had to struggle to make ends meet.

"Life is very hard for us here in Hungary, even under the Kádár regime. There are a few who have, and most who don't. National Socialism is not working, and sometimes we have shortages also in the stores that are reserved for the foreigners, even if you try to buy with Deutsch Marks."

She had married at eighteen but the marriage had not lasted since they all had to live together in a one-bedroom apartment with his mother and sister, so they were forced to sleep on a mattress in the living room for two years. Just out of high school, her husband had trouble finding work and had finally been conscripted into the Army where he learned to be a mechanic, but that was after they had divorced.

"Now he is doing so well for himself, living in Pécs, working for the Lada Auto Parts plant there. We thought of getting back together, but it would have been hard to leave my father, who is very lonely. Recently, my ex has met someone else and may be marrying her soon, I think." She said this as a matter of fact, though there was a slight tremor in her voice.

Aniko asked me about my life and about North America. I told her about New York and Broadway, Fifth Avenue, the Lincoln Center, the many museums, American culture, and fine dining. About the Rockies and the west, the great distances, the winter cold, and the beauty of the vast rolling continent that spreads before you as you drive for almost a week from one coast to the other. Aniko's eyes sparkled and she hung onto my words, filling in some of my sometimes-uncertain vocabulary in correct Magyar.

At one point, she asked me to speak to her in English just so that she could hear the sound and flow of the language. She had a friend with whom she listened to The Rolling Stones although their music was almost impossible to find and its "decadence" discouraged by the State. She loved to dance and she and her friend would put on the Stones and boogie to "Satisfaction" while the parents were out working. Aniko wanted to learn English and wanted more than anything to travel and to see the West, she told me. But here, I noticed the great disconnect between us. While I had the full possibility of my life before me, she only had dreams, and these dreams bordered on desperation. They were about everything she couldn't do and everything she knew she would never have.

She told me all of this as we were walking along the Duna Korzó across the Chain Bridge over to the Buda side. Somehow, she had twined her fingers into mine. It had happened quite naturally, as naturally as she brushed her flanks against my side as we strolled through that early summer evening.

We passed 12 *Döbrentei utca,* my home as a child, walked through the *Tabán,* a former park that I remembered where my father had told me our mother had died. Once, while digging among the leaves in the park, I had unearthed a defective landmine, much to my father's horror, that was left buried when the German's retreated from the Russian Army at the end of the war. We turned up a small street and came to an older block of tenement houses where she pointed to the third floor and said:

"This is where we live, but my father is not home now. He's working and will be away until his shift ends after midnight. Will you come upstairs? I want to offer you some poor Magyar hospitality, some small thanks for your kindness and good company."

We walked up the three flights hand in hand.

The flat consisted of two small rooms and a tiny kitchen. The bathroom was a shared space down the hall. While I sat down at a small table in the main room, Aniko busied herself in the kitchen, talking to me all the while. She told me about her work and her coworkers, about the obese head pastry chef who never shaved, smelled constantly of flour and stale cigarette smoke, and who was always pinching her ass when she was bent over some cake spreading on the frosting and decorations. She said that she hated him, yet had no choice but to put up with his abuse since she needed to keep the job, which had been hard enough to find.

Aniko came back with a plate of sliced salami, green onions, pickled vegetables, smoked bacon, and bread. She had also brought out a bottle of the *pálinka,* a local brandy made of peaches that burned like fire as you swallowed.

Aniko raised her glass: "To your health. You have been a gift today in my life. Please accept this small token of hospitality. May your path always be the less travelled, but the most interesting, as we say. *Isten Veled.* May God go with you."

We talked for a long time, mostly with me listening, though she did prompt me with questions about my life in the West. The *pálinka* had made me woozy and I started to slump in my chair until she asked me to sit with her on their old sofa that she said she used as her bed. Aniko went into the other room and came back with a book that she then inscribed to me. Its cover said *Biblia,* and its covering was of old leather with worn pages.

"So now you will have a Magyar Bible to read to practice your vocabulary. It is my gift to you and my thanks for your kindness. I give this to you from the depth of my heart and will always remember our afternoon."

I choked up as I thanked her, and she must have detected the catch in my throat. She bent over and kissed me tenderly on both cheeks as she adjusted a pillow under my head.

Some time later, I awoke with Aniko, asleep, nestled in my arms. She had one arms tossed back against the couch and I saw the blond tuft of hair under the armpit, something that had always aroused me. She smelled sweetly of sweat and peaches. Slowly, she opened her eyes, smiled, and looked into mine. We kissed deeply.

"Father will be home soon. We have little time." She said this almost desperately.

Quickly I unzipped her dress and pulled it off, tossing it by the side of the couch. Then the bra, and finally her panties. She tore at my shirt, pulling it over my head, pulled down my blue jeans, my Wranglers. As she straddled me, kissing me deeply, I ran my hands over her buttocks and thighs, feeling the fine down of hair along her legs and calves, finally moving my fingers deeply into her moistness. She started bucking hard against my hand and then grabbed for my penis and quickly inserted it, starting to ride me. I drove to the hilt again and again as she groaned:

"My God...My God...." I came almost immediately but stayed hard inside of her for a long time while we kissed, caressed each other with our tongues and started a slow rhythm that seemed to last forever until it built up to another violent climax. She came repeatedly and I tried to hold back until I couldn't any longer, crying out in both my languages.

After, Aniko went to wash up and put on a nightdress. She looked blousy with her dishevelled hair and the swollen lips that I had kissed, bitten, and feasted on. We didn't say anything to each other as I dressed and also went to use the bathroom.

Before leaving, I embraced her by the door and we kissed softly and deeply. We looked at each other for what seemed like forever until I stroked her entire body tenderly from the top of her head to where her nightgown met the cleft of her buttocks. I lifted the cloth gently, cupped her and kissed her again deeply as I felt her moan softly in my arms.

"*Viszont látásra,*" I said, the traditional Hungarian goodbye that is closest to *au revoir*. She said nothing as she opened the door except to stroke my face as I turned to go down the stairs.

Once I was outside, I looked up in the direction of her window, but there was only the light that shone through the curtains. I walked back down to the river, seeing the beauty of the Parliament Building all lit up on the Pest side and, above me, the dark Buda hills and the silhouette of the Fisherman's Bastion.

Aniko, with whom I found a space in the heart; Aniko, whom I never saw or heard from again.

CHAPTER 21

Back then, I believed in the holy contours of life, so magic happened, often. And now? The effort of living seems to be what creates so much of the distortion. When I was released from the Institute, they told me to live a meaningful life, to try to be happy, but I somehow knew that the "maintenance" they had prescribed was a way to survive my life, not to live it. As I am out today walking along Monkland Avenue on a grey afternoon, a moment of dizziness hits me and a feeling of slight panic. It's the occasional effect of the medication, and I almost trip on the pavement, accidentally jostling a young couple who glare at me with hostility and walk by rapidly, muttering to themselves. It strikes me how much we are alone in a big city despite its many people. We are not kind to each other.

As I get my bearings and the dizziness passes, I think of Frank O'Hara and remember one of his poems where he talks about reeling around the streets of New York. Frank, whose poems I love, and whose poetry inadvertently saved my life.

Years ago, while still a student at Dartmouth, I was in transit from Buffalo, New York back to Hanover, New Hampshire and had to stop in New York City to change planes with almost four hours to spare. I took the bus to the depot near Madison Square Garden and then rode the subway to The Strand ("18 Miles of Books"), a store I had always wanted to visit. Browsing in the poetry section, I found O'Hara's *Collected Poems* and sat reading. I laughed over his *Lunch Poems*, drooled over his description of hamburgers and milkshakes eaten along Broadway, and thought of the Olivetti in the display window of a shop where he used to stop to type casual poems during the course of his working day. I thought of the music of Billie Holliday—"*Strange Fruit*"—Frank, the strangest fruit of all, who, many decades ago had stood in the Five Spot (now gone) listening to her and Mel Waldron on the piano, her voice descending into a whisper, a sob, as he, the poem, and I all stopped breathing.

I, too, wanted to be like that, to see the world's mosaic unfold and to piece it back together through words. I continued reading, following the rhythm of the poems, losing track of time. When I arrived at La Guardia Airport, I found that I had missed my flight and would have to wait for the evening connection. Upon arriving in Hanover past dusk among the sharp smell of pines, country darkness, and silence, I hitchhiked along an unlit road in November drizzle that was quickly turning into snow. Finally, a car stopped to let me into its human warmth and the inevitable strained conversation between strangers.

"What do you do?" I asked my driver after telling him that I was a student at the college to set his mind at ease.

"I'm an insurance investigator, here to assess the crash."

"Crash? What crash?"

"Flight 764—the 2:30 flight from New York City. Everyone was killed on board. Just some miles from here."

The heat rose in my face, and I said: "I missed that flight earlier in the day!"

"Wait just a minute now," he answered, his voice filling the car as he pulled over to the shoulder and turned on the inside light. Rummaging among his papers, he pulled out a sheet that had the flight log and passenger list and shoved it toward me. "In the next day or so I will have to inform the families," he said, his voice breaking off.

There were seventy-three names on the list of those once living, now dead. Turning away from him to face the dark, I mouthed to no one:

"Seventy-two...with one still to follow."

Years later, I told Nico this story and many of the others. I think about the DVD he made for my sixtieth birthday where his friends, whom I had come to know over the years, all paid homage to me and congratulated me, giving their best wishes. Nico prefaced this with a short, humorous excerpt about how it was, in fact, a miracle that I had even made it to this age given that I had dodged Russian bullets while escaping from Hungary as a child, could have been blown up by a landmine at the age of five, had narrowly escaped death at the hand of a rapist who had picked me up hitchhiking on my eighteenth birthday in the middle of a March snowstorm, and, of course, the close call on this flight. He and two of his best friends then took turns reading a story I had written about the hitchhiking event, acting out the most dramatic and darkly humorous parts. It is the most precious document I have in my possession.

When I think back on parts of my life, I sometimes see it as a story of how life's extraordinary moments can come true, as the great Czech writer, Bohumil Hrabal discussed in his brilliant book, *I Served the King of England*. Hrabal's genius is not just in the way he fashions a story or in his use of language, but more in his acknowledgement of wonder. Would Dr. Rheinblatt understand this if I told him? I don't think so. Unfortunately, his profession is concerned with the practical aspects of life, of teaching people how to function well in society. What about diversity, I wonder? What if we all were these programmed creatures who did everything by the book? What would we say, then, was the final sum of our lives, that is, even if we ever had the time to take stock? Auden's .

"unknown citizen" as a final numerical statistic or perhaps some obscure epitaph on a tombstone?

In Paris early one morning, I had walked with Elizabeth in the Père Lachaise Cemetery. We had just gotten off the overnight train from Innsbruck, returning to Paris on our way home to Canada after five marvelous weeks in Europe. We had hours to kill before we could check into our hotel, so I had suggested making this pilgrimage, initially to see Jim Morrison's grave. The cemetery was like a small town with its own boulevards, crowded tombstones often in close proximity to each other as if they were the people themselves jostling for place in crowded Metro cars. Since it was just near 8:00 a.m. we had the entire place to ourselves.

It was not difficult to find his grave since people had scrawled graffiti of "Jim" with arrows pointing in the direction of his tombstone. When we did get to it, it was much smaller than we had expected, and part of the nose had been broken off, a souvenir for some desperate groupie, undoubtedly. On the grass by the bust was an ashtray with a half-smoked cigarette, a few stray and wilted roses near the stone, and a half empty bottle of what I presumed had been Jim's favourite whiskey. Jim, one of our heroes, dead at twenty-seven, indirectly by his own hand. What had he learned from life when the music was finally over? Did anyone, in fact, know anything, or did we meander through life like ghosts, haunting the spaces and lives we inhabited?

As I now head for home turning onto Sherbrooke after Harvard, I pass the Italian grocery store and see my reflection in its glass door: Ashbery's *Self-Portrait in a Convex Mirror* suggests how we reflect and, in turn, are reflected. Mirrors of love, of joy, or first hope and first expression. As a child in Hungary I remember when I first noticed myself reflected in the mirror after my first haircut, a too serious boy, head shaven, and later on a carriage in the Budapest

Zoo solemnly holding the reins of a horse, my sister in braids sitting beside me. I thought I had control then, that the world would yield to my whims and desires. Now, the same eyes, but an ageing face like seeing Rembrandt's famous self-portrait—an older man's face yet the same eager, youthful eyes, but these eyes now, hurt, sad. What has changed us? The encroachment of our mortality?

Remembering my time in Paris with Elizabeth that morning among the graves, we passed by the great Edith Piaf's and lingered by the tombstone of Oscar Wilde. Elizabeth had to put on her lipstick and planted a kiss, as had others, while I thought what it must have been like for him, dying in exile yet still departing the world with one last memorable quip. Later, in our hotel room we held each other and made slow love hearing the sounds of Paris' bustle in the street below. And after, we walked along the streets of the city drinking in the life and thinking of all the faces we passed, all the lives intersecting ours. What if all of us could intersect in openness? All relationships should be like the moments one has in a new city, eyes open in wonder to the stranger whose eye we catch in the street, a mother's warmth as she looks at her child in its stroller, a word of endearment overheard. I thought of Kerouac who had written about the acceptance of loss, about how we should walk with the imminence of death proudly erect, but not as romantic posturing—rather, life as our right to live it, death as our inevitable legacy, its constant shadow our shroud. For me, not the search for a god, but a search for the heart. Now, maybe too late to learn forgiveness—forgiveness of others, ourselves, our lives, and our inadequacies and to find our place on earth.

CHAPTER 22

After Elizabeth left, I decided to make amends. I thought of the women I had known and wanted to contact them, to thank them for having given me love and for having touched my life. Perhaps this was sentimentality on my part, perhaps guilt for the departure of Elizabeth, as Dr. Rheinblatt would undoubtedly tell me. Who knows? Maybe it was out of loneliness or out of some deep need to feel romance and love, albeit through memories. So, I embarked on this quest to connect with the ones who had had a special meaning to my life.

I had no real desire to meet them again, but just to maybe write to them. I wondered if they remembered me at all. I could never understand this about women, and those who were my friends would never disclose their truth.

Years ago, I had received a letter, a note really, from Maria, who was now a successful doctor in southern California. We had split up after almost two years together because she had slept with a mutual friend and later married another one who had known us as a couple, a tall, ex-basketball star named Peter. Peter lived in the apartment below ours and, once we got to know him, he came by daily, often at odd times, which now, in retrospect, makes sense. Maria loved to have him around, and I knew Peter found her attractive. He was six foot seven of sculpted muscle with one of those large, square-jawed American faces that seemed almost a cliché. He enjoyed it the most when we'd go play basketball at the local gym with Maria watching as he swatted the ball away, or into my face, each time I tried to drive on him, giving away almost seven inches. After, he'd grin and dunk on me and glance at Maria who was watching in silence. Shortly after I had moved out, Maria started sleeping with him and later told me:

"I have never been into muscular men, but he was somehow different."

"How so?" I ventured, during one of our awkward conversations when we crossed paths outside the Milton Gates at McGill, even though I didn't care to know.

"He shares so much of my interests in science, medicine especially. Also, when we first made love, I was impressed by his ardour and because he was able to recover so quickly and become erect." She paused briefly, looked at me, and then continued: "But now he's off studying in Vermont, and the times when we do get together, all he wants to do is make love constantly." She paused again, tears welling up in her eyes. He only wants to touch me when he wants to make love....no hand holding, no hugging, no quiet intimacy that isn't physical. At least you weren't like that..."

"At least...," I thought, thinking about her backhanded compliment. Maria had been an impossible lover, utterly selfish. I would spend an hour pleasuring her orally until she finally came and then rolled over into sleep. I would be left high and dry, as they say, groaning with unresolved desire.

Maria continued: "When I was visiting last weekend, we hadn't seen each other in almost a month. Peter was so anxious to fuck me (this was the first time I had heard her use this word—it was always "make love") that he tore off my clothes, jumped on top of me, and started thrusting violently. He was so aroused and I was so dry that he ended up tearing his foreskin so that he had to stop. Now, he has to get circumcised, I suppose...." She began to cry silently.

Unfortunately, this struck me as utterly absurd and hilarious, and she could tell I was about to laugh. She stared at me with abject hatred and stormed off.

When a letter came from her years after, I opened it, curious if it was an apology for having cheated on me, perhaps asking me how and what I was doing. This was something I had always wanted to do, the attempt to somehow reconnect with someone with whom I had been intimate, to find words to tell them that they had informed my life and even spirit, a kind of reconnection of the heart. Maria's letter went so:

I wanted to tell you that I now have my own practice, which is thriving, in Paolo Alto, California where I settled after doing a residency in Dermatology and Internal Medicine in Wisconsin and, later, at Stanford. After he finished his medical degree in Vermont, Peter and I were married though we lived apart for some time until he too got a residency at Stanford in Geriatric Medicine. The marriage didn't work out, and he moved to the Bay area where he has his own practice and also teaches at the University. We had no children, which I guess is good, all things considered. Our breakup has made me very sad, and I wonder if it is something I did. It seems to be, though he would never tell me. My mother also died last year, so I am left with the house and everything in it. She left me quite a bit of money, so I am well off and probably don't need to work, although I feel the need to. I don't know what else I would do. Travel? I don't know. I am sad most of the time. This is not how I thought things would turn out. My patients think I am wonderful, of course. I give them a lot of my time, but something seems to be missing. I never travel to Montreal and don't think too much about my time there, as it is where it all began—the painful part that is now my life. Peter told me when he left that I was a selfish person, not giving. I wonder if this is true, and if this is how others see me. Anyway, I have to go now. My waiting room is full, and my patients are anxious to see me.
Maria

I debated for a long time how to respond to this. Her words made me wonder if she was reconnecting just to be affirmed after all of these years. During her years in school when we were together, I had been her greatest cheerleader, encouraging her through all of the difficult times, cooking for her when she was prepping for finals, staying up and waiting for her when she was out (fucking her lab partner, I later discovered), forgiving her all because I needed to feel I could love and perhaps be loved in return. In retrospect I now realize that it was a symptom of my loneliness and fear of being disconnected from everyone, just as this had happened when I came to Canada by myself and had to make a new life.

For the tenth time I began a letter to her:

How strange that you are writing to me after all of these years. Stranger still that you never ask about me or my life. I'm married happily, if you must know, with a child we both adore. I finished my Ph.D. in English. I remember how you used to mock me about my interests in Creeley and Olson, calling them Creepy and The Owl, how you never once looked at or commented on the poems I wrote for you, how you never apologized for cheating on me, and how you took my stereo and my records and even our cats when you left, leaving me with nothing, though I was happy to be rid of it all, including you. You were a selfish bitch, absorbed only in your interests and studies, never caring about how I felt excluded from your life, excluded from you sexually, always taking your own pleasure and denying me mine. I realize now that you were emotionally crippled, and I feel sorry for you for that. Peter did right to leave you. Why would he have stayed? Why did I for so long? That's my biggest regret. And yours will be having to live with yourself. Don't write to me again or contact me. There is no point. It's finally over, and good riddance to all the memories.

I showed it to Elizabeth, who read it carefully, looked at me and asked:

"Is this the person you really are?" That's all she said.

I never sent a reply, and I never heard from Maria again. Strangely, I did see her one time on late night television on an Infomercial, of all things. She was the doctor giving a testimonial about some new product for wrinkles or varicose veins, I forget which. It was the same Maria, yet not the same. Older and heavier, she still spoke with articulate confidence, yet there was something haunted in her eyes, a sadness I had never perceived, perhaps the very sadness that for her had begun back in Montreal during her days as a student. Her cloaked grief weighed on me that night, making sleeping alone that much harder.

CHAPTER 23

Dr. Rheinblatt has been staring at me for a long time. It is our weekly session, and he mentions that he finds our conversations have become disjointed, unfocused. He asks me if I am taking my medication, and I lie and tell him "yes," though I have recently stopped. Almost instantly, my sexual desire has returned, though without any particular focus. For some reason, my memory of first meeting Elizabeth so many years ago has been haunting me. I want to tell him about it but the reference to the Borges poem will irritate him even though I believe it's the most important part of my self-evaluation. Instead, I start to tell him about walking along Laurier when I happened to look into a café with its loud chatter of people and there, after months of no contact and not having spoken except through the impersonality of email, mostly about details about Nico's education, I saw Elizabeth sitting at a table with a man. She was talking and laughing. How beautiful she still was, although there was something different about her: animated, alive, and perhaps even happy. I didn't feel jealous, but only sad, sad because I had taken away the joy from her life. I hurried down the street so she wouldn't see me, so that we wouldn't have to suffer the awkwardness of introductions and the banality of small talk.

"Tell me about how you felt at that point," Dr. Rheinblatt says as he sits back in his chair, poising his pen over his notebook.

"It was almost a feeling of panic. I didn't want to meet her, yet I also wanted her to acknowledge me. All the years of being together, of having loved each other, came back in a wave of some sort. I felt sad that the love we believed to be forever could be so fleeting. That the intimacy we had shared, the years together had ended in this way: two strangers passing each other, unseeing, on the street. I realized then that I had no more claim on her, that she had gone on and created a life independent of mine. And yet? What about all that we had once had, the joy, the love, raising a child together, the agony of loss...."

"Loss? How so?" Dr. Rheinblatt pounces on these words, though I myself wasn't even sure at first what they meant. I pause for a long time before answering:

"It happened when our son was around four years old. Elizabeth was always exhausted, for Nico was a demanding child, always alert and awake. One night, he had miraculously gone to sleep early. Usually, either my wife or I would lie down with him so that he could drift off to sleep, and inevitably one of us would fall asleep in bed with him. This made intimacy difficult and rare...."

"So, you were not having normal sexual relations?"

"What's 'normal'?" I reply. "Twice per week on work nights and perhaps twice more on the weekend? I never counted how many times we made love in the years we were together."

"Anyway, stick to the point," Dr. Rheinblatt says. "Tell me about this 'loss' you are referring to. I think you're skirting the issue about something important that you need to face. It may also give us a clue to why you did what you did."

"Again, the euphemisms?" I answer. "Well, then, what I was talking about... that night, when Nico had fallen asleep early, Elizabeth had come to lie down next to me. It was summer, and there was a cool breeze in our bedroom. She slipped out of her nightgown and lay there, naked, next to me. We kissed, and then, almost frantically, we started to make love... I remember the string of pearls she was wearing, her eyes pleading with me to take her, to see her again as a woman, desired...." I stop talking, wrapped in the memory of that moment.

"And after?" Dr. Rheinblatt prompts.

"And after? Nothing immediately, though some weeks later she started having nausea, so we knew it was morning-sickness, that she had become pregnant."

"Were you both happy about that fact?"

"In a way, I suppose, yes. We had spoken about having a second child, though we could hardly afford it. Still, we came to accept it, as one does these things. We felt it would be good for Nico to have a sibling. It was a testament to our love…"

"And what happened?" Dr. Rheinblatt, says, cutting me off.

"Well, Elizabeth had a difficult first trimester. She was constantly sick, tired, and often depressed. Still, we were preparing for the birth of our child. We had even spoken to a midwife since we wanted a home birth, something different from the misery of thirty-six hours of labour she had gone through."

"And then?"

"One day Elizabeth had gone for a checkup at our family doctor's office (he was to assist with the birth, even though he was a GP.) You see, we liked and trusted him and felt that with a midwife present, all would go well. When his Nurse–Practitioner examined Elizabeth, she suddenly began hemorrhaging in the examination room. She lost so much blood that her blood pressure dropped and she lost consciousness and had to be taken to the ER. Luckily, it was nearby. I don't know if I want to talk anymore about this…"

"But you need to continue. This is important. You've opened a door, and now you must pass through it to get to the other side."

I take a hard look at Dr. Rheinblatt. He's not normally a person given to metaphors. He looks at me blankly from behind his tinted glasses as I continue:

"Elizabeth spent two days and nights in the ER until they found she had stabilized. However, on the first day, the OBS Resident came by to examine her with a group of students. He inserted the speculum unceremoniously and asked the others to have a look without even asking our permission or even addressing either of us. He mumbled some words and then said: 'We will have to remove the conceptus.' I knew enough Latin to ask him if he meant to terminate the pregnancy. He said yes, and told us that otherwise it would result in further hemorrhaging and even cause irreparable harm to the 'mother,' as he called her. He quickly explained how they would have to perform a D & C and soon. We were both dumbfounded and silent."

"So, what happened after that?"

"We waited until our GP came by. He told us in detail the risks involved. He was an extremely kind man, his great liquid eyes wide and earnest. The next day, Elizabeth had the procedure, was discharged the day after, and began a week of bedrest."

"So, what were your thoughts on the risk to your wife after what they told you in the hospital?"

"Thoughts? A combination of things I suppose: fear for Elizabeth first, for her life. I wanted her to be all right above all else. I was willing to do anything necessary for that to happen."

"Surely you don't feel some guilt about what you had to do? Clearly it was the only viable medical alternative."

"Well, I had stopped a long time ago believing in a God of Judgment and Wrath. Still, I had been brought up in a religious household, with all of its sadness, fire and brimstone, and guilt. One can't shake that off so easily. Harder for Elizabeth since she had been brought up in a strict Catholic household."

"But clearly you are both highly educated and you must know that's all nonsense, no?"

"It's never as easy as all that. I consider myself a Hopeful Agnostic, or something like that. The possibility that there is a God who cares about human suffering, which I know is just basic wish fulfillment, is something that I can never quite relinquish. Maybe it takes some effort on my part to mitigate the darkness of life. Let me ask you this. You are obviously a man of science, yet born, undoubtedly, a Jew. Do you celebrate Yom Kippur with your family?"

"What has that got to do with what you are telling me? Let's stick to your story, please."

"Yet this is the very thing I find hard about our relationship...sometimes 'adversarial,' as you call it. Should there not be more of a give and take between us, at least on the human level? My question is related to my story and what I have said earlier. Yom Kippur, as I understand it, is the Day of Atonement, atonement for one's sins. You can't tell me that a part of you doesn't think about the concept of a God of Wrath and Judgment before whom all sinners must bow? After all, our traditions, Jewish and Christian, are predicated on guilt: in the case of the Jews, guilt about disobeying Yahweh and being punished generation after generation with exile and persecution, and for the Christians, guilt about Christ's suffering and His willingness to die to save mankind from sin. We are haunted by our historical past, and despite Santayana's warning, we are forever condemned to repeat this. Not an easy bind to get out of, wouldn't you agree?"

Dr. Rheinblatt looks at his watch and says: "We will continue this discussion next week."

CHAPTER 24

When I leave his office, I think again of Bruegel's painting and Auden's message–how we are all oblivious to despair and to tragedy unless they are our own. It must be difficult for a psychiatrist, inundated daily by the despair of others, to feel compassion–true empathy. And I think of the Buddhist edict of compassion for all living things, and how hard that truly is as a measure by which to live your life. Dr. Rheinblatt wants to "cure" me, to have me integrate into the world of social responsibility, of friends, family, and the so-called normalcies of ordinary living. What Dr. Rheinblatt can't admit is that there's no real "cure" for those who are acutely aware of the human condition, not that I posit this as something that makes me spiritually superior, so to speak. God knows, it's more of a burden and a yoke–an inevitable block to true joy and perhaps to even true living, somehow being self-condemned to wrestle daily with these perpetual questions and longings.

I think of when Elizabeth and I were at The Banff Centre visiting Nico, who was working there for a summer. We went to a reading moderated by Ian Brown of *The Globe and Mail.* Two others read before him: the first a woman who read about her adventures in the B.C. interior, and the second, an urbane, witty editor from Toronto, whose piece was all clever form without any real feeling. He was reading to an educated audience who understood and appreciated intellectual pyrotechnics but wouldn't know raw passion if it hit them. Brown read last from a work in progress about his mother, which contained a whole register of emotions from the clever, the humorous, the clichéd, to, finally, the poignant. It was this part that really worked, and he finished with the death of his mother as he choked up, and he left the audience wanting more of this, of the profound human expression of despair. Even the crowd fell silent at this part as we listened to his weighty self-exposure. I wonder why we are afraid of this?

Later that evening, Elizabeth and I spoke of this after I had mentioned that the reading reminded me of Kerouac's battle to get down the sacred yet ephemeral moments. She told me how the subject of mortality was a constant reminder of her own death and the fear that this produced. I tried to ease her anxiety by speaking about all we had to live for and about living in the moment. That was the best we could do. I should have listened more, engaged with her more at the deepest level. I now know that I was much too flippant most of the time, which undermined the dignity of her fears. Over the years, I had made a mental note to get her to talk about these feelings with Nico, who would have understood more than I did. Sadly, this never happened.

Walking in the direction of Parc Avenue through the McGill ghetto, a place that still draws me after all of these years, I pass down Lorne to Milton and pass the triplex where I first met Elizabeth, remembering all the nights we had spent making love before our lives became a burden, fraught with the inevitable complications of living. Before turning onto Milton, I look into an open basement window and see, to my shock and eventual amusement, someone squatting on a toilet in rapt concentration bordering between terror, ecstasy, and embarrassment when our eyes meet. As he hastily gets up to close his curtains, I think of Kant's observation: "*If a hypochondriacal wind storms in your bowels, it all depends which direction it takes. Should it go downwards, so a fart comes therefrom, but should it climb upwards, so it is a vision of holy inspiration.*"

I think of that guy's vulnerability at this moment, the absurdity of it all, his unwitting self-revelation in that most intimate of moments, and my own tendencies as a voyeur to capture these moments and store them, for what or when, I wonder? And I realize at this moment how unoriginal and disingenuous my own thoughts were and are, being filled with someone else's words to give ballast to my own experiences and to the experience of others.

The last words Dr. Rheinblatt said during our previous meeting come back to me as a revelation. We had once again strayed back to why every time I touched upon something personal or intimate in our discussions, I had put up a wall of words, quotations, fragments of poems, insights that I pretended were mine.

"Wasn't it that Norwegian writer you are always talking about who said something about writers failing to develop their own voice because all they hear is the voices of the others they have been reading? Maybe that is the very trap you are caught in. Think about that for a while."

It puzzles me that he has made a reference to Karl Ove Knausgaard, not without some measure of irony. It's his attempt to acknowledge my own way of looking at the world through the words of others and maybe offer me a key to pass through a door beyond that. When I get back to my apartment, I start removing one book after another, leafing through each one, looking for that specific passage. There is a mess of opened volumes on the floor when I finally stop, and I notice that there are a bunch of postcards, notes, and slips of paper all saved from my past, which I begin sorting neatly into a pile until I start examining one after the other, compelled to do so. Words from my past float before me, utterances that once had meaning and still obviously do since I saved them.

Putting the books back carefully on the shelves, I can't help but glance at some opened pages, hoping for some sign, some synchronicity, all to no avail.

CHAPTER 25

I thought that I had purged most of these letters and remnants after I had broken up with Elizabeth, that I had gotten to simplify my life, free from emotional encumbrances. Consciously or not, I had secreted these reminders, now held in my hand, both afraid to explore them, but also curious.

I don't know if these are reminders or simply affirmations of the value of my work as a teacher and my own self-worth. Surely, they must be a little of both. I hold a piece of paper in my hand from a student of ten years. She told me that back in her high school days she had been forced to write a letter of "thanks" to her teachers, that she had been cynical about it then, but she had come to realize it wasn't just a habit that had stuck but also a chance for her to reflect on the whole process of her education.

She had written:

It's also so unbelievably wonderful to have a teacher who still believes in passion and in art. As students, we are at a stage where our hearts feel like exploding and our brains feel like imploding. Postmodern society keeps telling us that love, passion and inspiration are sentimental nonsense, and cynicism pervades all. You've no idea how amazing it is to be told that beauty and love really do exist, and that we should all go out and seek them out to our best capacity. I'm often moved by the beauty of a metaphor or the splendour of an emotion, and hearing you laud the wonders of literature and life made me realize I may not be alone. The last class you gave us was just brilliant. Thank you for having faith in the young (as you should. Not all of us have ambitions of becoming soul-sucking accountants or anything of the like).

For some reason, my eyes fill with tears. Are they because of the genuineness of her sentiment, or is it more about the regret I have about my own cynical attitude toward life and the concomitant bitterness of loss, wishing somehow to retrieve this innocence and purity in my own life? I remember throughout my period of teaching that I felt it a duty, a moral obligation, to laud the virtues she mentioned though I came to believe in them less and less over the years. Had I really possessed faith back then, and, if so, what had happened to it?

Then another note, this one from Nico. I had initiated a correspondence with him via snail mail, believing that the pleasure of actually receiving a letter, a physical momentum that could be retained over the years, unlike emails, would make a difference to him, and they had. During his time away, working, travelling, or studying, we had written on a bi-monthly basis. Nico, who has the brooding artist's temperament despite his youth, sounds so chipper in the letter I open:

Dad, how's your writing going? Do you find that even when you don't have time to do it it's constantly on your mind?

I never told him that writing was a real chore, at times an agony. Yes, I did think about it constantly, mainly because I had dealt with writer's block most of my life. Plus, there was the added onus of teaching the work of others whose writing you knew was better than anything you could ever produce. Yet there was also the faint hope that somehow, sometimes you could produce something of worth, some statement of truth, a testament to a life lived with sincerity and joy, despite the imminence of the tragic.

I continue to read Nico's letter, skipping to the second page after his update about his courses, his daily life, and his living circumstances. He had instinctively learned that as a writer you had to save some gem for the last part to make the reader feel that the effort to read on had been worthwhile:

You've always been so humble and generous in your approach to publishing. To me, this confirms your deep respect for literature and the written word, which is such a noble attribute to have. I think you're one of the few people who approach writing as a great reader, more concerned with finding beauty and quality, even if it is the writings of others... You should know—if you don't already—that you've been instrumental in helping me locate something primordial that I'll always carry with me. This will always link us, even when physical distance separates us.

Nico's words bring me back to perhaps my only real passion: the days when I edited a literary magazine back in graduate school and, later, after more than two decades of teaching, telling Elizabeth that I wanted to open my own publishing house. She had been completely supportive, as always, so I had taught some extra courses to come up with the initial financial outlay.

Over the span of five years, I managed to edit and publish seven books, three chapbooks (those literary thongs writers wear so well), and a literary journal specializing in prose, followed by an on-line version. It was a thrill to see each book take shape, a testament to someone's perseverance and my faith in them. To have played a small part in it, to promote it through book launches, trade shows, and readings meant everything and built a palpable excitement where I felt there was a living network of like-minded souls who shared a belief that writing mattered. Like all things, though, it came to an end because the energy and money needed to keep it going got the better of my efforts. However, along the way Nico joined in the venture, and working with him and watching him deal with the everyday concerns of small-scale publishing brought us closer together. Thus, his words that I reflect on serve as witness to something I believed in then, the sacredness of the Word as testament, something that remains in my case still to be written.

And a homemade card from Elizabeth, wrinkled, yellow, the writing faded though her bold hand is still apparent: *Surprise!* she had written on the page facing her drawing of two cats hugging with a kitten attached to the father's tail. *Little He/She due Nov. 22-25, one month before Christmas! Happy Birthday...I Love You.* It brought me back to that moment when she announced her pregnancy with Nico and how she had kept it to herself in the days leading up to my birthday. I had wept from happiness and hugged her delicately, and later we had made love, gently, me touching her ever so carefully so as somehow to protect the child that was in her, touching her like some precious offering.

I can still remember the changes that had accompanied her body in the months that followed. She said she had never felt more beautiful, happier, or more desirable. I loved to touch the changing weight of her breasts, the tautness of her stomach, loved how she would look after a few hours awake in her first trimester when all she wanted was to sleep, fatigue overcoming her like a gentle dream, and lying together, spooning, with my hand on her stomach rocked by the swelling of her breathing.

When I was on my own, there was much truth in what I later wrote to a former lover about how memories "lie in the body" and how one can never forget someone you have been intimate with. Or maybe, thinking of what Dr. Rheinblatt had suggested, our memories are fabrication, not unlike the stories poets and writers make up to ease the pain of living.

It suddenly hits me how disconnected I am from others in my apartment amidst a pile of half opened books, old letters, scraps of paper, but no photos, so much missing from the home I once had among the cocooned security of a family life. I had written in a letter to Nico, trying to explain to him my own estrangement from North American culture, how I felt exiled, somehow ungrounded, yet had told him that embracing displacement is important since dealing with loneliness is something we all have to face. These sentiments seem like bravado, facile in the still air of early summer and in the empty silence.

CHAPTER 26

Slowly reshelving the scattered books and papers, I wonder why I am doing this. I come across the bound volume of my Ph.D. thesis and read at random. The voice is stilted, artificial, false, yet replete with all the appropriate academic jargon. It drones on repetitively, and I toss it aside, remembering the day of my defense.

Being so nervous that morning, I had asked Elizabeth not to attend. I had thrown up twice and suffered from severe bowel cramps, coupled with a hollow stomach. I entered the conference room in the Arts Building and was met by five indifferent gazes from the Examining Committee, plus a few graduate students and Ph.D. candidates who had come to view the bloodletting and to assess what they themselves would be in for.

The Committee was chaired by the Pro-Dean, a Professor of Anthropology who recited the rules of the examination and introduced the other members: my thesis advisor, a nice man, nattily dressed in a striped three-piece suit, the Chair of the English Department, a dour man who was clearly nursing a hangover. Two other examiners were also present: one of them a short, balding man, a specialist in critical theory, just then coming into vogue, known for seducing his graduate students and then throwing them a bone, so to speak, by way of introduction to scholarly journals or a gig as a research assistant on one of his many projects funded by SHRCC grants. Finally, there was the outside examiner, a member of another Department, in this case Political Science, a stocky, bearded man sporting a bow tie and wearing a perpetual grin, looking like a small, hairy ape.

After introducing me and reading my thesis abstract, the Pro-Dean told me that I had twenty minutes to summarize the essence of my thesis before the questioning would commence. He then settled back in his plush, high back leather chair, closed his eyes and feigned attention as I began.

Blood drained from my face and I began a rapid–fire summary of my thesis, promptly forgetting everything I had memorized. My notes swam before my eyes, a meaningless blur, and my voice rose by an octave and sounded to me like some high–pitched scream. Now and then I glanced at the faces around me and noted the bored indifference of the Committee. The Pro-Dean had fallen into a gentle sleep, and the Chair of the Department glanced briefly at his watch wondering, undoubtedly, how much longer it was before the cocktail hour.

Then suddenly, there was a loud, piercing clanging, and I realized it was the fire alarm. The Department secretary, a lovely elderly woman who was like a mother to all the graduate students, burst in and told us we had to evacuate the building at once. As we waited outside, the others huddled together while I was left on my own like some pariah. It was a beautiful spring day, and the sun held the promise of warmth. Students were gathering outside between their classes to enjoy the weather, and their eager chatter sounded strange after my drivel. The secretary, Mrs. Compton, came over to me and took my hand:

"How are you doing in there, sweetheart?"

"Not so great, I'm afraid . . . I'm dying in there and I have no idea about half of what I'm saying. One person has already fallen asleep, and two others have looked at their watches. To come all this way, and for what? I'm tempted to walk away from it all."

"Nonsense. You will be wonderful. And you owe me that lunch you promised after you are dubbed 'Doctor'." With that she hugged me and tousled my hair, the first human thing that had happened since the beginning of the proceedings.

Eventually we were able to go back inside and I was told to continue. By that time, though, I had lost whatever shred of confidence and enthusiasm I had entered with and just wanted it all to be over. I finished the remaining twenty minutes allotted to me in half the time, and so shocked the Pro-Dean that he asked me if "that was all," to which I replied curtly: "That's it." Then, the questions began.

The first person to address me was the Outside Examiner. His eyes, were bright and shiny and he said:

"I have only one question: can you tell us about the trends in poetry from Horace to the Black Mountain Movement? What are the major changes you have perceived?"

I was stunned. What in God's name was he asking, and why? Then, I realized that he had not read a word of my thesis and asked this question to test the depth of my knowledge of literature, undoubtedly feeling this would present him in a good light.

I addressed the Grinning Monkey, as I now came to think of him, saying: "What does that even mean? How can I begin to do justice to that question in the time allotted?"

"I'm just interested in hearing your theories on poetry, that's all," he replied, no longer grinning. He noticed the hostile looks from the other Committee members, though they followed the protocol of never siding against one of their own and remained silent. I then proceeded to bullshit, quoting tidbits from various poems that I remembered, granting each century a sentence or two at best. After, I felt spent, not remembering anything I had said during my rant.

Then Baldy, the theorist, followed, asking me how my thesis reflected on recencies in Canadian Literature and French critical thought. My response, again half-assed, was that the Black Mountain poets I had written about had once held a memorable conference in Vancouver that had initiated interest in their work north of the border and influenced a bevy of poets on the West coast. I made up some mad theory about how Olson's theory of "Projective Verse" echoed, or was echoed by Foucault, who talked against this idea of the "self" apparent in one's poetry when he wrote his complexly convoluted statement about how the interpreter of signs does not interpret a personal "truth," but rather engages in an endless interpretation where the interpreter himself disappears. I felt somehow ashamed that I was giving voice to this drivel and thereby condoning the very trend that I felt was maligning the study of literature. Baldy listened to my answer, shrugged, and then passed the baton to the Chair.

I believe the Chair had read up to page 83 of my thesis since he opened up to a few pages before that, the end of the chapter where I had written on William Carlos Williams' attack of Eliot's ideas on Impersonality. He read a passage from my text, prefacing it with: "What do you mean by...?" and then read the part about "how much more real and compelling the voice is in Williams' 'This is Just to Say' than the artifice of Prufrock comparing himself to a crab or bottom-feeder." He looked at me wryly and said: "If you have ever woken up with a hangover, you would not question the veracity of Eliot's insight." This drew a polite chuckle from the other Department members and a grin from the Monkey, and I strained to put a smile on my face before stammering some explanation.

The questions continued, mostly hostile, but some penetrating. My advisor, who had been a friend and drinking buddy during my five-year tenure in graduate school, turned into a Mr. Hyde, deciding to showcase his own knowledge of the subject and his familiarity with my thesis. He had borrowed two recent books by the writer who was the main subject of my dissertation, books that had just come out and did not figure in my analysis. He had never returned them to me but had them open in his hand, proceeding to read out selected passages, asking me to comment on them. This caught me completely by surprise, and the best I could do was improvise answers and try to lead back to the passages I had actually written about. I then realized he too had an agenda. I was, after all, his first Ph.D. student, and he wanted to prove to his colleagues not my worth but rather his own. It was a pissing contest, pure and simple, a chance to enhance one's reputation before one's peers, and there was no merit in the fact that I had argued there was some Truth in literature and that Goethe's dictum of *Dichtung und Wahrheit* lay at the foundation of the poetry of the Sixties.

Three painful hours dragged by and the oral defense was finally over. The Pro-Dean asked me to step outside while they deliberated. When I walked out, I was trembling, and the first person I saw was Elizabeth, who came and hugged me and asked how it had gone. I could tell that she had been worried and was still, but my gloom lay not so much in my concern about whether or not I would pass and be granted the degree, but in the subject of my thesis, which had been devalued by academic pomp and grandstanding. The personal connection that purported to exist in the Humanities existed in name only. It was all intellectual masturbation without any real substance. I had become part of this game and was thereby complicit.

After an interminable wait, Mrs. Compton came out from the Committee Room with a wide smile on her face. She took both of us by the hand and led us in, and now everyone was standing, holding a glass of sherry as Elizabeth and I were offered one.

"Congratulations, 'Doctor'," the Department Chair said, raising a glass and smiling for the first time, "to a long, academic career and a fulfilling life of scholarship!"

We drank and mingled for a half an hour or so. They shook my hand and mouthed empty platitudes, but I found I had little to say and felt numb. It did not help that I had been unable to eat anything for over twenty-four hours so that the sherry went straight to my head. Mercifully, the enforced socializing was soon over.

After, Elizabeth and I drove over to La Bodega on Parc Avenue, our favourite hangout, and enjoyed a light lunch followed by a bottle of Spanish bubbly she had ordered to mark the occasion. I had trouble swallowing the food, so I drank several glasses and immediately got very high and light-headed. As I was exiting the parking lot, I drove my car into the fender of a Mercedes parked close by. Immediately, I began to panic as the attendant came over to check on the noise. My rear taillight had been smashed, but the Mercedes had only a slight scratch, one that could be missed if you were not looking for it. The attendant, an older swarthy Greek man with a two-day growth of beard and salt-and-pepper hair looked at me and at the bumper of the Mercedes, then rubbed his thumb and index finger in the air.

"I no see nutin, I no say nutin..."

I understood all too well and gave him a twenty-dollar bill and drove slowly and carefully the rest of the way, falling into bed as soon as I got home. At night, I was troubled by dreams where I was being pursued by a monkey in a bow tie and Baldy having vigorous sex with Elizabeth, perhaps a response to how he had actually hit on her during the sherry party. For several weeks after, I'd wake up with night sweats, wondering if my crime in the parking lot had been discovered and if I would have my Ph.D. revoked. When I told Elizabeth about my paranoia, she hugged me and replied: "That's why I find you so attractive: you are a sexy criminal with a postgraduate degree who knows how to work a bribe."

My life as an academic was short lived. I make the distinction between being an academic and a teacher. I did have a long and full career as a teacher, but the posturing and the rabid competition that went with academia turned me off early in my career. At one point, I had a summer tenure at Dalhousie University in Halifax. Elizabeth was pregnant with Nico, so I was by myself. Although I missed her terribly, I also enjoyed the city with its quirky Maritime charm. It was a throwback to the Sixties, replete with cafés, vegetarian restaurants, European cinema evenings in warehouses, and a great art scene. The university life was less appealing.

The teaching was fine with a class of interested students, but the colleagues I met less so. There would be the occasional cocktail party or dinner, and it was always a case of competition and one-upmanship. The buzzword for everyone was "What are you working on now?" It was the publish-or-perish mentality with the actual teaching playing just a small part. Where you published, whom you knew, and what conferences you attended were the main, perhaps the only topics of conversation. There was little or no talk of actual literature unless it was prefaced by an insight or a quotable phrase. Everyone was on edge, and people looked at one another suspiciously, wary of where the next intellectual assault would come from. Inevitably, I too got caught up in the game since at that time I aspired to find a tenured job at a university, so I started taking pieces of my thesis and turning them into short academic articles, sending them out to journals and to potential conferences as papers. This was the only way to obtain academic credentials and add to one's list of achievements to pad the curriculum vitae.

I remember my first foray into the English conference circuit. The scene goes something like this:

Winnipeg in the late 1980s. It's 34 plus degrees out, a balmy day on the prairies at the University of Manitoba, during the annual Spring ACCUTE Conference, an apt name for the Association of Canadian College and University Teachers of English who have gathered to intellectually dry hump each other for four days.

I am a freshly minted Ph.D., teaching my first university gig out east. Though I am only on a contractual appointment, the university has kindly paid for my flight and accommodations since my paper has been accepted for one of their sessions. The conference is a job market, but it is also a giant whorehouse. Young prospects are prodded, ridden, abused, all in one great circle-jerk of posturing, sniping, and academic backbiting. A lucky few will be offered one-year positions; the rest will slink back into academic obscurity, hoping for some post-doctoral grant to tide them over for another year so they can escape from the real world of shit jobs and nine-to-five zombification.

I am standing on stage before fifty or so of the best minds of my generation, about to sweat over some paper I have written entitled "Phallic Exclusion in the Poetry of Sylvia Plath." The moderator, a benign, white-haired Professor Emeritus of Something, soon to retire from teaching, has introduced me, proclaiming my paper "brilliant," although he has never read it. In fact, he follows my droning voice, page by wearisome page, until he drifts into a peaceful sleep.

When I finish reading my paper, I feel relieved. My sphincter muscles have finally ceased to contract, and I anticipate the welcome prospect of my second bowel movement of the afternoon after the inevitable question period. I think of Oedipus waiting to answer the riddle of the Sphinx. Sphinx... sphincter; there must be an obvious connection. There is a smattering of polite applause, followed by long, awkward silence. No questions. It's twenty minutes to the Happy Hour sponsored by the Scholarly Society for the Appreciation of Suicidal Confessional Poets, and everyone is tired. I gather my papers without looking up and wait while the room empties.

CHAPTER 27

Things are not going well in my meeting with Dr. Rheinblatt. He challenges me on my career choice and on what he calls my "obsession" with the works of others. I tell him about my Ph.D. defense, but he listens, only half interested, with little or no empathy. I am struggling to articulate my feelings about the betrayal of my passion over the years.

"Whom do you feel you have betrayed? Your students, or yourself?"

"My students, of course, but not first and foremost," I answer.

"How so?"

"Well, it had become increasingly more difficult for me to go into class and sound genuine and enthusiastic about the material that I was teaching."

"Oh, and why was that?"

"For one thing, were I to return to the classroom, I don't know if I could go in day in and day out and genuinely argue that the "truths" they discover in literature have any real worth, or that it is all a panacea for all the ills of the world. What right do I have to come in with a smile on my face and talk about how this or that poet has articulated a profound emotion, which may mean nothing to these young people in the long run? I would truly wonder about the relevance of what I was doing and of what I have done all of these years."

Dr. Rheinblatt shifts quickly in his chair.

"Then surely you are saying that you have not only deluded them but also yourself. We are back to square one again. You set up your intellect as a defense against the hard truths that you have to face about yourself. Surely you must recognize that it's some kind of posturing, perhaps of the worse sort?"

This is the closest he has come to a condemnation, and he is not entirely unjustified in his criticism. Yet he doesn't see the entire picture and may, in fact, be missing the larger point.

"I guess I'd like to ultimately believe that literature does provide one with certain 'truths,' bitter as they may be, the recognition of which may make our lives worthwhile."

"Worthwhile? In what sense?"

"Simply in that the stories we read, the feelings and longings of others, provide us with a connection to the past, the present, to others, and to our humanity...."

He interrupts at this point: "So you are saying, in fact, that your teaching is of some worth since you provide inspiration to your students. Surely that means something?"

"It's more complex than that. Sure, it would be easy to pick books that offer the pat happy ending. Literature, unfortunately, has a ton of them. I'm thinking of Dickens who in a book like *David Copperfield* chronicles the life of a young boy coming to manhood, complete with tragedy, sorrow, and ultimately redemption."

"And what's wrong with that? Dickens, if I understand it, was a wildly popular writer in his day. You had said at one point that his novels were serialized and people couldn't wait to get the next installment."

"True, but that was before the next installment in our world view... The Lost Generation, Camus, and the Postmoderns, those who belied the worth of any genuine sentiment and said that all art was simply to be dissected, that human life was tragically meaningless, that there were no absolutes, and that the only authenticity we could experience was our own mortality, having been dropped into a world that held little coherence or order. Thanks to Darwin, Marx, and Freud, the "safe" world view of the Victorians was finally overturned; in fact, Tennyson wrote of his doubt when he penned "nature red in tooth and claw" as did Matthew Arnold in *Dover Beach* where he reflects on a world of confusing values. There is this wonderful parody by a contemporary poet, *The Dover Bitch*, that is a hilarious comment on. . . ."

"Yes, but now let's get back to the real point of this discussion. You digress again, as is your wont."

"And what is that?" I ask. I notice that I have briefly relaxed and am not gripping the arms of the chair, slumped back, away from his onslaught.

"You tell me."

"You see, that's what I find so difficult about our discussions. Whenever we touch on an abstract idea, you steer me back to an event or feeling I have discussed. It's becoming tedious to always walk circles around my so-called motives for trying to kill myself. To tell you the truth, I think it was some stunt I was practicing, a stunt without real intent. I knew almost at the very point of having taken those pills that I didn't really want to die. It was about something else entirely."

"And what was that?"

"It has something to do with the realization that we are surrounded by tragedy. When we get on the bus or the Metro, we don't know the weight of feelings people carry with them, the tragedy they have suffered or are suffering."

"You can't take the weight of the world on your shoulders. You are an intelligent man . . . surely you know that."

"And yet much of our civilization is predicated on the fact that someone did. In the Christian tradition, that Someone is Jesus, and we are all meant to feel guilty about his suffering."

"Now you and I both know that is nonsense, that religion is nonsense, no?"

"That may be true, but I can't entirely give up the notion that there may have been some poets, mystics, and others who wrote for the Greater Humanity, who had a connection to or awareness of the tragedy of life, of others, whose words are held as totally worthless in our utilitarian, materialistic world."

"So, that's it then? It is the fault of our society that people don't read or that they don't care about art? Is that knowledge worth trying to take your life for?"

I have no answer to this, so we just stare at each other, and I am not ready to tell him yet about the betrayal I came to feel over the years, a betrayal of everything I believed in and had once felt as that palpable excitement of youthful discovery, those moments that seemed to flow when one insight rode so quickly on top of the other that it was all I could do to keep from bursting open. Kerouac had written about this not long before he drifted off his own road into the embrace of alcohol and Florida's sunny silence.

CHAPTER 28

What had brought about this "betrayal," as I had called it, I ask myself after leaving his office and walking home along The Boulevard past the lush houses of the very rich, houses that always seem to stand empty, devoid of life? It would be all too easy to blame society, technology, urban isolationism, or any number of things. It would be wrong to say it was because we live in a world devoid of love or compassion, simply because this was missing in my own life, having lost love, having isolated myself into a cocoon of obscure resentments.

I try to recall the time when I began feeling that the platitudes I mouthed were just that: empty words to fill the hours, my hours, the hours of my students. Yet students, young as they were, did not ask for much apart from you being genuine and possibly passionate about what you were teaching, that you not bullshit them like the duplicity of the media that bombarded them relentlessly. Perhaps that's why most of my lectures contained wry humour and self-deprecating wit. After all, it would have been somewhat unseemly and perhaps even frightening to suddenly unburden my deepest thoughts and insecurities before them. I often wondered how they saw me. Surely someone old by their standards, yet also someone who was quirky in their eyes and charismatic, solely because I spoke out against all the things they themselves felt oppressed by: the need for success, wealth, the demands of familial expectations, everything that stood in the way of the spontaneous enjoyment of their youth, sexuality, and vitality.

The moment of disaffection may have come when I tried to explain to them something I had been wrestling with most of my life. We were reading Auden's poem, "*Musée des Beaux Arts*," a poem that has served as one of the great metaphors for our civilization, but how could I communicate that? I began by telling my class about the legend of Icarus, about youthful *hubris* contrasted with the wisdom of the father who chose the path of moderation, thinking that they could relate to this because of their own youthful impetuousness. I used the analogy of a person who has just received a driver's license and taken the family car on a joy ride on the highway, wanting to experience how fast it could really go, driving it into the dangerous red zone, feeling invincible in the glory of their youth and immune to tragic consequences. Few, if any, of them took this bait, so I sighed and continued more formally.

I projected Bruegel's painting on the screen and asked them to look at it carefully. What did they notice about the perspective? What was in the foreground, and what story did the background scenery have to tell? After being prompted, someone said that the farmer was plowing, and seemed to be working hard. "True," I said, but what else do you notice about him? Do you see his face? Is he aware of anything that seems to be going on in the sea below him?" It is always hard to explain how a work of art, be it a painting or a work of literature, has allegorical meaning. My students saw everything literally, which is why most were uncomfortable with trying to interpret a poem or a story, since the imaginative leap this necessitated took them into the territory of uncertainty. More than anything, they wanted assurances that their world made sense and their choices would lead to some certainty and order.

I couldn't blame them entirely, for they were a product of their generation and their time. Conversely, I had grown up as part of the generation that distrusted the imposed order of society and the world about me, believing in the more esoteric "truths" I found in Eastern thought or through the influence of the drug experience. My students, however, were much more stolid, conservative, and too timid to see life as an adventure fraught with chaos and uncertainty and the subsequent accompanying excitement.

I then went on to ask them why the painting had that name. Where was Icarus, after all, and what had happened to him? How did he fit into the allegory and what was his role in the seascape?

One astute student noticed that there were two feet sticking out of the water, that the splash and his "fall" were barely perceptible. I then asked what the merchant ship might symbolize as it sailed toward a large city. After much prompting, students came to see that this could represent commerce, wealth, and prosperity. Why then did the ship not stop to help the boy, and why was the farmer turned away from the tragedy that had unfolded before his eyes? What could this be saying about human suffering and how our world was structured in terms of its priorities? "That we don't care about what happens to others; that we are too self-absorbed with money and with the demands of our own lives," offered Nina, one of my most perceptive students. I told her that her insight was "excellent," something that I always did to encourage participation. Even in the case where what someone said was convoluted and unclear, I used this strategy since it gave them assurance that their ideas had worth. Certainly, hers did.

What did they think Auden meant by the lines "... *everything turns away/Quite leisurely from the disaster.* ..."? I prompted them by asking what most of them did when they came upon someone begging in the Metro while on their way to school. Many of the students were ashamed to state the obvious: that it was all too easy to turn away from the suffering of others and to go about our lives. I tried to explain how Auden might be implying that we don't turn away with a sense of shock, but "*leisurely,*" almost calmly, as if we were oblivious to it all. The hardest part for them to understand was the sense of Icarus' fall as "*something amazing.*" It had taken me years of contemplation to understand what this meant, and it was harder still to articulate.

I told them, prior to this, that Auden had been a Communist, active during the Spanish Civil War, and that he rebelled against the inhumanity of our society that created people who were clones of what society wanted, of how Auden, while criticizing our capitalist fervor that begat this obliviousness, also criticized the facelessness of a Communist society that made everyone be part of the cog of the machine and also made them lose their humanity, as in the poem "The Unknown Citizen" that we had studied in a previous class. That message had been more obvious to them, but they struggled, as I had, with the complexity of this poem.

In some of my evaluations, a few students had noted that while I was "interesting," I was also prone to digression, something that Dr. Rheinblatt is constantly pointing out to me. Yet for me digression was also my way to make aesthetic and intellectual connections, and it was something that I was able to put to good use at times to try to make a point. For me, such connections were a kind of creative exercise, and I had often felt invigorated after a class that had taken me on the tangents of discovery that I so prized in talking about literature. And so, after we had gone through the poem bit by bit, comparing Auden's interpretation to the allegorical nature of Bruegel's art, I began what could be classified as one of my many mini-rants, something that had become more frequent in my years of teaching to increasingly passive and apathetic students.

I digressed to Blake's "Nurse's Song," since we had studied him previously. This led me to my views on what I perceived was at the heart of most great literature, which was not just the acknowledgment of human suffering and the need for some vindication through a belief in beauty or the redemptive power of art, but to my mind the real cause of our suffering, which was the poignant acknowledgement of our mortality. Perhaps unfairly, I told my students after introducing some basic concepts of Buddhism to them in a previous class that the first Noble Truth was that "All of Life is Suffering." This was hard for them to grasp since many had not yet suffered in the way that most of us suffer in our daily relationships and tribulations that come to haunt all of us eventually. So, I told them that the basis of our suffering was the knowledge that we were all mortal and would one day die. I then told them that true compassion was realizing this and practicing it toward others, so when they took the bus or Metro home that night, they only needed to look at the faces of everyone around them and acknowledge that they were all suffering due to this chilling truth, and that subsequently we can see ourselves as totally equal to others and feel true compassion for everyone around us. Of course, I had ended this part with some humour to cushion this "truth," insisting that they should tell the stranger next to them how they acknowledged their pain, and to approach everyone therefore with true compassion.

Finally, my digression took another leap and I began to talk about the allegory of the Garden of Eden from Genesis. Most had not read the exact passages, yet they were vaguely familiar with the story, though few had approached it with any kind of critical insight or had heard it so treated. After reading them the first three chapters, I asked what had happened to Adam and Eve when they ate of the fruit of the Tree of Knowledge of Good and Evil. Some came up with the obvious, that they had been thrown out of the Garden due to their disobedience, but none were able to fathom the connection I made to how the fall into the postlapsarian state was also a fall from innocence. I remember becoming increasingly excited about this, telling them that our greatest tragedy was when we lost our ability to look at the world through the innocent eyes of a child, but looked at it from the perspective of experience and adulthood where the dichotomy of good/evil, life/death, youth/old age, etc. were ever in our consciousness. Thus, our tragedy was longing for innocence since we instinctively know that is the state through which we should view the world, all the while knowing that we are estranged from this most precious part of our selves.

Moving back to Blake, I read to them *Nurse's Song* and then played my favourite video on YouTube: Allen Ginsberg singing the poem while accompanied by a guitar and himself on the harmonium. I think most of my students were somewhat amused by the image of a balding, older man singing what appeared like a children's rhyme off key and with such obvious enthusiasm. The part that always got to me and made me tear up was his repetition of Blake's lines "and all the hills e-cho-ed," and a few of them may have gotten it since the class remained quiet. After an almost embarrassingly long silence, I asked them if they noticed how Ginsberg's voice had started to fade with this refrain until it seemed like the hills and vales were truly echoing something? And what was that, I asked? But then I answered my own question, as it had become my habit: the echoes were a reminder of the sounds of our own joyful childhood, faded, yet still perceptible, and the Nurse, a symbol of societal and parental authority, did allow the children to play despite the encroachment of the darkness. I don't think they got it, and, in retrospect, I ask myself why would they, as they were too far from that "darkness" in the glory of their youth?

When I asked what they thought of the video, there was total silence until one student spoke up, echoing the general sentiment of the class: "He's weird, sir..."

By which point the class had drawn mercifully to a close.

CHAPTER 29

Was that the beginning of the end? I now wonder. Or, was it the beginning of my own journey of doubt, disillusionment, and disappointment, a betrayal that I view now for the first time as a betrayal of my life's ideals? It's always easy to assign blame, but infinitely harder to acknowledge its source as oneself. Perhaps I had learned this in therapy indirectly from Dr. Rheinblatt. While his ultimate goal, I guess, was to steer me on a path toward a productive understanding of my limitations, and acceptance of living with the norms of society, not to see myself as a victim or depressed by the injustices of the world, I had slowly come to realize that to reenter the world fully needed a drastic step, some action that would stand beyond the intellectual constructs I had set up throughout my life. Yet, there before me, stood what seemed the barrier to the very truths I had been struggling to realize: my books, containing what I had always thought of as the wisdom of the centuries. There were many I had not reshelved when I went on that frantic hunt to find the Knausgaard quote, and now they all sat pile upon pile, silent. I think of my last days with Elizabeth when she confronted me time and again to engage with her honestly about my feelings, to voice my years of jealousy and resentment. I had crept off to my study to read and to hide behind them. She had told me:

"It's so hard to live with someone who looks at me constantly with hurt in his eyes. I want to swat you, to draw some feeling out of you, some action, some emotion."

"But I always stood by you and supported you, no? Wasn't I there for you through all the 'dark nights of the soul' when you doubted your talent and nothing was coming together for you? Wasn't

I always there to pick up the pieces as both a parent and as a source of support, both financial and emotional?"

"Yes, but it always came at a price...of you judging me and becoming ever increasingly separated from me. I needed someone to be there, who could yell back when angry, who could tell me I was a shit, who could *blame* me for my needs, my self-indulgence, yet also accept me for who I am."

As always, I had removed myself, not wanting to argue, and I had crept off to read while she cried herself to sleep, alone in our bed.

And sometime soon after—was it days, weeks, a month?—she left, as I watched her pack her things and move out. There seemed nothing to do or say except, days after, the practicalities of putting our house up for sale, and most difficult, telling Nico.

When I told Dr. Rheinblatt about the end of our relationship, I had spent most of the time talking about selling the house, skirting around the emotional turmoil of informing Nico, who was away studying. To this day, I remember telling him over Skype, the most awful way of doing it, and learning that he already knew, that Elizabeth had taken it upon herself to travel to see him and had spent a tearful and wonderful weekend with him while she unburdened herself. I think Nico truly forgave her for any part she may have played in our divorce. I also believe that he came to realize that I was cursed with this darkness of depression that kept me frozen in silence, isolated.

"How are you doing, Dad?" he had asked me. His face swam in and out of focus on the computer screen and it was hard to read what he was thinking, though his eyes seemed bright and moister than I remembered them.

"What can I say?" I answered, trying to keep the tremor out of my voice. "Please know that your mother loves you very much, that it is no way her fault, that it is one of those sad, sad things that happen to people. You will always be the first in our hearts, and even though we may not be together, we will always have that special connection through you. One day we will, hopefully, be able to sit down together as a family, or, at best, as friends and even laugh together again. Being together for as long as we have has left an imprint on our souls, and we will always have a deep love for each other, despite everything." At this point, I had run out of clichés, and we turned off our monitors, perhaps both grateful and relieved.

I got used to living on my own with Elizabeth gone and all of our affairs finally sorted. I suppose it had something to do with how I had spent so much of my past few years with her, isolated, having to fend for myself, alone. Dr. Rheinblatt had tried to delve into this in one of our sessions, prompting me to uncover my feelings. I told him that from early childhood, my sister and I had been taught to hide our deepest feelings, following the example of my father who had suppressed his own agony about the loss of his wife, our mother, his country, his roots, and his past. I told him that it was normal for us to all sit in our living room in separate chairs, reading, seldom speaking, or listening to music. We'd sit there in silence until my father emitted a profoundly sad sigh that shook us to our depths. No doubt it was to call attention to his grief, but it also served to make us feel both empathy and guilt. Even my aunt had said to me when I was twelve: "You are always so serious and seem never to be happy. What is it with you?"

What indeed? This was a question I could not easily answer. I realize that this melancholy pervaded my life, and became so much a part of my disposition that it undoubtedly wore on Elizabeth, especially since it kept me socially and emotionally isolated. During my darkest times before our split, I had confessed to Dr. Rheinblatt, when Elizabeth and I barely saw each other, I had been so crazed by loneliness and despair that I spent most of my evenings on the

Internet in chatrooms, assuming different personae in a pathetic effort to engage with others. He had pointed out, correctly, that this was a safe haven for me since there was little chance for real emotional involvement.

I never told him that I had met a woman who called herself "Apate" in one of the chatrooms devoted to books and writing. I had awakened her interest when I told her I caught the reference to the Greek goddess, who was the personification of deception, which had fascinated me. In turn, my handle of Icarus had aroused her curiosity. I immediately noticed how witty she was, bold, and highly literate. We soon developed a rapport based on our mutual love of poetry and art, and soon after she started sending me private messages that included her attempts at poetry. The poems, while rough, were poignant, raw, yet somewhat skillfully crafted. I'd anticipate her messages and would take great care to elaborately critique her work, offering suggestions and, at times, rewriting entire passages. I remember she had one piece entitled "Icarus," probably written at the height of her obsession with my *nom de plume* and what she thought of as our "relationship." It went something like this:

Father, artificer,
you have taught me much
of kings, monsters, maidens—
a labyrinth of words
snails through my shell.
You have taught me
the mastery of air, waves and sun
but of love—
nothing, or too little.
No wonder now

my wings, soused
in sea foam are heavy,
no wonder I fly
upwards, blinded
by Her delight:
the soul's high adventure,
only to fall,
again.

Despite the first line being lifted almost directly from Joyce's
Portrait, and near the end, a phrase from Joseph Campbell, the
beauty of her words moved me. There was such genuine longing
in her words that I foolishly fell under their spell and responded
to her with a poem of my own, despite having had writer's block
for many years:

'For you
I will be
a mirage
of disappearing riders
on a wide plain,
the sound of ice
in your Scotch,
the eyes that never meet
yours in mirrors,
the shapeless form in your
cigarette smoke,
the ash of your desire.
'For you
I will be
no other lover
than he who

meets you
in the forest of stars,
the mountain of sky,
the faceless one
who sighs
the whisper of
your sad heart's murmur.
For you,
I would make
a garland of words
and hang thereon
your joy.
For you,
I am a mask
of all longing–
the lick of the lover's
tongue, a whispered
endearment, rain
on a November night.
For you,
I have walked
in dead winter
burned fires,
lit lamps,
waited,
only to sing
again words
the wind takes away
and scatters like leaves
into the silence.

I learned that she had two children, was unhappily married, and was living somewhere in Ontario with her husband, who was in the military. There was an increasing desperation in her messages, and she asked to meet me or at least to talk on the phone. I knew that my literary game had gone too far, that there was a human price to be paid for my cheap gratification, but I had become addicted to this game I was playing, too addicted to the power afforded by her attraction to my words, to give it up so easily. My poem had so touched her, she wrote to me, that she needed to meet me, to be with me, to share the "sentiments of the heart," as she called it, in a more real, physical way.

The urgency of her need frightened me, and I didn't know how to extricate myself from what I now realize was a terrible game. I had to invent something that gave me a way out without hurting her, and I felt guilty about how I had led her on through the duplicity of my words. Yet, perversely, it was a game I had begun and now had difficulty halting. The persona of the poet and man of letters I had created suited me, or at least suited the person I wanted to think was me.

Like many relationships, this one eventually ended in boredom. "Apate" was a thrill junky. As long as I appeared mysterious to her and unattainable, she wanted me. She thought she was in love with my intellect, but actually it was with the idea of who I might be and how I might affect her life. And there was that other element: her desire to be with me physically, a clear indication of the frustration with her own marriage. This was finally what doomed things. Her emails became increasingly sarcastic and abusive, emotions I felt she was directing at her husband, using me as a sounding board. I stopped responding to her, and she stopped sending me poems. The great literary romance, like that of the Brownings', was over. The last email I received from her simply said: "Since we have sunk into silence, I am unable to write a single word. Goodbye, to you, Icarus, as you fly off into the sun." As I sit with my piles of books, I think about "Apate" and this bitter game we had played, which had also helped me endure my darkest hours. How was what I had done different from what writers do, I had asked Dr. Rheinblatt when I finally came clean about all of this? He told me the obvious: that it was a kind of displacement of my own need to be loved and to feel self-worth, due to my own crumbling relationship with Elizabeth. He also equated my need to lie outright with a kind of impotence in my own life. "After all," he had said, "You never sought to physically connect with her even though she gave you every opening." I ignored the unintended pun and replied: "It would have ruined everything, I'm sure. Psychological foreplay, coupled with anticipation is the greatest aphrodisiac. Just look at Kierkegaard's *Diary of a Seducer.* When the woman finally succumbs to him, he is disappointed and immediately ends the relationship."

"So, again you have built a literary construct in a relationship only to watch it come tumbling down?" he asked.

What I could not tell him was something I had been wrestling with as a lover of literature all along. Writers create characters and a world that is immensely attractive to the reader. But why? Is it because they tell beautiful lies to alleviate the pain of everyday living? Are books ultimately escapism, an aesthetic rendering, or a bit of both? I remember as a child I had escaped my sad world through books, escaped the sorrow of my family life and the losses that went with it. I would devour books far into the night and vicariously lived through the lives of all the different characters. Was it now somehow different? I don't think so, but it was ultimately less satisfying. They say that writing is the "sullen art," yet surely reading is too. I know that I have used books as this kind of aesthetic escape from facing the events of my own life, yet I had learned something from them too, though when I think back on specific works I have read and studied, it all becomes a blur—one large, unfinished, interminable novel that is peopled with different characters somehow all sounding the same refrain.

I regard the spilled books on the floor in front of me and think back on the events of my life. When had I faced people and matters head on? When had I truly reacted from the heart without the intellectual constructs that I had elaborately set up as my course of studies and my career? Is it possible to live in the world and see it not through the eyes of the dead, as Whitman had written, but take things from one's life only? I feel a desperate need to do something *now* as I see myself for the first time as a true fraud, someone clinging to a hopeless ideal, who has worked at establishing a distance from the life I wanted to live through some real or unfounded fear.

This realization hits me so profoundly that I sit in my chair for a long moment, shaken and confused. Gradually, I feel some clarity and, stronger still, a desire to make a change, to act in some concrete fashion. I sit and stare at the books that fill the room—the vestiges of what was my life. They make me think about the relationships I have had and still have—the tenuous threads that have held me to this world. What if I were to cut them all? Would any of it matter? I think of Elizabeth somewhere, getting on with her life, without me. Does she ever think of me, I wonder? I think of Catherine, wondering if she is sleeping now in a morphine dream. Why had she phoned that time? To say what? Finally, I think of Nico, and I can barely remember his features from the last time I saw him. For a moment, it is tempting to boot up my laptop and look at all of the pictures, but then I remember it was Elizabeth who had meticulously labelled each file, and that they were probably all gone, deleted, memories on a USB key.

And then I do what I maybe should have done long ago, pick up the phone and dial. After three rings I hear the familiar voice, can see him there sitting among the stacks of books, bespeckled, bearded.

"Hello," I answer, "this is Stephen. I have some books you might be interested in; in fact, all of them, over a thousand, lots of hard covers, all in good condition..."

"Yes, of course, Stephen," he replies. "I can always count on quality with you. Will this afternoon do?"

"Why not? This afternoon is fine."

And later that day when he enters my apartment, he asks politely, "Which ones?"

"All of them."

He walks around my living room, scanning the shelves and the floor, occasionally picking up a volume and deliberately leafing through it, then replacing it, reverently.

We don't talk much, if at all. Both of us have long moved beyond the need for banalities. Finally, he takes out a small notebook and writes down a price and hands it to me.

I stare at it for a long time, staring at the absurd price. He never ceases to surprise me by giving me top value for books. He is, after all, an expert, a connoisseur.

Then, he disappears down the stairs to his van and returns with his assistant and several boxes and starts packing. It takes a long time, but finally the shelves are empty and there are only a couple of books left on the table. Gordon looks at the table, stroking his beard, but is too polite to ask. He makes out a cheque and says:

"Is that everything?"

"Yes. Everything."

"Well then, goodbye."

It is almost twilight, and the room seems strangely empty.

When I clear my throat, there is an echo from the bare walls that sounds hollow.

I look at the cheque again and feel some relief and smile for the first time that day, then move over to sit in the green armchair that has the imprint of my elbows from the years of sitting there holding books, reading. Despite a sense of relief, I feel strange sitting in the silence without the comfort of books.

As I look around, I can almost see the indentations they have made on the shelves from the gathered dust, all the once familiar spines, all the stories of those lives. Surely, the authors of these works had to put it down–their words to bear witness to their lives or the lives of those they had imagined.

I think back on everything that has happened, and it all seems somehow unreal, like some vast dream. When I was ten years old, I used to pinch myself at times to see if I'd wake up, if I was dreaming. That's what it feels like now, to finally be alone, to be rid of a lifetime of accumulation. But can one ever be free, unencumbered, really? Even without the books, I remember flashes of phrases I have read, ghosts that trespass in the chambers of memory. Auden's words and Bruegel's painting, those feet disappearing in the water, the ship sailing on to someplace where it has to be. Then, I move off to the bedroom.

There is a large bottle of the pills I have saved and stored next to a carafe of water and a glass turned upside down. Immediately, I remember the poem by Williams, "Nantucket," and can see the actual sentences grouped upon the page, can almost see the flowers dancing through the stark, white curtains, the bed, empty.

Flown.

I get up with purpose and sweep the bottle into the garbage can by the bed, the tricoloured pills spilling into the bottom of the basket. I turn the glass over and fill it with water, drinking long and deeply, finishing every drop.

CHAPTER 30

Each day unfolds in its mundanity. So, this is how most people live: shower, breakfast, an eight–hour day (mercifully absent from my life since it is now the summer and I am officially "off" on vacation for the next two months), home, supper, sleep? One of the luxuries of being off work for me has been the ability to let my day unfold as I wish. And there were always the books to offer diversion. I remember being able to read at times for four to six hours on end, transported into the world of the author, oblivious to my own. But without my books, I feel restless, at loose ends. I will myself not to think about them and spend a lot of my time thinking about the life I had compared to what I have now.

I also try to meditate, to still the mind, as the Buddhists say, but to little avail. It creates an anxiety that makes me wish for some of that knowledge I had spent so much time reading about. In fact, I recall one of my favourite books, Krishnamurti's *Commentaries on Living*, a book that had informed my youth. Krishnamurti has a wonderfully lyrical style, and the first part of each chapter is a poetic/allegorical preamble to the eventual "lesson" with which he infuses the rest of his dialogue. Each of the chapters leads back to the ultimate point about freeing the mind from preconceptions, of how truth could only be perceived when we view the process of our being and becoming in an unencumbered fashion. I remember wanting to hear him, to be guided by his presence toward the state of mind I believe he possessed, forgetting that this very desire was the antithesis of all that he was trying to teach.

As a nineteen-year-old travelling in Europe, I heard that he was giving a lecture near Lac Léman in Switzerland, a place so famously cited in Eliot's *Wasteland,* and since I was staying in Innsbruck,

Austria at the time, I decided to hitchhike there to hear him. The gathering was in the spa town of Évian-les-Bains on the southern part of the lake across from the palm-studded area known as the Swiss Riviera that stretches along the north shore between Lausanne and Montreux. A huge tent that could accommodate over three thousand people had been set up, and there was a simple stage with a chair and a microphone.

Finding a place near the middle of the packed venue, I noticed several people, mainly Western women, sitting in the front rows, all similarly dressed in Indian saris. Many of them had removed their chairs and sat in the lotus position in anticipation. There was a palpable excitement when Krishnamurti, a small, slender man dressed simply in slacks and a Nehru shirt walked out. Even from where I was sitting, I could see that he exuded presence. He was calm, measured in his speech, speaking in a British English laced with a slight Indian accent. He would sometimes switch into French, which he spoke correctly albeit haltingly, depending on the questions from the audience.

The chief topic of the afternoon was dependency. K, as his "followers" called him, though he had disbanded the Order of the Star that Annie Besant and the Theosophical Society had originally founded, talked about how people follow a guru, and how this creates a dependency on an idea that is ultimately antithetical to true freedom. Using the Socratic method of questioning, and sometimes answering these rhetorical questions, he explained how we are all dependent on ideas, religious figures, societal norms, etc. The man of intelligence, he said, was free from society, yet still a good citizen since he asked for nothing but had everything to give. He said that society sought to make "citizens" of men by claiming their freedom and turning them into automatons who quickly lose the capacity to think critically and to make decisions based on their own perception of the truth, depending on others to make their decisions for them.

At one point, he looked directly at the people in the front row and asked:

"How long have you been following me, most of you? Why do you do so? What have you really learned about yourself? Are you enamoured of the truth, or of the guru? If you have heard or understood anything I have said, you would all get up and leave and never come back. You would strike out on your own path of discovery, difficult as that may be."

When he said this, an extraordinary thing happened. Everyone was sitting in their full lotus, seemingly happy just to be in his presence, but at that exact same moment, a tremendous force almost physically invaded me and compelled me to rise from my seat, as if an invisible hand had grabbed me by the hair and forced me to act. I stood up, walked down the aisle, and left through one of the flaps of the tent, driven by an absolute compulsion to leave, even though I found his lecture fascinating, but it was as if his words had seared a hole into my being, and I felt he was addressing me directly, someone who had been so happy to be one of the supplicants beforehand.

I walked out into the beautiful afternoon, strolling along the lake, and thought of what he had said, the feeling more than the words etched into my consciousness. There was no one there that I knew, and I felt truly alone for the very first time, yet it was aloneness, not loneliness. The excitement of the possibilities of my life swept over me, wave after wave of pleasure that made me grin in a way any passerby must have thought of as idiotic, making my way away from the gathering.

As I sit here today remembering that moment, I think how ironic that this message is the very one indirectly echoed by Dr. Rheinblatt who has questioned me on my dependence on books and words, although his intentions are perhaps less noble than K's were.

I look out through my window onto the tree-lined street below, hear the buzz of traffic and the murmur of voices, and marvel at the beauty of this moment. I try to preserve it as a memory, not of the mind but of the senses beyond logic and thinking, and to retrieve the excitement and passion of my youth.

CHAPTER 31

In a drawer of my desk is a batch of random letters in a box at the very back. Hand-written in my cramped and stilted writing and addressed to different people, I leaf through them. Why had I never sent them, I wonder? Many of the unfinished letters are my failed attempts at making amends to so many people and to the circumstances of my past life.

One of them stands out. The ink somewhat faded on lined, yellow legal paper; I must have written it several decades ago. Squinting to decipher my terrible penmanship, I can see that I had composed it slowly and carefully in Magyar, which bears the signs of my arduous wrestling with the nuances of that language that's so much a part of my cultural consciousness. English having usurped my original tongue, my Magyar is stilted and awkward in my attempt at an apology for something I had perceived as a wrong I had committed, though I strenuously denied to myself any wrong doing at the time.

The letter is dated February, 1978, and it brings me back to Ágnes, a girl I had met during my graduate studies, shortly after I had started dating Elizabeth. At that time, Elizabeth and I were on the "outs," she having stormed off, calling me emotionally aloof and unavailable, unwilling to be open and trusting in our relationship. There was much truth to what she had said. Both of us had just gotten over unsuccessful and wrenching relationships. Approaching that point of intimacy all new lovers experience, of needing to know everything about the other, I had shut the door and told her something vague like how everyone needs to remain a mystery to the other person, that too much knowledge of a lover's past does nothing more than create a kind of dependency and violates the true mystery of another's self.

After our argument, Elizabeth had shed angry tears and gotten on the Metro, deciding to spend the weekend at her parents. I had followed her to the entrance on Peel and then turned around, feckless in my retreat, making my way up McTavish to Thompson House, the Graduate Student Centre of the university. I knew the place well, as I had spent the last three years there after lectures drinking cheap beer and playing pool with friends. It was a dreadfully cold January evening, and the streets were covered with snow and dangerous ice patches. I slipped and almost fell several times as I wound my way up the steep climb toward the Allan Memorial, a place that I have come to know all too well since my incarceration and my subsequent appointments with my doctor.

I sat at the bar nursing a beer and chatting idly with David the bartender when Ágnes entered, seemingly flustered. She was a cute girl, a bit on the chubby side with short, dirty blond hair that produced a shock of curls crammed under one of those Russian type aviator hats with what looked like real rabbit fur. Draped over her arm was a faux fur coat that had seen better days. She made a pretty but comical figure, and were it not for my relationship with Elizabeth, I would certainly have shown more than a passing interest in her.

She was a bit tipsy, slurring her words, as she said to me in rapid Magyar:

"Thank God I met you tonight. We had a get-together over drinks upstairs with members of our department (she was a graduate student studying Geology), and this new professor they had recently hired was hitting on me mercilessly. Can you keep me company for the rest of the evening or at least until they leave? Please?"

I told her it wasn't a problem, and she sat down next to me on one of the barstools so close that her leg brushed my thigh. She made no effort to move it, and as her conversation grew more animated, she would occasionally touch my hand to emphasize a point. I had ordered a pitcher of sangria, and she continued to pour it down, glass after glass, while she told me a strange story that I attributed at first to her inebriated state.

"Do you know when I first noticed you?" she asked.

"No, ... but tell me."

"It was when we were in old Fuckhead Faludi's graduate seminar and you gave a brilliant paper on Füst Milán's poetry."

I strained to recall the event. We had met a few months back in a seminar on Hungarian Literature that was an elective course we were both taking. Professor Faludi taught Russian, and he was the head of Slavic Studies, a department that had inexplicably included Hungarian Literature as one of its offerings. He was in his early fifties and had studied in Moscow, one of the bright peasant boys sent from Hungary to study in the then Soviet Union as part of the Russian attempt to create educational equity for the masses. Faludi's specialty was Tolstoy, and he lived on a farm in the Eastern Townships trying to emulate the lifestyle of the great Count, despite his socialist background and leanings. Some of us had speculated that Faludi was working for the KGB, recruiting impressionable university students. He was not without charm and charisma, and he had treated me as a friend and had even invited me down to his farm one weekend where we spent most of our time drinking vodka while he took out his balalaika and played and sang some poignant Russian songs and others in Magyar that I could understand. Faludi had an eye for the ladies. Despite a seemingly happy marriage to his Russian partner who lived full time on the farm, he was a notorious womanizer who had blatantly tried to seduce Ágnes, albeit unsuccessfully. In fact, he had asked me at the beginning of the term if he could occasionally use my apartment in the McGill Ghetto as his love nest to bring women on the days that he taught in town.

Ágnes and I had had some interaction in class and afterwards, and we would sometimes talk in Magyar over coffee at Gertie's, the Student Union café. She told me that she had emigrated from Hungary with her parents when she was sixteen. They had headed out to Edmonton, where her father worked as a field geologist mostly exploring prospective mines for different companies in some of the more remote areas including a stint in Churchill, Manitoba. She was mad about her father, who fancied himself a bit of a poet, and she had even shown me a type of epic poem he had written in Magyar in Whitman's style that I politely affirmed at the time as "interesting."

Ágy, as she asked me to call her, had graduated from the University of Calgary and had been briefly and unsuccessfully married before she came to McGill to pursue graduate work in her father's discipline after her divorce. She missed living in the West and missed the beauty of the Rockies, a few hours' drive from her home. She also told me a bit about her former husband, a fellow student who just didn't seem to be able to understand her "European ways," as she called them. They had parted amicably, and spoke occasionally on the phone, though she emphasized that there was no chance of them ever getting back together.

As we continued to talk and to drink, she slurred her words more and slipped into a maudlin state:

"You understand me because you are also Magyar. You know what's in my soul."

This was hardly true, though it felt good speaking the language with her, even though her command of it was far superior to mine. I did manage to hold my own, though, and I even remembered lines of József Attila's poetry, which I quoted at one point.

"I have to ask you something," she mumbled, grabbing both of my hands in hers.

"What's that?"

"Faludi told me that I shouldn't be interested in you because you're obviously gay. Is that true? I just need to know."

This struck me as highly amusing. "The bastard. And I thought we were friends! He'd say that, knowing that it would make most women less interested. And no," I continued, "I'm not gay, though what difference would it make in either case?"

"I want you to sleep with me, then."

"What? To prove it? I don't think it's a good idea, especially not now."

"Why not? You are a Magyar like me. We should be together tonight."

"Well, you're a bit drunk... in fact quite a bit so. I don't want to take advantage of that. You will regret it tomorrow, and I might regret it as well."

"Don't you find me attractive?" she cried out, raising her voice. "I won't regret anything... unless you can't for some reason?" At this, she burst into hysterical laughter.

"I find you very attractive. And under better circumstances, I would want to at the drop of a hat." I thought of Elizabeth, of how I was drawn to her, and I also saw before me her angry face when she had stormed off into the bowels of the subway. "I have to tell you that I am in a relationship of sorts with someone, even though we are on the outs at the moment. It may not be fair to anyone in the long run. I certainly don't want to hurt anyone."

"Well, well... aren't you noble and altruistic? Sounds like you are bullshitting me now... You know what? I like to be hurt sometimes," she said, laughing and looking at me provocatively.

This was too much to bear, and I blurted out to her awkwardly:

"Ok then... if we both understand that this is a one-time thing and that there will be no regrets or expectations afterwards."

"None at all. Just a Magyar lass and lad doing what comes naturally. Can we go to your place? I know you live close by, or is the other one there?"

"No... my place then."

We went out into the bitter winter cold and she linked her arms into mine as we slipped and slid down McTavish and made our way through the campus, up University, and across to Prince Arthur to my basement apartment.

Once inside, Ágy had a hard time standing up, but she reached out to kiss me wildly. I was somewhat tipsy myself, so I forgot all of my inhibitions and doubts, and I realized that I wanted her badly. We kissed deeply and frantically, and I tore the rest of her clothes off until she stood before me, naked and swaying, clutching the cheap Formica kitchen counter near the bedroom door.

"I want you to take me now. Do whatever you want to do."

She said this, just as I was grabbing her delicious body and covering her breasts with my mouth as we clutched and bit each other. Suddenly, she looked at me helplessly and stammered: "Oh my God... I think I'm going to be sick..." And with that she ran to throw up in my bathroom. I followed her, naked, still aroused, and helped her finish her business in the toilet, took a wet face cloth and wiped up the strands of vomit and mucous that covered her mouth and hair. She looked sad and vulnerable huddled by the toilet, and she kept apologizing profusely in between bouts of retching.

I offered her a toothbrush and held her upright while she used it, gagging all the while. Then, I made her drink a large glass of water with two Tylenol and led her to the bedroom, covering her nakedness with my duvet and with the faux muskrat coat of hers as I crawled in beside her. It was a completely innocent moment, devoid of any eroticism, just two people looking out for each other, lying down together to offer up some comfort and solace. She looked at me, her eyes rheumy from the alcohol, gently stroked my face, and kissed me softly on the cheek saying:

"Thank you....and I'm sorry...thank you."

She then turned on her side away from me and fell instantly asleep.

I was wedged tight against her buttocks, and I felt my desire returning fiercely but ended up just holding her closely as she snored beside me, her breath smelling of sour sangria and toothpaste. Unable to resist, I slowly moved my right hand over her exposed breasts, softly stroked the nipples until they became erect, and then moved my fingers into the cleft of her armpit where I felt the outline of hair that she hadn't shaved. I was struck by how European this was and how erotic. Still, ashamed of thinking about taking advantage of her in this state, I resolutely turned away from her, my tumescence a throbbing hurt, and tried to will myself to sleep.

It must have been some hours later that I awoke, feeling the draft of cold air from the old windows of my apartment invading the bedroom. I got out of bed, turned up the heat, closed the bedroom door, went for a glass of water, and crawled back, bleary eyed and exhausted. There was a small sliver of light from an outside street lamp that illuminated her side of the bed, and I thought she was looking at me for a moment, speculatively. To shut out her image, I closed my eyes tightly and threw my right hand over my head and tried to nod off again.

At the point of drifting off, I had that weird sensation of falling and kicking out in my dream, when my hands were forcibly grabbed and then fastened to the bedpost with the cord from my dressing gown. Confused, I opened my eyes to see Ágy poised above me, naked, her erect nipples brushing my chest and my cheeks as she firmly secured both of my arms.

"What the....?" I murmured, but she just smiled and whispered: "Sh...sh.... just lie back and enjoy it..."

She started nipping my skin from my neck down to my belly, raising the flesh periodically and letting it retract so that I was soon covered in goose bumps as she continued running her tongue between my navel and groin. I began to breathe heavily, and my penis rose fully erect, a painful throbbing. She seized it in both hands, one of them caressing my sack, while the other began a steady rhythm up and down my shaft. She then continued nipping at the exposed glans, running her tongue up and down slowly, excruciatingly, as she glanced up into my face to weigh my reaction.

By this time, I was straining against the cords that pinioned my wrists to the bed, wanting to reach down and grab her and urge her on to further pleasure. I began moaning loudly, and as if sensing my need, she sped up her oral manipulation until she brought me to climax, the lower half of my body bucking in response to her mouth and hands as wave after wave of pain and pleasure washed over me.

She stopped to look at me as she untied my hands, smiling, and then she snuggled against me, laying her curls across my chest and gently tonguing my nipples until they stood up pointed and erect. I was overcome by a fierce desire for her and felt a sharp stirring in my loins, feeling her hand squeeze my revived erection. No longer caring about propriety and consequences, I turned her onto her back, parted her legs, and slid down to inhale her strong odour and to plunge my tongue into her dampness.

Soon I was deep inside her, and as we sped up our rhythm, I asked her:

"What about protection? Are you using any? I haven't."

"It's ok...I will be ok.... don't stop, PLEASE..."

It was a bit disturbing to hear this, so I stopped moving and raised myself above her, saying:

"Come on...this is serious. What if....?" I didn't finish the sentence.

She just laughed for a moment and replied:

"Then, we will have a little Stephen...now come on, for God's sake!"

At that point, I withdrew from her and sat up, looking at her in the dim light.

"This is so wrong...you know that, don't you?"

She leaned over and kissed me fiercely, saying:

"Stop thinking about it all. Be in the moment. I want nothing else from you but for you to make love to me. Here. Now." She then grabbed my erect penis and guided me into her and kissed me deeply until I too became lost in the moment.

We made love repeatedly that night. She abandoned herself so much to the pleasures of the moment while I, although delighting in her body and loveliness, was never able to fully let myself go. I thought of what she had said before, about her romanticizing our common heritage, and also of how this would play out the next morning and maybe even in the days to follow. I also felt guilty about having "betrayed" Elizabeth though we had parted on such bad terms. Yet the body knew no logic, and frantically excited to be with Ágy, I took her again and again until we both fell exhausted into a deep sleep.

When we woke up late next morning, it was not in that intimate, relaxed cocoon that new lover's share, but remote from each other. Our conversation became awkward, and I was overcome by panic and the desire for her to leave, which I think she sensed. However, I put on a brave face and offered her breakfast, which she didn't refuse. As we sat over bacon and scrambled eggs, I in my bathrobe with the sash restored to its moorings, she wearing an old flannel shirt of mine, I hesitated before asking:

"Now what? What is this thing between us?"

"What do you want it to be?" she responded.

"I don't know. Can we be friends still?"

"Nothing more?" She looked away, and I saw her eyes grow moist, although she tried to hide this from me. I felt a deep pang of remorse, yet she seemed so vulnerable and infinitely desirable that against my better judgment I took her in my arms and brought her to the sofa where I frenziedly tore off the flannel shirt and made love to her wordlessly. She was more vocal even than the night before, but I saw that she was crying despite her abandon. After we had finished and lay together, my face buried in her neck, she stroked my hair and shoulders gently, gently and clutched me with her thighs as if she never wanted to let me go.

Avoiding my eyes, she asked if she could shower. She drained the last of her coffee and moved to the bathroom, naked, unabashed, and lovely. I heard the water running, and I had a wild desire to run in and join her, but instead I tidied up the dishes and threw on my clothes.

After she emerged wrapped in one of my towels, she went into the bedroom and closed the door behind her, returning some minutes later dressed and ready to leave. I noticed that she had put on a bit of lipstick and eye shadow, and I thought again how beautiful she was and how I still desired her, wanting to both be with her, yet also wanting her to walk out of my life.

"I can find my way home. I'm sure you have things you want to do," she said. I tried to read something in her tone, but it was neutral, and she gathered her belongings as she put on her aviator's hat and coat and finally her red, hand-knitted scarf.

"No, wait. I want to walk you back to your place."

"You don't really have to do that you know," she replied. Then, more sullenly: "I can show myself out, and I don't live too far."

"I insist," I answered, and quickly put on my hat and coat as she made for the door.

"Always the gentleman," she answered. I couldn't tell if this was meant as sarcasm, though I suspected as much, and, again, the overwhelming feeling of having done something that I knew I'd regret came over me. As we exited my building, she was a few paces behind me, and once she caught up, I didn't know whether I should take her hand or what. We compromised, and she awkwardly held on to my arm as we traversed the snowbanks along Prince Arthur, making our way to Ste. Famille where she lived with her roommate.

Once at her place, she asked me if I wanted to come in, but seeing my hesitation, she said:

"I understand, really I do. Go. But before, there is a book I want to give you that you might like. You told me last night that you found it difficult to read Magyar since you had left while still in the first grade, but this book is easy to read and will tell you about contemporary Hungary." She hurried into her room as I stood awkwardly in the doorway until she came back with the novel by Fejes Endre, *Farewell to Summer, Farewell to Love*. "You can bring it back when you finish. There is no rush. I think you will really enjoy it." And then she smiled at me shyly, grabbed my face in both of her hands, and kissed me full on the lips before closing the door.

Weeks passed. Elizabeth and I had made up and were together again, happy. I sometimes thought about Ágy, mostly about how I wanted to avoid her since we lived close to each other, but our paths never crossed in either the McGill Ghetto or on campus. Then one day I received a call from her. I think it was late spring, on an especially warm day. She asked me how I was and then asked if I had read the book she had lent me. I told her I had, and then felt too embarrassed to say much more. However, I finally apologized for having kept it for so long and asked her how I could get it back to her.

"You can even mail it to me if you want," she replied. "Or, you can drop it off at my department on campus. There is a drop box for grad students near the main office."

"All right then," I answered. There was a long silence, and neither of us had anything more to say.

I did this the next day, and as I passed one of the laboratories, I saw Ágy inside, working at a desk on her computer. I knocked on the door, and she rose up to meet me, smiling. She was dressed in a flower–patterned dress that was low-cut and gathered at the bosom. I was immediately struck by her allure, and felt a stirring of desire for her that I tried to will away. For some reason, she eased herself onto a desk before me, and as she did so, her dress rode up on her thighs. She made no effort to adjust it.

She was impossibly attractive, and I knew I had to leave, though we both knew that I did not want to.

"Bye, then. Thanks again," I said and made a move to peck her on the cheek, but she held up a hand as if in warning, looked deeply into my eyes, and said:

"Magyar women don't just turn heads; they break necks.... And maybe even hearts."

Then, "*Minden jót....* all the best." A last, definitive farewell.

CHAPTER 32

Ágy and I never met again, so why do I think of her now so vividly? Is it the false nostalgia of erotic recollection? My loneliness? Or the need to right a wrong? And who was in the wrong, and if me, how? The letter in my hand seems strained and false, conveying none of the moments we had spent in each other's arms on that fateful evening. It was written in a moment of haste, and I suddenly realize that her memory has everything to do with me wanting to know if she thought of me a little bit or even at all, as the remembrance of her body is still so much alive in my own.

Some years after Elizabeth and I had gotten married, we had tuned into the CBC News, and there was a special on anglophones living in rural Québec. I was shocked to see Ágy's face fill the screen as she was being interviewed, though she hardly qualified as an anglophone. She was with her two young boys, living in Chicoutimi, or some such place. Her husband, a McGill graduate, had gone there after finishing medical school as part of the government's efforts to place doctors in rural areas, and they had liked it and decided to stay and bring up a family. She was articulate and intelligent, explaining how she found life in a French speaking community, what she missed about Montreal, and how she had adjusted culturally. She looked different, heavier, more matronly, but still the same sparkle in her eyes when she smiled.

"I know her," I muttered.

Elizabeth had responded, only half interested: "Oh yeah, who is she? How do you know her?" I thought about telling Elizabeth about Ágy, but then I was struck by a pang of remorse about my betrayal in the past. It's true, as they say, it's easier to betray a second time and thereafter.

I wondered if Ágy was happy and sincerely hoped that she was, and if the man who was her husband had understood her Magyar "soul," what that even meant, and if I still had one.

Why would I want to communicate with her after all these years? Would it be a desire for affirmation, or to assuage my guilt? Was there still a part of me that felt we could have had something together, or was it simply to know if our encounter had meant anything to her, and was it something she remembered over the years as I did? I also wondered if she had somehow given me permission to be intimate without consequences, and if in fact such indiscreet intimacy is ever really possible, tampered by the weight of our sense of morality.

My thoughts also drift to Elizabeth and other women from my past. Women were a great mystery, and I had always felt a certain awkwardness in their presence, which I often tried to mask as bravado through my intellectual discourse. But beyond this, being with them was coupled with the excitement of discovery. Catherine had once told me that she could sense that I loved women, though she also said she could never understand my reticence in relationships, always letting the other instigate things or control the relationship. For me, each woman was a new, unique being, and each relationship started a new pattern with its own intricacies and demands. In my own naïve way, I had been in love with each one I had known, and that's why I sometimes wanted to connect with them, years later, one by one, and find a reciprocated affirmation. Was it a question of pride, I wondered? Again, the need to be thought of, well-regarded, or simply the need to feel that love had been a part of my life? And had I ever been able to give them something, love them in a way that was passionate, palpable, and real, albeit never enduring? Was this within our nature, the desire to love another only to be left with memories false or fabricated? It is sad going down this dark road, alone in my place that echoes of hollow and perhaps false memories.

I walk out to check the mail, for what reason, I wonder? Most of what I get are circulars and the occasional bill. No one writes letters anymore, so I am completely surprised, curious, and excited when I open my mailbox and find in it a small package enclosed in a bubble envelope. There is no return address on it, and the shaky handwriting bearing my name and address seems tentative, albeit familiar. I tear open the package, cutting through the plastic bubbles and shreds of orange-tinted paper.

There is a USB key inside and a simple note:

"I thought you should see this, you who knew me once, for better or for worse. Catherine."

I boot up my computer and insert the key and wait. There are only two files on it, and I realize they contain a series of jpg. images in the form of a PowerPoint. The first one is entitled: "The Adventures of Cancer Girl."

I look at the first image, and it is Catherine, but a different Catherine than the woman I knew. She is gaunt, almost emaciated, and her hair is shorter and thinning. Staring directly into the camera, her eyes reveal great sadness. Her long fingers seem at rest, draped over one another, and she is wearing a long dress that closes high up on her neck, which is covered by a colorful shawl. I suddenly recall that it's the one I had picked up for her years ago in the boutique of the Montreal Musée des Beaux Arts, the one patterned with the vivid Picasso print of a face that incorporates all of the body parts disjointed and randomly arranged. I had given it to her as a parting gift before she left to study Lieder in Germany.

It was the day before she had left that I met Catherine and Paul, her old friend, who I later surmised was her patron and/or lover, who had paid for her trip and had continued to support her during her three-year stint overseas. Paul, with whom I had spoken briefly on the phone; Paul who had told me about Catherine's illness. We had sat over dinner at Carmen's, speaking awkwardly to each other in German, neither Paul nor myself wanting to acknowledge the inevitability of her departure. At the end of the meal, Paul, ever the gentleman, solemnly shook my hand and helped Catherine on with her jacket. We walked out into the humid air of a late, rainy summer evening and they hailed a cab on the corner of Stanley and de Maisonneuve. I watched the taxi disappear into the night as I headed back to my apartment, passing through the dimly lit campus.

Catherine and I did meet nearly a year later, and it was through the most unusual of circumstances. We had exchanged letters, with me writing the lion's share. As the months passed, her letters came less frequently, and when they did, they were largely newsy, telling me about her studies, her performances, and about her life as an artist, for she was now performing regularly throughout the country, and about life in Germany. Her birthday was approaching in July. I had finished my graduate courses and finished teaching a summer session at a college in Montreal, so I was officially free. Whether out of boredom or out of some desire to do something poetic, I decided to make the Grand Gesture.

In early July, I flew to Munich to surprise her. I knew from a previous letter that she would be performing a solo Lieder recital at the Schloss Nymphenburg near the Munich Music Academy on a Friday, a few days before her birthday. My flight arrived in the early afternoon, giving me time to have a quick shower in my hotel and to change. Afterwards, I took the *S Bahn* to the city center and spent a couple of hours before the concert strolling through the *Altstadt,* enjoying a beer that immediately went to my head, and finally stopping for a short foray into the *Frauenkirche* before making my way by tram to the western part of the city and walking to the castle.

I had about half an hour to stroll through the oddly symmetrical Baroque gardens before finding my way into the Fest Hall after purchasing standing room tickets for the performance. The hall was beautifully ornate, and decorated in the French style with blazing chandeliers, which were suddenly dimmed at the start of the performance. A polished, black Steinway occupied the stage, and as the accompanist walked out in his frock coat and tails, I felt embarrassingly underdressed. Then, Catherine came out, dressed in a floor-length green velvet gown, her blond hair cut shorter than I remembered it, falling just above the shoulders. Even from the distance where I was standing, I noticed that she was clutching her hands together, a sign of nervousness and anticipation I recognized from having attended several of her performances in Canada.

The recital began, and I was struck again by the power and beauty of her voice, which seemed to have grown richer and more mature in the months since I had last seen her. The repertoire, even though I knew little of it, was mainly Schubert, and she finished with two songs from the *Winterreise,* a cycle of twenty-four songs, one of them about a man who journeys far in order to be with the woman he loves, only to find out that she rejects him. The music is composed almost entirely of minor chords that carry with it a sharp, poignant sadness that she put to excellent use, never hesitating in her phrasing. When the last note was struck, the appreciative audience gave her a standing ovation, and after she had received a bouquet of flowers, she bowed once more and walked triumphantly off stage.

Somewhat nervously I pulled up at her address in a taxi an hour later, clutching a handful of roses I had quickly bought at a *U-Bahn* kiosk despite the lateness of the hour, since it was close to midnight. I swallowed hard as I made my way up to the third floor of an older building where just a few of the windows were still lit. Was she even home, I wondered, or out celebrating? But I had come this far, and I was both hesitant and eager to see her. I knocked on the door softly. There was no answer. I knocked again. I almost felt relief and turned to go away, when the door slowly opened. Catherine stood there in a short, silk robe, looking at me in complete surprise. She had removed her makeup, and she was not the glamorous diva I had witnessed performing, but more the Catherine that I knew from our days together, which gave me the courage to smile and offer the flowers.

"*Ausgezeichnet!*" I said in German. "You were amazing tonight, and you looked stunning. They loved you!" I said this a tad weakly as she was looking me up and down, speechless, not knowing what to do with the roses in my outthrust hand.

"My god, Stephen, I don't know what to say..."

"Well, are you going to invite me in?" I joked, though the words were quickly turning to ash in my mouth.

"It's just that I...anyway, come in, of course...."

I followed her, hesitantly, into her large flat. A cello rested on its stand next to the small piano that she must have used for practice. She saw me looking at the instrument curiously and stood gazing at me silently for what seemed an interminable period. Just when we were both about to speak, the bedroom door opened, and out came a tall, disheveled man in his early thirties in a bathrobe and bare feet. He was obviously naked underneath it.

"What's wrong! Who is it?" he asked her in a strong Bavarian accent. Catherine made the awkward introductions:

"This is Stephen, a friend from Canada." She continued in German, telling him I could speak and understand the language well. We shook hands almost formally and Werner, as she called him, welcomed me politely into their home. There was a long silence, and I looked around for some way to escape my discomfort.

He offered me a drink but I declined and told him that I had to be off, making some weak excuse about meeting a friend for drinks, saying that I had just come by to offer my congratulations to Catherine. We shook hands, and as I was walking toward the door, he asked me how long I would be in Munich and that maybe I would like to have dinner with them sometime. He shook my hand firmly and gave me an encouraging smile as Catherine walked me to the door.

She followed me out, shutting the door to the flat behind her, so that we were both facing each other on the landing.

"God, I don't know what to say, except that I'm with Werner now." She spoke rapidly, obviously wanting it all to be over. There was no hint of an apology in her voice, just some vague annoyance.

I asked her why she had never said anything to me. However, the more I spoke, the more I felt like the hapless cuckold, and as she had nothing much by way of a retort, I stopped speaking in order to preserve what little dignity I had left. As I turned to depart, I reached out, took her right hand, slowly brought it up to my lips, brushed her fingers gently and gave her hand a soft squeeze.

"Goodbye then," I murmured. "I wish you and…Werner all the best."

And then I walked into the empty streets looking for a taxi on that crazy July night.

Some months later, I received a letter from her telling me that she and Werner had split. Most of the letter was devoted to her feelings, and she made no mention of my visit. I read the letter twice and then threw it into the wastebasket, resolving not to contact her any more.

More than two decades later I saw Catherine again. She was in Montreal visiting her niece and had decided to phone and say "hello." Elizabeth was working in her studio and wouldn't be home until the evening, so I agreed to meet at Pizzadelic on Monkland for lunch. She had asked me to pick her up at the Villa Maria Metro, and after I had found parking a couple of blocks away, we walked along the busy street in the early summer warmth. She linked her arm to mine and told me that it was good to see me, but I felt uncomfortable, almost guilty as if I were somehow betraying Elizabeth through this seemingly innocent gesture. Over lunch, Catherine filled me in on her life, telling me she had been living and teaching on the West Coast until an opportunity arose for her to take a full-time job teaching voice in Toronto where her mother now lived and where she had bought a house. She told me I looked good, very "European" with my beard and greying hair, but she never asked me about my relationship with Elizabeth nor about my son, nor much about my life.

Instead, she began to dissect our relationship. We were really not suited to each other, she said, but she admired how I had treated her with respect and, she laughingly said, "reverence." I realized then how selfish she was, how egotistical and self-centered, something I had romanticized as a manifestation of her artistic temperament when we were together. At one point, she said:

"Don't you miss that time in our lives when we were always so horny that we'd fall into bed and just maul each other?" Against my better judgment, her words aroused me, and I remembered our moments together, so much so that I felt a sexual pang. I then knew that it would be all too easy to suggest a few hours in some motel, that Catherine, ever willing to seize the moment, perhaps wanted me to ask her, uncaring about the circumstances of my life, or of what a moment of lustful infidelity would do to my relationship or to my moral compass. We had run out of things to say, and she looked at me teasingly, waiting for me to take the initiative when I blurted out:

"Remember that time I came to see you in Munich? You know, after your Schubert recital when I came to your flat with the dozen wilted roses and you introduced me to Werner?"

She laughed, saying: "Oh, yes… that was so long ago. I thought of you that night, wondering how you spent your evening after you left. You seemed so hurt, so much in despair… it was too much for me to take seriously."

"Was it now?" I said in a cold, deliberate tone, clenching my teeth. "You know I had come across an ocean to see you, and it was like some clichéd romance novel about the jilted lover. Well, I followed through, true to the script. I went to the Schwabing district, drank myself into a mellow state, and then visited a brothel I knew about from my student days in Innsbruck. In fact, I was surprised to see it still there, though it took me some time to find it."

Catherine looked at me, her eyes twinkling with amusement: "So you saw a whore to exact revenge on me for not welcoming you back into my bed? My God, we had been apart for over ten months. What was I supposed to do? Live a life of cloistered celibacy, or what?"

I knew that she and I were talking at cross-purposes again. I had told her several times in the past that I loved her, but she had never said these words back to me, even though I desperately wanted her to at the time. I now wonder if it was due to some innate wisdom on her part, knowing that my idealization of her was a romantic fabrication, or whether she was incapable of such a simple, genuine statement. At any rate, I continued:

"Not exactly revenge, my dear. More like self-flagellation or retribution. I took no pleasure with the lady I hired for the evening; rather, I should say a girl, for she was surely no older than nineteen. Instead, I took out my copy of the Pocket Rilke, which I had purchased the day I arrived at a local kiosk and asked her to read to me parts of the *Duino Elegies,* telling her to use her best *Hohdeutsch.* I think she actually got into it and maybe even felt sorry for me as I buried my face in the pillow on her bed to avoid having her see my tears."

"Wow. Now that is some story...that is so...YOU...," Catherine answered. She may have remembered how much I loved Rilke, or she may have truly felt something akin to remorse at that moment. However, I would never know, and I soon realized that this story had been very hard for me to tell, and that it had come to form a fabric of my imagination and being over the years. *"Und jetzt?* And now?" she asked me, in German, hesitating, waiting for me, still teasing. I looked at Catherine and wondered who she really was. I thought about my past infatuation and tried to summon a memory from that time but soon realized that I was different now, not the youthful lover from so long ago. I said to her formally, firmly, albeit gently:

"Now is when I take you to the Metro and we part ways. Now is when we kiss each other goodbye on both cheeks in the European manner like old friends. Now is not then, not the forever I thought my moments would be a long time ago. We will go our separate ways, and if our paths cross again...well, that will be another new moment that will declare itself as it unfolds."

And with that I went to the bar to pay the bill while she waited outside for me on the terrace. We said little as I drove her the few blocks to the Metro. Leaning over to kiss me, she paused for a moment, and then brushed my cheek and lips with hers. She got out, smiled at me quizzically, and walked to the doors of the subway. In my rear-view mirror, I saw her glancing back at me as I turned the corner and headed for home.

CHAPTER 33

I shake off the web of memories and continue to the next slide on my computer. Once again, I am shocked by her drawn and emaciated figure from the effects of the chemotherapy and radiation. The slide is in colour, and her hair, once blond, is in short white curls cropped randomly on her head. What stops me though is her torso, for she is naked in the picture, and her left breast seems mangled, inflamed, and mutilated with purple and black bruises. The expression on her face I had never seen before: pain, suffering, frustration, and fear. Looking away from the camera, she seems to be in profile, almost as if she's trying to hide from the ruthless, interrogating eye of the lens.

The slides continue, the next series showing Catherine naked in various poses, dramatically rendered in black and white. Most of them are profile shots, focusing on her inflamed breast. The lighting has been cleverly manipulated, so that her face is in the background, covered in shadow, and her body is more prominent. Her lower torso shows the tuft of pubic hair, which appears to be somewhat faded and sparse, a hint of light spread upon it, illuminating it so that the viewer's eye is drawn to it, in spite of himself. One arm is extended, clutching her neck just at the base of the skull, while the other one rests on her thigh, her long fingers seeming to caress the flesh although the veins that are prominent on her hand indicate both a tension and strain.

In the next few slides, her face comes more into focus, and her body is increasingly in shadow. The photographer seems to have understood her intent, or perhaps created it himself. There is a story here: an attempt to move the focus from the ravages visited upon her body to her person, emphasized by her face coming into clearer focus and the tilt of the camera moving from profile shots to a full shot that finishes in the classic Richard Avedon photo of Catherine looking into the camera, one leg lifted so that it artfully covers her pubis and her hands open, palm upward in a gesture of acceptance or supplication. Her eyes are a deep liquid, perhaps from the morphine she has been taking, and they are beyond sadness, conveying a plea as if beseeching the viewer to take the time to look at her in all that she is and all that she has become.

The last slide of the PowerPoint is simply the words SEE ME in huge, bolded letters that swallow up the frame.

Before continuing on to the next folder, I think about Catherine, of the indignity she must have felt when posing for these photos: the betrayal of her body from the cancer. She had always been conscious of ageing and the fading of her beauty, and when we had met for lunch on Monkland, she had spoken about how women become faceless when they enter menopause, unnoticed by men on the street. When we were together as she told me this, I knew she wanted some affirmation from me that I still found her desirable, but I remained silent because what she had spoken of was all too true. I did not want to tell her the terrible truth that men lose interest in older women through some kind of biological imperative which presents the newer flesh of younger ones as infinitely more desirable simply because they carry within them the promise of fecundity, something that she had long passed. It seemed horrible to voice this truth, but I also could not lie to her at that moment since the flesh only speaks truths. So, I remember looking at Catherine then, her face lined from the years, her body still alluring, though the loose dress she was wearing clearly was a concession to the sag of her years.

The second file is entitled "Further Adventures of Cancer Girl" and begins initially as more playful. The first slide was taken shortly after her mastectomy, I surmise. It shows her seated naked in a velvet armchair, her legs crossed almost demurely, and one arm covering her left breast, her hand cupping her chin, as she looks directly into the camera. There seems to be a glint of amusement in her eyes. The next few were taken in various poses, most of them shot in places I could only guess were in the lobby of a plush hotel, as the chandeliers, rugs, and antique furniture suggest as much. The pictures are vaguely erotic, with Catherine striking suggestive poses, often times revealing full shots of her buttocks and the exposed cleft of her pubis although there are views of her full right breast only, the other obscured by the light or by the furniture surrounding her.

As the slides progress, what had been the playful adventures of someone exposing herself in a public place become more plaintive and somewhat more urgent. There is her reflection in the mirror, the expression on her face as if she has been startled and caught unawares. In the foreground is a door, its massive oak façade an ominous warning and Catherine, or a reflection of her, almost ready for escape. The next slide makes me catch my breath. Her left arm raised and folded over her shoulder behind her head, she exposes the long surgical scar where her breast had been. Her eyes are almost closed as she appears to be glancing downward, focusing on that one spot. I look at this image for a long time, feeling the gamut of emotions from shock, to sadness, and finally to despair.

It strikes me like a blow how someone must feel when they have been physically mutilated but are still struggling to affirm themselves and hang on to the impossibility of who they once were while trying to accept who they are not. I feel for Catherine, and again I am reminded of Bruegel's painting, of the splash that no one hears or is attentive to: the fall from our youthful beauty into the cold indifference of ageing, of illness, and of the final cruel embrace of our mortality.

The last slide is Catherine fully naked, her arms out, a gesture of embrace or of entreaty looking full into the camera, her scar now not so prominent but just a part of her. The picture is almost wanton, disturbing in its strange eroticism, and I know that it is one that will haunt me in the days to come. I think of the words on the previous series of slides—SEE ME—and understand what she may have meant by them. It is a plea to be noticed, to have someone look at her mutilation and to see her as a sensual creature still. It is also a demand to be seen as herself, not as just a martyr to her cancer but as an affirmation of her human self, aside from the disease, pain, and gross indignity she has suffered through the removal of her breast, which is inextricably connected with a woman's sense of her identity shaped by the world. I am overwhelmed by this knowledge as I look at the slide for a long time, trying to surmise what she must have felt when the photo was taken, what she must be feeling now if she is even capable of this scale of anger, desire, and pathos that shows in her story. She, who had had multiple lovers, been a diva in Europe, and seen her life and career change from that of a fledgling star singer, to a teacher, to this finality: someone wrestling visibly with her mortality, coming to the end of her life.

And then I know what I must do—the only thing I can do—so I pick up the phone and dial.

CHAPTER 34

After six rings, Paul picks up the phone. I identify myself and ask if Catherine is there and if I can speak with her. He hesitates and then asks me to wait. He is gone a long time before I hear him say: "It is too trying for her to come to the phone. Yet she says she would like to see you. So...yes, you may come here. When shall I say? I think mornings are the best. She is better awake then." We agree on a time the following day (he seems somewhat insistent that it be soon). I automatically look toward my shelves, but they are empty now, no help there.

The next morning, I shower and dress carefully–anointing myself, so to speak. Paul lives in the east end, in the older part of Rosemont near the Maisonneuve-Rosemont hospital. Many of the cottages and larger houses across from Parc Maisonneuve are the homes of exiled Romanians. He answers the door, a frail, old man, yet he comports himself with dignity as he shows me into the foyer. He looks at me long and hard through rheumy eyes and points to the stairs, his hands slightly trembling.

"It is the second door to the right after the landing...she is perhaps sleeping now, as she is most of the time." He then pauses for a long moment and pleads: "You must be kind to her...now more than ever. It will not be very long for her. She has suffered much."

"Thank you, Paul, I will." He then grips my hand as if to restrain me, but then eases up and pats it. He moves toward the door and picks up his fedora from the coat rack and without turning around departs.

I take the stairs slowly, my thoughts a confused jumble, wondering what I am doing here, whom I will see, and how I will address her. Why have I come? Out of guilt? Empathy? Friendship? Finality?

Then I think of her images on those slides and her words—SEE ME, so I turn the brass handle and enter the room.

The room is large and airy but dark in the half-light. It is a grey day, and the heavy curtains are partly drawn so that almost no light falls on the bed. It is sparsely furnished with a large, antique cherrywood armoire in the corner. A towel covers the mirror at the top of it that points directly at the foot of the bed. Next to the bed is a night table with a portable CD player on it and many prescription bottles, and by them a pitcher of water with the glass upturned. A commode sits next to the bed, its seat turned down. A strong smell of liniment and antiseptic pervades the room: the hospital smells of death.

She is lying in an old, four-poster bed on carefully positioned pillows, the duvet arranged neatly to cover her body, reaching almost up to her neck even though it's a warm day and the windows are closed.

I stand next to her, hesitating, and then reach out to take her hand that is resting on top of the covers. It's cool to the touch, and the veins stand out, a greyish hue, leading to the knuckles.

Opening her eyes, she sees me through the fog caused by the drugs and tries to smile:

"So, you have come," she whispers, straining to sit up.

"Let me help you." I reach behind her shoulders to arrange the pillows, and for a moment our bodies touch.

"I knew you would come...that you would understand my story, the pictures I sent you..." Her voice is stronger now, and she tries to lean forward toward me, looking at me intently. "Thank you for this."

"How are you?" I ask, knowing it's an insipid question, but I'm unable to say much else.

She pauses for a long time, then says with great intensity and bitterness: "Dying."

"Is there anything I can do for you...something you need...anything at all?"

She raises her hand, points to the CD player, and asks me to turn it on. Then, she makes space beside her on the bed and gestures for me to come closer.

I press PLAY, and it is set to Schubert's "*An die Musik*," his great piece that is his thanksgiving to the divine art of music. It is sung by Elisabeth Schwarzkopf, one of Catherine's favourite Lieder singers. We are both overcome by the music, the singer's voice, and the words, both of us feeling no need to speak. I stroke her face gently and I notice that Catherine is silently weeping as the song unfolds:

Du holde Kunst, in wieviel grauen Stunden,
Wo mich des Lebens wilder Kreis umstrickt,
Hast du mein Herz zu warmer Lieb entzunden,
Hast mich in eine beßre Welt entrückt!

The "better world" Schubert writes of is the world of art, of the artist, and I know that while it speaks uniquely to Catherine with its own, special poignancy, I too feel the reverence of his sentiments toward all that has sustained him in his craft.

We remain silent for a long time. She has wrapped her arms around my neck and has nestled herself on my chest. Finally, I speak to her slowly, deliberately:

"That night in Munich...you sang this, I'm sure of it. It was no less beautiful."

Without a word she smiles, and throws off her sheets with a surprising energy. She is wearing only a short silk night dress that has ridden partly up her thighs, which are still full despite her otherwise emaciated appearance. She looks at me, pleadingly and whispers: "See me..."

I hesitate but then slowly lift the nightdress above her arms, shoulders, and head as she props herself above me, naked. I sense that she is in great pain, and I gently place her back onto the bed, caressing her face, and brushing my lips over hers, softly, until she returns my kiss with a fiercer passion, drawing me down to her.

Slowly, I touch the spot where her breast had been and run my fingers across the scar, back and forth, ever so gently like a caress. I bend over, kissing the scar, running my tongue along its jagged, sharp edges, and only after do I touch and kiss her other breast, the unafflicted one, as she closes her eyes and begins to moan softly.

I remove my clothes so as not to disturb her reverie, and Catherine, her eyes closed, reaches out to caress me, weakly at first and then more firmly, more insistently, bringing me to tumescence, drawing me into her with a sharp sigh that is one of pain, pleasure, and longing. I try to bear most of my weight on my arms in order not to hurt her and move slowly, ever so slowly, deeply into her until I feel her shudder and grip me. We are joined together for a very long time until she finally pulls me tighter, moving more urgently, urging me on to my own climax.

After, she asks me to pour her some of the liquid medicine that must be the morphine, and she slowly strokes my face, my lips, my eyes, and the outline of my jaw as if to memorize my features. Eventually, she drifts off to sleep, and I lie with her until I hear her shallow breathing moving into its own weak albeit steady rhythm.

I dress and close the door silently, so as not to wake her. The flat is empty, and Paul has not yet returned. I think of Catherine and then the verse from Philip Larkin's "Faith Healing":

In everyone there sleeps
A sense of life lived according to love.
To some it means the difference they could make
By loving others, but across most it sweeps
As all they might have done had they been loved.

Thus, to Catherine I bequeathed love so that she could feel before the emptiness of death to have been loved and she, surely for the last time, to have lived her final hours or days according to love, having been accorded love.

CHAPTER 35

I am sitting in Dr. Rheinblatt's office, and for the first time I do not feel the dull edge of his censure. I speak slowly and describe my meeting with Catherine–all of it except for the intimate parts. He occasionally nods to me and says, "go on." And I do. I tell him about discarding my books and how I miss them but realize they are best gone, that by emptying those spaces from my shelves I have tried to empty my pretensions and beliefs, somehow to try to begin again.

"What is it like," he asks me, "to be without them?"

"Strangely empty. I am bored at times, footloose, not knowing what to do or who to turn to in times of doubt."

"And how do you cope?"

"I spend a lot of time reflecting."

"On...?"

"My life...my past...relationships.... things and people that I miss...learning to miss them again, perhaps."

"And your attempt at suicide?" He is no longer speaking in euphemisms, I think, again for the very first time.

"I am somewhat ashamed of the histrionics surrounding my suicide attempt. I now realize that it was a romantic longing for escape, for some vindication of everything I felt was wrong with the world. I think I have come to realize that the weight of our lives is something we have to carry with us to the end as our own private and special burden...."

"And Auden's poem...the one about the Bruegel painting of Icarus? How do you see that now?"

This surprises me, for now I know that he has been listening to me all along.

"I read it too, you know. It is a poignant poem, and I think I see how you have interpreted it during our sessions." Dr. Rheinblatt has never been this voluble. He looks at me directly as he speaks. The Mont Blanc pen lies on his desk on top of an unopened notebook.

I say to him: "I think I understand the role of Icarus better in that great painting. Maybe it wasn't hubris–the hubris of youth–that led to his fall, but, more tragically, curiosity... that desire to know the world in its first light, the world behind the veil. My son, Nico, said it best one day as he was telling me about his experience taking LSD. He said: 'I began to see the world again like a child... it was so overwhelming... a kind of mystical experience... something I was afraid of feeling since I might be stuck forever in that place.' I knew what Nico meant, what he had felt: the inability to articulate wonder, so Icarus too flies toward the sun, the source of it all, and it is this very wonder that destroys him." I think back on Nico and my heart opens in gratitude for what he has given me... how I too, briefly, was able to see the world through his child's eyes.

I pause for a moment, as my voice is trembling, but Dr. Rheinblatt makes no attempt to stop me, just nods to me and says: "Go on."

"Yes... so the tragedy of Icarus' fall–the father, the architect of the labyrinth, that great puzzle... him, the wise creator always second-guessing his own decision to send his son on his flight. So that's the paradox: the state of wonder we have lost but know is still there–that state we all want to return to, but for the burning sword barring the path back to the Garden."

As I say these words, I think of Catherine, of how she, dying in my arms, still clung to me with passion. In her moment of climax, she had an ageless face, that of a young woman or girl. Even dying could not claim that mystery. Through her, I had wormed out death.... her death.... mine.... the death of all others. Death as not the finality, but death as consummation, the loss of light, the fall into the chaos of the waves, on bent and flayed wings, feathers eroded–the splash no one hears but is the world's consummate cry: *"About suffering, they were never wrong"*–the secret heart of all art, the "why" of my own love of words–the sound of wings breaking the silence of earth, water, air, and sky–one last time to hold the blue.

I begin to weep as I think of this, weeping unashamedly, and Dr. Rheinblatt offers me some water that I gratefully take and drink. At the end of our session he shakes my hand. His face remains expressionless, though there is warmth and an answering pressure in his grip. We both know this will be our last meeting, that my journey will continue alone, as it must.

I walk for a long time through the streets of Westmount by the empty, manicured mansions, behind their curtained windows–other lives–past the huge Baptist church with the burnt copper dome, down Claremont, along St. Antoine to Girouard Park whose trees have been devastated and still lie bare from a freak summer hailstorm. I drop into one of my favourite bookstores and, against my better judgment start to peruse the shelves. I take down a volume, then another, and it is like holding onto the arm of a wise, old friend who had once offered solace and support.

I open the *Collected Fictions* by Borges and realize with a start that this was once my book, my familiar. Leafing through the pages, I come to a piece I know so well, "The Immortal," and read:
Words, words, words taken out of place and mutilated, words from other men–those were the alms left him by the hours and the centuries.

I leave the bookstore and walk east until I come to Café Shaika, an old hangout. I enter, order a coffee, and sit down by the window that looks onto avenue Marcil. Directly opposite from me sits a young woman, writing intently in her notebook. She has short auburn hair and is dressed flamboyantly in a loose blouse, gathered skirt and high laced-up boots that cover half of her calf. She is beautiful–strange–a mystery, as all women are. She has that intensity I recognize–the intensity of rapture coupled with doubt, which is the province of any wordsmith. I wonder about the contents of her journal, about the flow and scope of her thoughts. She looks up for a moment, worry and uncertainty creasing her features, and meets my eyes. I look away quickly in order not to make her self-conscious and wish her a silent "Godspeed" on her own journey. Then, I take out a copy of the small notebook I still carry in my jacket pocket, though it has been some time since I have written anything in it.

I reflect upon my life's journey, on this, maybe my greatest passion, the love of books, of words. I think also of those I have loved, those I still love, and all that I may love about my life and all that I still to have to learn along the way. There is always a new beginning, a new possibility if one looks hard enough, I think. If I have learned anything in my sessions with Dr. Rheinblatt (and I have to now admit that I learned much more than I had initially thought), it is the simple adage that you don't just survive your life, but you have to live it, and that when all is said and done, words remain, perhaps a poor choice and incomplete, but a choice nevertheless. There is also that abiding need, the need to tell our own story that fits within the eternal lexicon of all those others who have felt the need to groan out their own.

I thought I could never do this again, would never want to, but I find myself writing in my notebook filling the pages, quickly and steadily. Soon, I am lost to the others in the café, forgetting the time, place, and circumstances. And write:

He is dreaming.

He dreams of women he has known.

Now that he is alone, he wonders if you dream differently sleeping alone or with a woman? Someone he once knew had told him before he had experienced it himself that a woman's presence in bed made dreaming different. For instance, thighs draped over thighs. Does flesh tell its own story? And does each new body tell its own, unique story? Is that why some lovers never stay with the same person? The body on the lookout for new bodies, new flesh, new stories?

He remembers sleeping with Maria, with Elizabeth, with Ágnes with Catherine, with others but doesn't remember his dreams with them or without them. He wonders if they remember him at all and, if so, how?

In most of his dreams he sees them naked, wanton—he dreams them into being wanton, into apparitions of his lost desire.

He dreams of loving them, of being in love, but those moments don't live in his flesh, only in his memories and the memories of their bodies.

He recalls standing at the corner of Pine and Doctor Penfield, standing with her, Elizabeth, the one he loved, the one who no longer loves him, standing across from the Royal Victoria Hospital, waiting to cross. They held hands and said little. They were comfortable in their silence. The newness of each other's body, touching, spoke volumes. As she turned toward him, smiling, he felt a lightness, almost a dizziness as if the earth on that spring day was turning and calling to him. He felt hollow, lost, happy, not saying anything, just being with her. This was love, though he did not know it at the time, nor call it that. Only afterwards. Only then. Then, not now.

He thinks, he wonders, he dreams. He feels the rhythm of his heartbeat, the sweat along his skin, the pulse that throbs strong against his temple, and knows that one day it too will stop. Stop as love stops and as other lovers fill that corner and cross that same street, happy, in love, holding hands. Not yet betrayed by the flesh, which is still youthful, which they think will abide forever.

He knows in his dream that the moment of love was timeless, was a brief moment, then lost, is remembered now, in time, to be lost again and found again, timeless.

He dreams of love, of being in love, of wanting to be in love. What does love feel like if you have never known it? He wonders if he has ever been truly in love. But how can you long for something you have never known?

And when love is gone and disappears? All that remains then is shriveled and empty, legs suspended in empty air, a sleeper without form left to dream his life, his past, his longings over and over and over....

PERMISSIONS AND EXTRACTS

Zsolt Alapi was born in Budapest, Hungary, lived in the U.S., and came to Canada as a Vietnam draft resistor in 1971. He finished a Ph.D. at McGill University and taught English both at Marianopolis College and Concordia University. He founded and was editor of Siren Song Publishing and *The Loose Canon,* and his fiction, reviews, and criticism have appeared throughout Canada and in the UK as well as France. His most recent work of fiction was a collection of stories, *The Dance of the Seven Dwarfs.* Zsolt lives and writes in Montreal.